A Gift of Poison

A Gift of Poison

ANDREA NEWMAN

MICHAEL JOSEPH
LONDON

MICHAEL JOSEPH LTD

Published by the Penguin Group
27 Wrights Lane, London W8 5TZ, England
Viking Penguin Inc., 375 Hudson Street, New York, New York 10014, USA
Penguin Books Australia Ltd, Ringwood, Victoria, Australia
Penguin Books Canada Ltd, 2801 John Street, Markham, Ontario, Canada L3R 1B4
Penguin Books (NZ) Ltd, 182–190 Wairau Road, Auckland 10, New Zealand

Penguin Books Ltd, Registered Offices: Harmondsworth, Middlesex, England

First published in Great Britain 1991

Printed in England by Clays Ltd plc
Filmset in $11\frac{1}{2}$/$12\frac{1}{2}$pt Sabon

A CIP catalogue record for this book is available from the British Library

ISBN 0 7181 3344 7 (hardback)
ISBN 0 7181 3504 0 (paperback)

The moral right of the author has been asserted

To N.S.
with love

ACKNOWLEDGEMENTS

My thanks are due to Sara Barrett and Carol MacArthur for their enthusiasm and encouragement during the siege, Peter Wright for playing the Godfather, Colin Cina, John Hoyland, Dr Prudence Tunnadine and Dr Jesmond Woolf for providing information, Anne Askwith, Caradoc King and Susan Watt for the carrots and the whip, Yasmin Murray-Playfair for the massage, Susan Cowell for the moral support, Barnaby Jago for the high-tech advice and Carol Clewlow for the phone calls.

PROLOGUE

Sometimes they are almost happy.

Watching television in the evenings, sitting in separate chairs, or reading and glancing up now and then, each with a look of such tentative hope that the other is forced to smile back in reassurance while the boys' heavy feet and heavier music thump above their heads. This is normal life, he thinks. Or in the supermarket, wheeling a trolley full of drab necessities and loading them into the car; or round the kitchen table at supper, Inge ladling soup into their plates while the boys chatter or grunt. They are doing what other people do: this is how families behave. At times like these Richard can nearly convince himself it is going to work. He is back where he ought to be, if not where he belongs, and he is willing to make the best of it. He has the satisfaction of knowing he is doing the right thing. He wants it to work, or else all this pain has been for nothing. And Inge is desperate for it to work; he can see the desperation in her eyes, her smile, her patience. They are allies in hope, fellow-conspirators. If it doesn't work, they have nowhere left to go. They will have tried everything, and what do you do after that? So they have made a decision not to put pressure on each other and he can feel the weight of that decision pressing on him every day.

It presses at bedtime most of all. She has been patient with him while he left the probation service, patient while he found a job supply teaching, patient while he tried to readjust to the old discipline of marking and preparation, staffroom politics and classroom control. So much patience. She knows it's not easy for him. Living with her and the boys again, teaching again, he has gone back ten years; he is surprised to see a middle-aged man

9

in the shaving mirror and his sons behind him, taller than he is. She understands all that. In return he has hugged her a lot, kissed the top of her head, bought her bunches of flowers from street vendors, told her she looks pretty. It is true: she does indeed look pretty, even beautiful, but it doesn't make him want to make love to her and they both know it.

So they both ignore it. At night he wears pyjamas and she wears a nightdress where long ago they both slept naked. They behave like conventional strangers: it would be indecorous rather than exciting to let their skins touch. Safely dressed for sleep, he feels it is permitted, even essential, to cuddle her, feels she is a child to be comforted. They hug each other politely in the darkness and turn their backs, settle down for the night. Another day gone, another crisis averted.

At first he wakes forgetting where he is, expecting to see Helen beside him. In a few seconds he remembers Inge, what has happened, what he's done. He dreads that moment, so he doesn't want to sleep and he doesn't want to wake. His doctor gives him pills to perform these tasks for him and more pills to calm him down when he feels great surges of panic wash over him during the day, battering him like waves in which he might drown. Temporary measures, his doctor calls them with a reassuring smile. Everyone treats him like the invalid he feels himself to be. Everyone means Inge and the boys and his doctor, even his colleagues at work, all circling round this sick man in their midst, handling him delicately, as if he were a dangerous device that might suddenly explode.

Everyone except Helen. She doesn't react to him at all, greeting him stony-faced at the door when he goes round for suitcases full of clothes and small, insignificant possessions, feeling like a refugee. At first he went when he knew she'd be out at the studio or college, then found a note on the kitchen table saying R, could you leave your keys please, H. Who are these people who know each other only by their initials? He doesn't recognise them.

Anger fuels him for a while, then to his alarm he feels it beginning to ebb. They both have white marks where their wedding rings used to be. She looks pale with fatigue, dark shadows under her eyes, and he wants to comfort her, wants her to comfort him. He is terrified by these feelings which have come too late. He tries to coax the anger back into life like someone struggling to revive a fire that has nearly gone out: he meditates on her treachery, her selfishness, her deceit. It doesn't work. Instead he feels a great flood of pity for her and for himself. She is so beautiful. What has he done? The terror fills his throat, making it difficult for him to breathe.

'D'you want a divorce?' she asks one day as he is leaving.

The word is a profound shock. He realises he has never thought of such a thing. He shakes his head. He longs to touch her but he does not dare.

'I thought you might want to marry her again,' she says, and slams the door.

Sally is like two people now: the seductive child he remembers, who used to adore him, and a new tough person who uses swear words to shock. She says *fuck* a lot where previously she said *make love* and he is both excited and repelled. It had been erotic fun for him to coax a shy teenager to use forbidden words in bed, but he finds it oddly alarming to hear them flung at him by a woman who is out of his control. It is as if she is beating him about the head with words. 'Please fuck me, Felix. Now. Fuck me to death, can you do that? Please. Just go on fucking me till I pass out or something.' It unnerves him. It sounds like desperation not desire. It sounds like anger.

He has to admit the first time after the abortion is supremely exciting. Putting back what was taken out.

Going into that place where all the damage was done. Sliding into her body with the terrifying thought that it could all happen again (and remembering the mistress in his past with whom it did) both shocks and arouses him, though in reality it's the last thing he wants to happen and they've already discussed how careful they must be. It's a harmless useful fantasy, he tells himself, that's all, but Sally seems to pick up the thought. 'What if I got pregnant again? I'd have to have another abortion, wouldn't I? Now we know how easy it is.' He can see fear and disgust in her eyes but her body feels already more open to him. 'What about all the other times, Felix? How many were there, d'you know? All your unknown sons and daughters sluiced away or bunged in the incinerator. I wonder what they do with all the bits – I never thought to ask.' The only way to shut her up is to kiss her.

'I screwed around a lot last term,' she says when he stops kissing her. 'I just wanted people to fuck me. I didn't care who they were, I just went on a sort of binge. Sometimes I didn't use anything, just did it. It's more exciting that way, isn't it? I mean the risk makes it more exciting. I expect you find that too. Then I'd be so scared till I got the curse. But it was all right. I got away with it.' She starts to cry. 'We must have been really unlucky that weekend in Cambridge, don't you think? Or d'you think it means I'm infertile now? They say that can happen after an abortion, not often though, they're so expert, well, think of all the practice they get, isn't it sad? If you got me pregnant again, Felix, at least we'd know I'm not infertile. But I'd only have to have another abortion, wouldn't I, and then I'd start worrying all over again, so what's the point? D'you ever want children, Felix? I do. I want a baby so much sometimes I don't know how long I can bear to wait. And other times I think not ever, how revolting, and God, what a burden, twenty years of having to be responsible for someone else.'

Perhaps she's making it all up, he thinks, just a fantasy to annoy or excite him. He remembers the mistress who had the two abortions and then, mercilessly fertile, couldn't face another so had the baby next time and passed it off as her husband's. She got herself sterilised after that but the affair was never quite the same and she and Felix drifted apart. He felt sad about it for quite a long time: he had been fond of her.

Sally comes violently now, clawing at him, sobbing and screaming. Making love, which is oddly how he thinks of it now that she calls it fucking, is more like a fight than it ever was. Sometimes it turns him on, but it can repel him too, making his mind stand back and watch her while his body does its work, looking at this wild animal in his arms, fearing perhaps she's gone past him and he'll never be able to satisfy her again. She comes over and over again like a revenge while he waits and holds on. Then she comes again with him, when he finally comes. 'Yes, now. Come now. Fill me up. Oh Felix. Oh God.' Giving him orders. She's a changed person.

He's not sure if he likes the new Sally but he doesn't want to believe he's corrupted the old one. Sometimes she cries like a child in his arms and nothing he can say or do will comfort her. Then she starts to laugh. Gets up, says she's hungry or thirsty, puts on her clothes while he's still lying there exhausted, makes a sandwich, opens a can of some disgusting fizzy drink, says, 'Oh God, look at the time, I've got a seminar in ten minutes, I'll have to throw you out.'

She doesn't want the champagne he's brought. Hasn't even bothered to put his flowers in a vase, just left them in the sink. Surely she can't still be that upset about the abortion, he thinks, not really; it was last September, for God's sake. Has she been saving all this rage just for him? When she came to see him in hospital she was sweet and forgiving, said it was all worthwhile and she'd never be sorry. How can she blame him when she brought

13

it on herself, letting him think it was safe when it wasn't? If he'd done that to her, she'd have good reason to be angry. Then he might deserve to be treated like this.

'It would have been born in April,' she says. 'Did you think of that, Felix? You should have come to see me then. I'm very popular with guys here, you know, especially when I suck them off the way you taught me. You'd be proud of me. They're not so good at sucking me as you are, though, not nearly. I have to train them but I can't always be bothered.'

She's beating him up with words again. He doesn't want to listen. He hasn't driven all this way to be abused for something that was not his fault.

'It's a funny business, isn't it, Felix?' she says. 'You can get so close to people, sucking them or fucking them, bits of people inside other people and nobody feeling anything except pleasure, and sometimes not even that. I mean, getting right inside someone doesn't make you feel anything for them at all, isn't that odd? Only sometimes it does.'

He wants to hold her, comfort her, but she's pulling on more clothes, some of them quite disgusting and not very clean, leggings and T-shirts and layer upon layer of strange stringy garments. Even her hair isn't newly washed. She's changed, how sad, though nothing can mar her beauty and her youth. 'Don't hug me now, I'm late,' she says.

'I'll wait for you,' he says, 'wouldn't you like that?' though he also longs to run away.

'No, I've got to lock up, a lot of stuff gets nicked around here, and I'm sure you don't want to be locked in, do you?'

'I could guard your stuff for you.'

'I've got to go to a rehearsal afterwards, didn't I tell you?'

So now he can run away with a clear conscience and they are both relieved. Yet such a tender kiss in the doorway, it nearly breaks his heart.

And at other times it's all caution and you must use a condom, I'm so frightened; and she doesn't come at all, just lies there tensely saying, 'Oh, it's not the same, I want to feel you splashing inside me, I really need that. It was lies about those other people, I wanted to make you jealous, I haven't had anyone, I've been too scared, oh Felix, hold me, just hug me, please hug me.'

Safe sex always seems to him a contradiction in terms. If sex isn't dangerous, it hardly counts as sex. He can't bring himself to use the word condom: it is as ugly as the wretched thing itself, somehow sounding both leaden and soggy, which he supposes is appropriate, rather like wet concrete. It could be a term from the building trade. Sheath is slightly better: at least it suggests a sword and a scabbard. There is a touch of danger there, he thinks, reminding him of the swashbuckling films of his youth. But he does whatever she wants. Uses a sheath or doesn't. Comes or doesn't. Screws or hugs. Or both. Or neither. Sometimes she just wants to talk. Sitting cross-legged on her bed or the floor. What does he think of Blake? Reading aloud from a paperback in a self-consciously serious voice:

> 'O Rose, thou art sick!
> The invisible worm,
> That flies in the night,
> In the howling storm,
> Has found out thy bed of crimson joy;
> And his dark secret love
> Does thy life destroy.'

'I think it's all about you,' he wants to say, as she recites with a solemn face, in her poetic voice. 'You and me.' But he doesn't speak.

'Words are there,' she says. 'People come and go, but words go on for ever. Or nearly.' She laughs. He wonders if she is taking drugs. 'Words last. The last shall be first.' He feels out of date. Is she on something?

'No more than anyone else,' she says when he asks her.

And then: 'Oh, don't be silly, of course I'm not, I don't even smoke. I'm just a bit crazy, Felix, aren't you? Aren't we all? You people think we're all on dope but we're not, you just think that because maybe you all were twenty years ago.'

By you people she means older people, middle-aged people. She's never called him that before. People of his age. She's finished abusing him with sex and now she's hitting him with the generation gap. Their bodies a bridge but her arrow-words zinging across the gulf, aimed at him. He's wounded, as he was meant to be. Realistically he's in his prime, of course, isn't he? He knows that really. Doesn't he? But all the same . . .Twenty years. The blissful sixties. Pot and the Pill. No Aids. Short skirts and happy faces.

She's not his Sally any more. And yet he still wants her. And he also doesn't. He goes home to Elizabeth, who is comfortable and real and eleven years older than he is, and he feels restored. He feels young again, the way Sally used to make him feel. He knows who he is, as they say. Leaving Sally to return to Elizabeth is sometimes more satisfying than leaving Elizabeth to return to Sally. There is no challenge to meet. And he can get on with his work.

It's confusing. The girl in the book is young and adoring like the old Sally, but crude and outspoken like the new Sally. It's as if Sally is imitating the girl in the book without even knowing about her. So now there are several Sallys: the one he used to know and the one on the page, the angry swearing one he visits and her *doppelganger* who cries in his arms. He doesn't want so many.

'They made us stop just like that, didn't they?' she says. 'Mum and Richard. Well, they can't win. If we want to be together we will be. Till we've had enough. Till we're ready to have our own ending.'

She doesn't talk about love or permanence any more; she knows it will end again. He should be relieved at her realism but instead he feels disappointed, even slightly insulted. He wonders who will have enough first. He's tired. Well, perhaps not so much tired as over-stimulated. It takes a lot of energy writing the book and keeping Elizabeth happy and driving up and down to Sussex. The campus depresses him, although Sally seems to like it. It's filled with the young in their ugly clothes; they all look grubby and about fifteen. The red-brick buildings offend his sensibilities. The greenery is pleasant, of course, but he can get all that and better in Richmond Park. And the journey is a drag. To Brighton and back in a day, eating and drinking and screwing and still finding time for work. It's too much. Her room depresses him too. He didn't know she was so untidy. Seeing her only in his flat or Helen's house or the hotel in Cambridge, he had no way of knowing. The heaps of clothes piled up on the floor, in a chair, on the bed. The posters blu-tacked to the wall, including one of Helen's ghastly show. Unwashed coffee cups and glasses on the table along with books stacked high and unfinished essays. The wash-basin with a ring of grime around it. Did he ever live like this as an undergraduate? He must have done. He doesn't remember. He can't have done, surely.

Elizabeth knows. She's quite shocked by her own certainty, as if she had diagnosed a fatal illness by intuition and didn't need to go to the doctor. She doesn't want such an advanced skill.

She knows there is someone again and she knows it's Sally. Even before she checks the milometer on Felix's car. She's never done such a thing before and she feels soiled by doing it, guilty of going through his cheque stubs or his wallet, searching his desk or his pockets, looking for evidence. She never used to behave like this: it would have been beneath her dignity. Now she has no dignity left. Not since she saw Sally in her hospital corridor, that child who wasn't a child after all, but

Felix's mistress (that old-fashioned word), blushing and telling lies, pretending to be there on behalf of Richard.

So she looks at the milometer. She doesn't need proof but she wants it. Yes, there are days when he does over a hundred and twenty miles, just right for Brighton, and comes home late, complaining of long hours at the word processor. The knowledge makes her feel quite numb, as if she's beyond pain, like a dead person. She doesn't want to feel like that. She doesn't want to be someone who searches for clues. She doesn't like her new self.

She waits. She doesn't want to believe it. She so much didn't want to believe it the first time that she managed not to, a considerable achievement. But now she must: she has no choice. This is the second time. This is real.

It explains a lot. Why Richard tried to kill Felix. Why Helen doesn't want to be friends any more. She has telephoned Helen, sent her cards, even gone to the house to invite her out, but all with the same result: Helen wants to be left alone. She has said this in various ways. 'I'm not very good company at the moment.' Or: 'Sorry, I'm really trying to get a lot of work done.' Once Elizabeth went round with flowers (as a bribe, she later realised, but it had worked in the past) and Helen still wouldn't ask her in. 'Thank you so much. I'm a bit of a hermit these days, I'm afraid.'

Elizabeth doesn't know what to do. Only Helen knows the whole story, knows more than Elizabeth. Helen holds the key, but she won't hand it over. In a way this is a relief. Elizabeth doesn't have to do anything until she has proof and only Helen can give it to her. She is almost grateful to Helen for refusing to co-operate. She doesn't want proof. She wants everything to be the way it was before any of this happened. She looks back to the idyllic time when Felix merely had affairs with people she didn't know. She is amazed how painless that time looks to her now, although she clearly remembers suffering through it. No wonder Helen thought she was pathetic and ridiculous.

And there is something else. Some skeleton in the closet. It wasn't just an affair, was it? It was more than that. There was some extra dimension of horror. She can't tell how she knows this but it is part of her skin, her bones. There is some awful additional secret that she needs Helen to tell her, but which in some deep hidden place she already knows.

And yet, such is her respect for Felix's work that she doesn't challenge him; she lets the months go by and watches him work and reads what he lets her read and tells him, truthfully, that it's good. Even now, she doesn't want to sabotage the book. She knows how hard it is to do, how much is riding on it. Felix has had to destroy Tony Blythe to get to this book. It's his only option now; he has manoeuvred himself into a necessary corner. So she's supportive: she has to be. And in a way she finds comfort in her familiar role. She reads, listens, praises, cooks. She lets the time pass without recrimination: she remembers when she sat by his hospital bed and thought he might die and promised God anything to let that not happen. And God heard her. Felix is still alive, still here, and still unfaithful. And they still make love, only now sometimes she weeps and he doesn't ask her why.

Helen learns more about loneliness than she ever wanted to know, and she thought she already knew everything. She feels she has gone back in time and all the love and security of the past ten years have never existed. When she wakes she doesn't at first remember whether she has lost Carey or Richard; she only knows she is alone again and has to re-learn all those arid self-sufficient survival skills that she thought she had put away for ever.

Sally treats her gently but with slightly distant sympathy, as for a relative who has had an embarrassing accident like falling down in the street, a misfortune, certainly, but perhaps one that could have been avoided with a little extra care. Helen feels she has let Sally down. She has turned back into a problem after being a tower of strength. Their roles are reversed, as if Sally were the patient disappointed mother and Helen the errant daughter returning home after yet another failed marriage. Helen hears unspoken criticism. 'First my father leaves you, then my stepfather. What is the matter with you that you can't get a man to stay with you and let me off the hook? I'm very fond of you but I can't be responsible for you for ever, you know.' Sally watches her now where once she would have hugged her. She brings her drinks and snacks. She often asks if Helen is all right, but she clearly wants the answer yes. And there is a certain detachment in her manner, as if she were saying, 'Look, I'm sorry, but I can't get too involved this time. We've been here before and I've got to look after myself.' She goes out with her friends a lot and when she comes in she looks at Helen apprehensively, as if hoping not to hear of any fresh disasters. 'I hate Richard,' she says one day. 'I think you're better off without him.' Helen wants to say, 'Now you know how I feel about Felix,' and having made up her mind not to, suddenly hears the words coming out of her mouth. She is surprised at herself. Sally stares at her for a moment, defiantly, then shrugs. 'Just don't talk about him, all right?' she says. 'I don't ever want to hear you mention his name again.' She goes out. She slams the door hard behind her, shaking the house.

The abortion weighs heavily between them: at any rate Helen blames Sally's detachment on that. They get through the Easter vac as best they can but when Sally goes back to Sussex for the summer term Helen feels certain they are both thinking that now is the time the baby would have been born. She can see the thought in Sally's face, but she still believes she did the right thing and she has to hang on to that belief, or else all this pain is for nothing. They have a chilly farewell, although they hug and kiss on both cheeks. And then Helen is really alone.

20

She tells her friends: 'Richard and I have separated. And I don't want to discuss it.' The few friends she has, that is. She has never had much time or need for friends. They got in the way of work. They made demands. They drained her energy. She couldn't spread herself so thin, not with two days a week at college and the other days in the studio ... time with Sally ... time with Richard. Where could she fit in friends?

Now perhaps she would like some, although she doesn't want to be an object of pity. Now she seems to have a lot of time. The days are hard to fill and the studio feels as empty as the house, which puzzles her. She expected it of the house, where she lived with Richard, but not the studio, which has always been hers alone. It's ten years since she lived there with Sally, since Richard came and found them. She almost used the word rescued. Though at the time she thought it was the other way round, that it was she who rescued him from Inge.

Inge. He's living with Inge. She knows anyway, but he leaves her a note on the kitchen table along with his wedding ring. An address, a phone number, just to hurt her. He doesn't love Inge. It can't last. It's just cheaper, somewhere to hide, to punish her, to punish himself, to atone. She understands all that.

So she tells herself. But she takes off her wedding ring too and leaves Richard a note to stop him coming round for clothes and things while she's out. She wants his keys back: after all he doesn't live here any more. Why should he walk in as if he did? It's like being burgled by a close friend. After each of his visits there's a wounding gap in the bookcase, the wardrobe, the record collection. But she's also surprised how few possessions he has. How easily he can move from one home to the other. How she and Inge each have a complete home waiting for him to enter. She remembers him saying bitterly that he was only a lodger in her home and not even a very good one: he couldn't pay enough rent. She imagines Inge's joy, and it makes her feel sick. She remembers the crazed creature on her doorstep shrieking, 'You've lost him for ever,' when it seemed like a curse but not a reality.

When she sees him she imagines he will say he's made a terrible mistake, will plead to come back. Each time she waits for these words. But he is polite and distant. Seeing him gives her a terrible pain in the heart as well as a sense of disbelief. And then the visits stop. He's finally taken all his books and clothes and records. She's really alone. She keeps the two wedding rings in an old empty biscuit tin in the kitchen because she can't bring herself to throw them away.

Only Elizabeth pesters her. Is Elizabeth perhaps her only true friend? She takes bitter pleasure in rejecting Elizabeth, using up all the anger meant for Richard, who has left her unjustly. Or for Sally, who has cost her the marriage.

She tries to work but often only succeeds in going to the studio and sitting in front of an empty canvas, pulling bits of horsehair stuffing out of the old armchair. She tells herself that salvation lies in work but she can't do any. It's as much as she can do to get herself through the day. She is so tired. She sleeps and sleeps and always wakes exhausted. The more she sleeps, the more exhausted she gets. When she does work she finds she doesn't want to paint any more: all she can do are charcoal drawings of the skull she keeps in the studio, dozens of drawings, at first just the abstract shape, then gradually becoming more representational, each drawing only marginally different from the previous one, as if for an animated cartoon. The drawings are good, she can see that, but she hasn't drawn like this since she was a student. In the final version, as realistic (lifelike, death-like?) as a photograph, she draws the skull in a suit, complete with collar and tie. Then she sits and laughs out loud at it, rocking backwards and forwards in the disembowelled chair. She thinks she is going mad, but it doesn't matter.

So she drags herself through the spring, the summer. In

the long vacation Sally rides around the States on a Greyhound bus. When she comes back she goes to visit her father. Finally coming home in September she seems to have run out of places to hide. Now she sits in the garden sheltering behind a book, or stays in her room playing loud music. And occasionally she goes out to lunch or dinner, always looking her best and never saying where she is going. And suddenly Helen knows. And she also can't believe it.

She says to Sally, 'You're seeing him again, aren't you?'

Sally says insolently, 'Who?'

'Felix.'

'I thought we agreed you wouldn't mention his name.'

'Are you seeing him?'

'It's none of your business.'

Helen screams. They are both shocked by the sudden loud noise, more so by such embarrassing, uncharacteristic loss of control.

'For God's sake,' Sally says.

PART ONE

Inge tells herself it is only a matter of time. If she is patient and loving. If she can wait. If she puts no pressure on him, eventually he will turn to her.

At first the triumph of his return carries her through. The thrill of victory, the knowledge that he has left the cow and come home makes her feel very powerful. Just having him in the house every day and lying beside him every night is enough. At first she can hardly sleep because knowing he is there keeps her awake to marvel at the knowledge, like a mother checking to make sure that the newborn is still breathing. She remembers all the nights she slept alone, the desert she lived in for so many years while he was happy with someone else. She has to stay awake to assimilate the new reality of her life, to absorb how much it has changed. Small mundane things, like seeing post arrive addressed to him, please her vastly, proving that he lives here again.

But as the weeks pass and he doesn't make love to her, her confidence ebbs away. How long does she have to wait? What if he never does? When patience is exhausted she tries provocation: new scent and seductive underwear, rubbing her naked body against him in bed instead of accepting routine hugs and kisses and clothing. He doesn't respond: he ignores her and then moves away. He says, 'I'm sorry, Inge, it's going to take time.'

She says, 'How much time?'

He says, 'I don't know.'

She says, 'But Richard, I can't live like this, I've tried so hard but it's killing me.' She hadn't meant to be so dramatic, but all the frustration and disappointment of the past weeks wells up and spills over. She doesn't believe he has any idea how much it has cost her.

He says, 'I know and I'm sorry.'

She weeps and he comforts her. They fall into uneasy sleep. Over the next few weeks it happens again and again. A pattern is created that torments her and she can't leave it alone. Knowing she should let him be, she keeps on and on, worrying at him, until one night he actually starts to cry and says, 'I'm sorry, I can't help it, there's nothing I can do about it. Not yet.'

She says, 'It's all right, it's my fault.' She tries to comfort him and he pushes her away. She is terrified that they may live like this for ever.

The boys don't help. Karl doesn't speak to his father at all. He talks across him directly to Inge as if Richard isn't there, even when he is sitting next to him at the table. It gives her an eerie sensation, as if Richard really is invisible, as if only she and Peter can see him, as if he is a phantom of their joint imagination who might actually disappear at any moment. 'Talk to your father, Karl,' she says, alarmed. 'I'm talking to you, Mum,' Karl says, eating. 'My father left home years ago. Don't you remember? He went off with another woman.'

Karl is only present for meals and sleep. If he's not at the kitchen table, he's out or in his room, while Peter hangs around Richard asking for help with homework ('D'you know anything about Bolivia, Dad?'), trips to football ('Can we go to the match on Saturday, Dad?'), anything to get his attention, behaving as if he were much younger, perhaps trying to turn back the clock, Inge thinks. He watches Richard's face anxiously to gauge his mood. It breaks her heart to see him try so hard. He reminds her of herself.

One day she hears him asking, 'You won't go away again, Dad, will you?' She holds her breath for Richard's reply and when it comes it sounds frighteningly burdened. 'No, of course I won't.' She doesn't know how Peter feels about it, but it doesn't reassure her at all.

The harmony between the boys is disrupted: they quarrel with each other because Peter is nice to Richard and Karl ignores him. If Peter says, 'What d'you think, Dad?' Karl will say, 'Why bother asking him? He may not be here tomorrow.' Peter thumps Karl. Karl shoves Peter. Inge says, 'Oh God, please don't.' Richard says, 'Karl, if you're angry with me tell me how you feel, don't take it out on Peter.' Karl stands up. 'I'm going out now, Mum, okay?' he says pleasantly. 'I won't be late.' He goes out. He is taller than Richard, heavy, threatening. He is seventeen now and growing into himself; he is a powerful presence in the house. Inge is distraught at his hostility yet also somehow thrilled by his arrogance: it is like having a champion in the lists, a lover to spring to her aid, Lancelot defending Guinevere when Arthur is cruel.

She goes to her doctor, who is also Richard's doctor now. She values him. He has known her for many years, coped with her tears, prescribed many drugs, listened to her, talked to her, seen her through everything. She says, 'What can I do? I can't live like this. It's three months now. It's torture. We're living together and sleeping together and we don't make love. I can't bear it. Why did he come back? It's almost worse than being alone. At least then I knew I was alone and I could have other people. But now he's with me and not with me. Can you help me? How can I make him want me? Or how can I stop wanting him? I've got to do one or the other.'

She says bravely to Richard, 'I've talked to Dr Shaw and he was very nice and understanding about it.' Seeing his shocked expression she rushes on before he can interrupt her. 'There are people who can help us. We can go to marriage guidance. Or he can send us to see a therapist. It's all right. There's someone he recommends who has a private practice in Hampstead, only it's too expensive, but that doesn't matter because he does one evening a week at the health centre and we can see him there for nothing, except there's a waiting list, of course. Will you come with me?'

As she talks her nervousness goes and she begins to feel hopeful and excited.

His eyes close, as if to shut her out. He says, 'Oh God, Inge . . . can't you let it rest?'

'But we have to do something. I can't live like this. And the boys . . . If we were happier they might be too.'

'That has nothing to do with sex,' he says wearily. 'Karl won't forgive me for being away. He got used to being the man of the house and he doesn't want me taking his place. And Peter wants me to make up for all those missing years. Those are two opposite things, Inge, it's hard to do them both at once.'

'They know we're not happy,' she says, 'and it makes them worse.'

'And I'm still trying to get used to the new job,' he goes on as if he has not heard her. 'It's a tough school and I'm rusty. It's not easy getting back into teaching. I want to make you happy but I've got a lot on my plate and I'm very tired.'

'Are you still in love with her?' she says, shaking with fright, not knowing where she finds the courage to ask, or what she will do if he says yes.

'I wouldn't be here, would I?' he says. It's not the positive denial she needs to hear but she senses she won't do better.

'Well, we have to wait for an appointment,' she says, 'so maybe it will be in the summer holidays when you're not so tired. And if you won't come with me I'll go by myself. Perhaps he can teach me how to bear the pain of living like this and I won't have to bother you any more.'

He doesn't answer.

Weeks pass. Then Dr Shaw offers her a cancellation before the end of term. She tells Richard. He shakes his head. She thinks he looks relieved.

'I can't – it's a parents' evening.'

She looks at him incredulously.

'I can't miss it. It's part of the job. You know that.'

'But Richard, how can you say that? This is our marriage. Isn't that more important? What did you come back for if you don't want to make it all right?' She is so shocked. And she senses she is on firm ground. 'You're glad to have an excuse, aren't you?'

He says, 'Look, Inge, I will come with you, but it'll have to be another time. I can't miss a PTA meeting. What would I say to Kate?'

'Kate?'

'My head of department. How could I explain it to her?'

'You could say you want to save your marriage. She's a woman, she would understand.'

'Perhaps, but she'd also tell me to choose some other evening to do it. Inge, be reasonable. It'd be very embarrassing. It's too short notice.'

'Of course it is, it's a cancellation. We're very lucky to get it.'

'And I'm very lucky to have this job. I've been out of teaching a long time. Another evening, all right?'

His tone makes it clear that's the end of it. She supposes it's a kind of victory that he's promised to go with her at all. She says, 'Yes, all right. And this time I shall go by myself.'

Inge likes him on sight. Perhaps she is so desperate, she thinks, that she would like anyone who might help her. But it feels like more than that. There is something reassuring about him, even something familiar. She has never met him before yet he seems like someone she already knows. It's a strange feeling.

31

'Hullo,' he says, in a very casual, friendly way. 'I'm Michael Green.' He is rather thick-set with dark receding hair that is turning grey. She thinks he must be about fifty. When he stands up to shake hands with her he is scarcely taller than she is, so she doesn't have to look up at him. They are on a level with each other. His eyes are dark behind horn-rimmed glasses.

'I'm Inge Morgan,' she says, and they shake hands. He has a very firm handshake, but then so does she, perhaps especially so today. Even as she shakes hands with him she thinks it is like grabbing hold of a life raft.

'Have a seat. Maybe Dr Shaw has explained, I'm not a doctor, I'm a counsellor and psychotherapist. I'm not here to tell you what to do, but sometimes it can help to talk about how you feel, and look at the choices you have, maybe make some changes if you want to. How would you like to start?'

'I don't know. I'm very nervous.'

'Take a deep breath.' He smiles encouragingly. 'That usually helps me when I'm nervous.'

She tries but it doesn't. 'Well, it's my husband. He couldn't come tonight, he's a teacher and he had a meeting at school. But he'll come next time. He promised.'

'So you're hoping you'll both be here in future but tonight you have a chance to talk to me on your own.'

'Yes. Only I don't know what to say. I've been so anxious to get here but . . . '

'How are you feeling right now, apart from being nervous?'

Suddenly tears well up and spill over. She's so surprised she can't speak.

'Yes, you're very sad, aren't you?'

She nods. She cries for what feels like minutes and she can't say anything at all. It is such a relief. She hadn't realised how hard she had been trying not to cry.

'We don't make love at all,' she says, when she can

finally speak. 'There's been nothing since he came back. That's three months. That's too long, don't you think?'

'Well, it's too long if it makes you unhappy and it obviously does. What I think doesn't matter. Some couples make love every day and others never do. There are lots of variations in between. The feelings are more important than the frequency.'

'I don't think he loves me any more,' she says despairingly.

'You sound really hopeless when you say that.'

'Yes, I am. Did Dr Shaw tell you about us? I told him he could, I thought it would save time.'

'Just the basic facts. Tell me if I've got them right. You were married ten years, you have two teenage sons, you separated ten years ago and your husband remarried. Then you got back together in April.'

'I don't know why he came back,' she says.

'Have you asked him?'

'No. I'm afraid. He said he didn't know if it would work. I thought if I was patient . . . But I have been and it doesn't help.'

Michael Green leans back in his chair. 'D'you have any physical contact at all? Are you affectionate with each other?'

'Oh, he hugs me sometimes. Or he kisses the top of my head. That's all. He never touches me as a woman. There's no desire.'

'And you feel very sad about that. D'you feel anything else?'

'Yes.' She hesitates. 'Sometimes I hate him. He came back but he doesn't want me. It's not fair. He shouldn't have come back if he doesn't want me.'

'You sound very angry with him.'

'Yes, I'd like to kill him sometimes.' She's quite shocked to hear herself say that. 'That's a terrible thing to say, isn't it?'

'It would be a terrible thing to do,' he says calmly, 'but it's all right to have the feeling. Any feeling. You're not actually going to go home and kill him, are you?'

'No. But I tried to kill myself twice. I cut my wrists when he left me and I took an overdose when he married the cow. But it didn't work.' She smiles faintly. 'Here I am.'

'Did you really want to die when you did that?'

'Yes, I was so unhappy but I wasn't very efficient. I wanted to die but I wanted him to come back more, so maybe . . . I don't know. It's a long time ago now. I've waited so long for him to come back and now he has but he doesn't want to touch me and I can't bear it. I know you can't make him want to but if he never does we're going to break up again, aren't we? I mean we can't live like this for ever. It's not a marriage. And I'll have been through all this for nothing.' She hears herself sounding desperate and she's terrified. 'I don't know what to do. You're my last hope.'

'Well, some people agree to have marriage without sex. But you obviously don't want that.'

'No. It's like being tortured.'

'So sex is very important to you.'

'Yes, I love it. I think it's magic.'

'Is it just with your husband you feel like that?'

'No, it's special with him, well it was, it's so long ago, but I had lovers after he left me and I always thought it was wonderful, even though I didn't love them. But I can't do that when we're together. I don't want to. So I'm trapped. I have to live with nothing.'

'So you've got a lot of intense feeling invested in this marriage. And the way you see it, if you don't make love you're bound to break up again.' He looks thoughtful. 'That must put a lot of pressure on both of you.'

'Yes, it does, but what can I do? That's how I feel.'

'Well, is there any way we can take a bit of the pressure off? Say we had a time limit, another three months perhaps, when you knew there was no chance of making love?'

'There's no chance now.'

'No, but it sounds as if you're constantly hoping and being disappointed, and your husband must be aware

34

he's disappointing you, on a daily basis. It's very hard to live like that. You need time to build up some goodwill, don't you, instead of all this pressure. And at the same time you could be thinking about the options. If you start making love again and you stay together, fine, that's your ideal. You say you don't want a marriage without sex and you don't want lovers, so those are two options you've considered and rejected. What about the final option of breaking up, because there are only these four options, really, aren't there?'

She shivers. 'I can't bear to think about it.'

'I can see it's very painful for you. But is it the worst thing that can happen? After all, it's happened before and you survived. As you said, you're here.'

'You think it's going to happen again, don't you?'

'I think it's too early to say. But it might be a relief to you if you could think about it as something possible that you can tolerate, although it would be very sad. Otherwise it's a bit like thinking about death all the time, it stops you doing anything else. You're so sad and angry about not making love and you're so frightened of breaking up that you're sort of squashing yourself to death between these two options.'

'Yes,' she says, amazed. 'That's exactly how it feels.'

'It's quite natural to feel like that, of course,' he says, 'but it doesn't leave you much room to manoeuvre. D'you think you can ease up on yourself a bit?'

'How?' she says. 'How can I do that? I don't know what you mean.'

'Well, your husband has agreed to come with you, so that's hopeful. And there's no time limit on this, you know. You're not going to be shot if you don't have a sexy marriage within a certain time. And if you do break up eventually you're not going to kill yourself, are you?'

'No,' she says. 'I suppose not.'

'So your life must have some value to you, even if it's not very happy at the moment. Can you hang on to the idea of that value, of you as a person, quite independently of your husband? Can you try doing that, as an exercise? Concentrating quite deliberately on the idea that you are important, whether or not you are having sex or staying married.'

When she gets home Richard is already back from the PTA meeting. She wonders how long he has been in and whether he could have come with her after all. He doesn't say anything when she comes in so she says, 'Aren't you going to ask me how I got on?'

'I can see you've been crying, so he probably feels very sorry for you and thinks you're married to a pig. I expect you had a lovely time telling him how badly I treat you.'

She's shocked. 'It wasn't like that. He was very nice. He's there to help us, not to take sides. He said at the end that you can go by yourself next time if you like, so that we'll both have had some time alone with him. That's very fair, don't you think?'

'I don't want any time alone with him. I said I'd come with you and I will but I don't want to talk about it now.'

'Well, we have another appointment in two weeks. You'll have broken up by then, won't you, so you won't have another PTA meeting.'

'When you've been apart for ten years,' Richard says, 'three months doesn't seem very long to get used to each other again. At least it doesn't to me. I can't perform to order. I thought you as a man would understand that.'

'Is that what you feel you're being asked to do – perform to order?'

'Isn't that why I'm here?'

'I thought you agreed to come with your wife to talk about how you feel in the marriage.'

'Oh really? You make it sound like a tea-party.'

'You sound very angry,' Michael Green says calmly.

'That's probably because I am.'

'And you felt I as a man would understand.'

'Well, you obviously don't.'

'What are you angry about? What exactly d'you want me to understand?'

'Christ, you know what this is all about, so don't pretend you don't. My wife wants me to make love to her and I can't. All right? It's very embarrassing and very humiliating, but it's a fact, so there we are.'

'Have you actually tried?'

'What?'

'Have you tried to make love to your wife?'

'No. I'm sure she told you that. Didn't she?'

'She is here. You could ask her.'

'So I could. Inge, did you tell him I haven't even tried?'

'Yes.'

'You see? We actually agree about something. Are you playing games?'

'No, I'm trying to find out if you think you have. If maybe you feel you've made an approach and been rejected, either of you. Sometimes two people can see these things very differently, particularly when they're emotionally involved.'

'Which you're not, of course.'

'Well, I'd like to be able to help you help yourselves, that's what I'm here for. It doesn't actually make much difference to my life if you make love to each other or not, if you stay married or not. But it might make quite a big difference to your life.'

There is a silence in the room. Richard feels his anger has nowhere else to go. He can feel it wearing out, like an insect battering itself against the glass.

'You see,' Michael Green says, 'there's an obvious difference between trying and failing, or being rejected, and not trying at all. Between being afraid to try and not wanting to try. I'd like to get a clear picture of what's

37

actually happening before I make any assumptions. If you haven't tried then you haven't failed and you haven't been rejected either. Inge, have you tried to make love to Richard?'

She hesitates. 'Not really. Well, he knows I want to. I've tried to be affectionate, of course.'

'Well, so have I. For God's sake, Inge, be fair.'

'D'you actually feel affectionate, Richard?' Michael asks.

'Not always, no. Sometimes.'

'Inge?'

'Yes, usually. Well, sometimes I feel angry and miserable. It's hard to feel affectionate all the time when you're not touching very much.'

'Have you talked to each other about how you feel?'

'Well, not really. It's difficult. We've had rows more than we've talked, haven't we?'

'Yes, I suppose we have.'

'Well, rows or silences.'

'All right, hold it there a minute. That's only the second time you've actually spoken to each other this session without me asking you to. Is there anything you'd like to say to each other here that you can't say at home?'

'No.'

'Yes. I'd like to ask him—'

'He's here. Ask him.'

She turns. 'Richard, why did you come back?'

A long silence. He knows he has to lie. He feels the lie screaming into the silence, announcing itself as a lie.

'Because I wanted to try again.' It could have been worse. She might have asked him if he still loves Helen. He might not have been able to manage that lie. He wonders if the slimy therapist can tell he's lying.

'Then why don't you ever make love to me?'

'I don't know. I'm tired. I'm not ready. It's too soon.'

'So at this stage we don't really know if it's fear of failure that's stopping you, or lack of desire, or something unresolved from the past. There's no question of blame

38

in any of this, of course. It's not anyone's fault. D'you see that?'

'Oh, sure.'

'Some people feel sex in marriage has more to do with duty than pleasure, anyway, and that puts them off. Do either of you feel that?'

'No, never.'

'Perhaps.'

'D'you notice how often your answers are opposite – when one says yes, the other says no? And yet you're here together. Might there be a positive side to this conflict? D'you think perhaps you need each other to express things you can't quite manage for yourselves?'

'D'you mean like attraction of opposites?'

'Something like that. D'you remember why you got married in the first place?'

'We fell in love.'

'It was a very strong sexual attraction. A bit ironic now we're here.'

'And I got pregnant, of course.'

'So maybe you got married faster than you would have done?'

'Well, obviously. And we were very young.'

'Is there anything Inge could do now that would help you, Richard?'

'Yes. Leave me alone. Give me a bit of peace. Give me some space, some more time. I don't know how much I need. I had a sort of nervous breakdown earlier this year.'

'That must have been tough. Would you like to tell me some more about that?'

'No. It's private. It's irrelevant to all this, anyway. It just explains why I haven't got much energy. As well as the new job, of course.'

'So that's an area you'd like to keep to yourself. And you're feeling quite burdened at work. Okay. Inge, if you try to ease up on Richard a bit, what could he do in return to help you?'

'I need him – sorry. Richard, I need you to touch me more often. If I really thought you cared about me, maybe I wouldn't even mind if we don't make love for a bit longer.'

'All right, so you want very different things from each other. You, Inge, want loving and touching more than anything, and you, Richard, want more time and space and peace. Those are very different things and yet you're together in the marriage and you're both here. Is there any way you could meet each other, so you each get a little of what you want? If we rule out the possibility of sex for the moment, to take off the feeling of pressure, could you trade each other a bit of peace and space for a bit of touching? We're coming up to the August break, so I'm going to suggest a few things you might like to try in the meantime, things some people find helpful. It's entirely up to you, of course. Nobody can force you to do anything you don't want to do. But you wouldn't be here if you didn't want something to change.'

He outlines his suggestions and they both listen in silence.

'How does that sound?' he says when he has finished. 'D'you think you could manage any of that and let me know how you get on?'

'Yes, I'm sure we could.'

'Worth a try, I suppose.'

When they all stand up to say goodbye Richard notices that he is several satisfying inches taller than Michael Green: he could even spit on his head.

'He's nice, isn't he?' Inge says on their way home. 'He really understands. And he doesn't mind if you're rude to him.'

'I think he's revolting,' Richard says. 'He probably gets off on other people's sex lives.'

'Oh Richard, please don't hate him. He's trying to help

us.' She puts her arm through his. 'I'm so glad you came with me.'

August passes slowly. The boys are out a lot or away staying with friends, so they are often alone in the house. It feels strange, like being young again, before they were parents.

When Inge caresses him he thinks of Helen and feels the stirring of desire. He has to tell her to stop before she notices what is happening. Reluctantly, when he can't put it off any longer, he strokes Inge's back, her neck, her shoulders, her arms. Safe in the knowledge that she can't see him, he looks at her helpless human body with pity not rage, her freckled skin, her brown hair spread out across the pillow. She could be any woman, not just Inge, whom he has injured. If he shuts his eyes he can imagine she is Helen, and waves of longing and loss sweep over him. He opens his eyes quickly.

'Oh, that's so nice,' she says. 'It's so lovely to have you touching me again.'

He thinks of all the harm he has done her and he feels sad. None of it is her fault, that she was too much for him, that he wasn't enough for her, that he fell in love with Helen. Perhaps it was not even his fault either. It was all an accident, and they are paying for it with their lives.

'Well, we tried and it didn't work,' Richard says.

'Is that why you came with me?' Inge says. 'So you could say you'd tried and it doesn't work?'

'What did you try?'

'We did the exercises, the way you said. Well, some of them. The massage. We stroked each other. God, this is embarrassing.'

41

'I thought it was nice,' Inge says. 'It was lovely to be touching again.'

'How often did you do them?'

'Enough.'

'Not very often,' Inge says. 'Maybe twice a week.'

'It felt very artificial,' Richard says. 'I told you it would.'

'So you were right,' Michael says. 'Is that important to you?'

'What?'

'To be right?'

'God, what are you trying to prove? Any fool can see that stroking you ex-wife after a ten-year separation is going to be embarrassing. Not to mention reporting on it afterwards to a perfect stranger.'

'Yes, none of this is easy, is it? In fact it's quite painful for you, isn't it? So you're feeling pretty angry about the exercises. Did they have any erotic effect?'

'If you mean did I get a hard-on, no.'

'Did you want to?'

'What d'you mean?'

'Were you hoping the exercises might give you an erection and lead to making love? Or put you in the mood for making love without an erection perhaps?'

'No. I don't feel ready for that. Anyway, you said we didn't have to try.'

'That's right. The exercises were only meant to get you both used to each other's bodies again. Perhaps help you start to feel more relaxed and playful.'

'It would have been nice, though,' Inge says. 'It would have been a lovely surprise. Sometimes I thought maybe it was going to happen. I was very excited and I thought you were just a little bit excited too.'

'Were you, Richard?'

'No.'

'Did you try any of the other things I suggested?'

'Such as what?'

'Well, you remember I said you might like to read

some of the books on the list, or watch an erotic video together, or use fantasy, or just talk to each other about your feelings.'

'No, we didn't do any of that.'

'We did talk a bit about the past,' Inge says. 'It was very sad. I think maybe that put us off making love.'

'I think we just need more time,' Richard says. 'A lot more time.'

'And yet you're still here,' Michael says. 'You've both come back. You didn't cancel, although you both sound a bit disappointed. It's early days yet and none of us thought anything would happen very fast. So what would you like to do next? What would feel helpful? Do you want to go on with the exercises? Or is there something in the past that's blocking you and stopping you moving on? Maybe we need to talk more about why you broke up and why you got back together.'

Richard feels total panic. He had thought it was bad enough already, being asked intimate questions and given embarrassing tasks to perform, but far worse horrors suddenly open up in front of him. If I walk out now, he thinks, I'll be in the wrong, but if I stay, he'll get to Helen. I'm not having Helen brought into this.

He thinks grimly to himself that there is only one thing, no matter how difficult, that will get him out of the whole ghastly mess, that will shut her up and allow him to stop going to the godawful therapist, but with honour, not as an admission of defeat. And that is what he will somehow have to do.

He must try to accommodate her. With a morning erection sometimes, a brief coupling when they are both half asleep and he can pretend it's not really happening, or

43

stay lost in a dream of Helen. At night after drinking a lot but not too much. In the dark or with his eyes shut, so he doesn't have to see her eager, loving face; or from behind, so he doesn't have to kiss her and it's easier to pretend she's someone else. Sometimes with a violent fantasy of Felix, of trying to kill him, not just with a blow but close in, hands round his throat, choking him to death. Or thinking of Felix with Sally. Pictures of Felix and Sally together, uncensored. The sicker the fantasy, he finds, the harder he gets. It still isn't very hard but it's enough. Honour is satisfied and Inge is happy. He hears the words he dreads, over and over again. 'Oh Richard, I love you so much,' followed by the ultimate self-sacrificing gift: 'It's all right, you don't have to say it.'

And he doesn't say it. He can't. He's already done all he can by coming inside her. Not well, not often, and not for long, but he's done it. That's his gift to her. It's all he can manage and more than he wants to give. He feels relief that the long struggle is over but also disgust that he has the sort of marriage where only ugly fantasies can excite him. The therapist has told him that this is all right, even normal, it seems, whatever that means, but Richard still doesn't like it. He wants to be excited by love.

'It's all right,' Inge says. 'I don't know how to tell you. I'm so happy. It's all right. We – we're actually making love again.'

'Ah,' Michael says. 'I'm glad.'

'It's embarrassing, it feels very private. But I had to come and tell you. It's all right. I'm so grateful. We needn't come and see you any more. I can't believe it but it's all right.'

'Well, that's splendid. I'm very pleased.'

'Thank you for helping us.'

'You helped yourselves.'

'Well, I don't know what to say now. I feel so silly being here. I don't have a problem any more. I should have cancelled and written you a letter. I'm using a space that someone else needed.'

'And that's all right.'

'I just feel so happy, I wanted to tell you in person.'

'It's really nice to hear good news.'

'Well, you can cancel our other appointments and give them to other people now.'

'Yes.' He pauses. 'Unless you'd like to go on coming by yourself for a while. Would that be helpful?'

'Yes.' She's surprised. 'Could I do that? I know how busy you are.'

'Well, you might like a bit more time to sort out your feelings. These are big changes happening very suddenly. You might like a little support while you go through them.'

Afterwards, walking home, she wonders why she was so eager to accept, why she didn't just say no, I don't need that. But something about the offer seemed reassuring, like a safety net. Richard need never know, she tells herself.

After a while Helen starts to get used to the pain. It feels familiar, almost comforting, like a child's rag doll or piece of luggage, giving her a sense of security. Tentatively she begins trying to direct the pain into her work, use it as if it were an actual implement. She isn't quite sure how to do this, but she does it nevertheless. She is surprised by the extra dimension it gives her, this new sharp etching tool inside her. She experiments with technique, colour, texture, shape: she feels freer, she now realises, than she has for years, like a student again. She even dares to be excited by the change of her work. If she can be a different kind of painter, perhaps she can be a different kind of woman. Locked into a marriage that was ailing more than she knew, perhaps her work was landlocked too, without her realising it. She takes to arriving earlier and earlier at the studio, sometimes sleeping there as in the old days when Sally was a child and they were alone together. She feels a little crazy in her isolation but the knowledge that she is working again comforts her.

It is autumn. Perhaps that too gives her renewed energy, the cooler weather, the supportive structure of the new term at college. She has to accept that she can't control Sally, who will see Felix if she wants to. Sally can't be protected indefinitely. She is a grown woman now and entitled to ruin her life in her own way, just like Helen. Felix may not even be the worst thing that can happen to Sally, incredible as that seems: she may be doing drugs at college or sleeping around and catching HIV or getting herself raped and murdered by an intruder: any nightmare that Helen cares to imagine. It's a hard fact to swallow, the hardest fact of parenthood, that you cannot save your own child from pain or death, not even by laying down your life. The anxiety she feels about Sally, which could turn into an obsession if she let it (another pregnancy would be the end of the world, she thinks) can be transmuted into anger. Anger is safer. Anger mobilises her. And anger with Sally leads her to anger with Richard. Perhaps finally it is the anger that saves her, not the autumn energy or the experimental work. Pure distilled rage sets her free.

Magdalen phones while she is safely in this mood, not on one of the evenings when she still has a relapse, goes home and cries and gets drunk. Magdalen, who has never been married, has left her alone through the summer, announcing, 'I'm going to give you time to get over it,' as if this can be precisely measured. Perhaps Magdalen is right. Helen isn't sure of anything any more.

'Helen, I want you to come out with me next week,'

46

Magdalen says abruptly. 'It will do you good. You've been mouldering away far too long.'

Helen opens her mouth to say something sharp and resentful: she loathes having good done to her, especially by Magdalen, who should know this by now. It's an uneasy relationship at best between painter and dealer, a mixture of friendship and necessity and financial bitterness, but she has been too long with Magdalen to change now: it would be like another divorce and she lacks the energy for it. Besides, she knows Magdalen believes in her work and that is all that really matters.

Just before she has time to be rude Magdalen says, 'Jordan Griffiths is back from New York and he's having a retrospective. I think he's grossly overrated but I know you like his work.'

Helen hesitates. She hasn't seen Jordan for fifteen years and he was the only person who meant anything to her after Carey and before Richard, though Magdalen can't know that. It would be fun to see him again and he is still one of the few painters whose work she respects. It seems ages since she has had any fun.

'How is he these days?' she says. Magdalen usually knows any gossip there is.

'Well, he's getting ridiculous prices, as even you in your ivory tower must realise.'

'You know I don't read the papers any more,' Helen says. It seems an inadequate summary of her life over the past few months, with everything fined down to mere survival: work and sleep, rage and tears. Learning to be alone. Waiting for something to happen. She has been inside as truly as if she were in jail, locked up in herself. She hasn't let in any extraneous information because there didn't seem to be any room for it in her head.

'Well, if you lived in the real world you'd know he's hit the jackpot in the States.'

'That's not the real world,' she says, defending herself. 'That's the art world.' Besides, what she meant was, How is he in himself?

'Well, you're part of it, like it or not, and it wouldn't hurt you to turn up occasionally, see what's going on.'

Now she would like to refuse because she responds badly to bullying. But she wants to see Jordan again, now that Magdalen has planted the idea, although she had not thought of him for years. Magdalen has been very clever.

'Well, of course I know he's successful,' she says. 'I just didn't realise he's filthy rich. I'm glad. He deserves it.'

'His wife died of cancer last year,' Magdalen says. 'I think that's taken the shine off things a bit.'

The gallery is crowded and noisy and Helen sees lots of people she knows. But she can't concentrate on any of them. Her eyes are searching for Jordan even while she is looking at his paintings, vast slabs of interrelated colours and shapes which dominate the space. Jordan has never lost his allegiance to Hans Hofmann while developing his own style. She would like to come back and look at them quietly with no one else there. It would be a rare pleasure to examine Jordan's progress over the past thirty years.

Memories of the affair come back to her as she stands in front of each painting. It hadn't lasted long, six months perhaps, because he was still married to his second wife at the time and Helen was still mourning the loss of Carey. She had thought Jordan was unreliable, even a rogue, and she was trying to cure herself of rogues. He had seemed like Carey, only much more talented, and she had said goodbye to him because she didn't want a messy life any more. Then a year later she heard he had divorced and gone to live in New York where he remarried. The news had hurt her more than she expected.

Now she finally sees him at the end of the room, talking to people, and she walks towards him. He is standing near a large charcoal drawing of an emaciated woman, hollow-eyed and almost bald, lying in bed propped up on pillows. She is smiling slightly but she looks very close to death. It is the only representational picture in the show, the only portrait, the only charcoal drawing, the only black and white and grey object amongst all the colour and he is standing beside it as if they were a couple. Helen shivers; she feels a real shock. She notices that although people cluster round him they avoid this picture and there remains an empty space in front of it like a charmed circle that no one will enter.

As she approaches him she realises that the attraction she once felt so strongly is still there. She is amazed: she had imagined herself to be sexually dead after all that has happened. She had thought that if Richard never came back she would put all her energy into her work for the rest of her life, but now she is near to Jordan she is looking at him with actual desire.

It's not that he has improved with age, as some men do. In fact he is falling apart. He has put on a lot of weight, so that he needs all his height to carry it, and his hair has turned grey and quite a lot of it has fallen out. He also has the look of a man who has gone through a great ordeal and only just managed to survive. There are lines of endurance around his mouth and deep puffy shadows under his eyes. People would say he has gone to seed. She thinks he looks wonderful.

He sees her then and comes across to her, saying, 'Helen,' as if they had met recently. He sounds pleased to see her but not surprised.

She says, 'Hullo, Jordan.' She remembers that they had never talked very much, just spent a lot of time looking at each other's work and a lot of time in bed. She wonders if he remembers that too. She sees Magdalen watching them curiously from across the room and she wishes they were not meeting in such a public place as the gallery. But without Magdalen's intervention they would not be meeting at all.

She says, looking round at the paintings, 'All this is pretty impressive,' a vast understatement, but he would understand.

49

He smiles and says, 'Not bad. Not bad for an old man.' The residue of Welsh that she remembers in his voice is overlaid with American now.

She makes a quick calculation. He must be fifty-five. 'I'd say you were in your prime.' Then she hesitates. 'Jordan – I'm so sorry about Hannah.' Somehow it seems important to go in bravely at once rather than wait for a suitable moment that may never come. It had been one of those legendary marriages, his last and his happiest; they had been a much photographed, much interviewed couple at one time, so that it was impossible for her not to know they were happy. She remembers envying them.

His face clouds over, closes down. 'Yes, it was bad.'

'I didn't know, till Magdalen told me. I'd have written.'

'It's a bad way to go,' he says, almost thoughtfully. 'That's why I decided to hang the portrait. I thought she'd like to be here. But I can see it freaks people out. I did a whole series actually, towards the end.'

She thinks this is the most intimate conversation they have ever had, and it is fifteen years since they met. Perhaps he thinks so too, for there is sudden silence between them.

'Well,' he says, 'I'd better go back to the fray, I suppose. Let's keep in touch, Helen. I'd like to hear your news. I hope it's better than mine.'

'Not much,' Helen says. They exchange cards.

'He's on the skids, if you ask me,' Magdalen says as they leave the show. 'I never liked his work as much as you did, but even you must agree he's painting too much. The latest stuff is like self parody, it'll never sell. Well, maybe it will in the States but he can't get away with it here.'

Helen is silent. She doesn't want to be disloyal to Jordan but in fact the same thought had occurred to her when she walked round the gallery a second time after her conversation with him.

'Don't you agree?' Magdalen says.

'Maybe the last two or three paintings. I'm not sure. I'd like to go back when it's quiet, I can't evaluate it properly with everyone there.'

'I can,' Magdalen says. 'And so can you, you're just being diplomatic. Why, is he a friend of yours?'

'Oh, we knew each other slightly fifteen years ago,' Helen says casually. 'He had a studio near mine when he was married to Laura.'

'I gather she never forgave him for running off with Hannah Levinson,' Magdalen says. 'Well, she's got the last laugh now. I suppose he's been overworking to pay all the medical bills. It must cost a fortune to die of cancer in New York even if you're insured.'

Helen dislikes Magdalen's brutal tone: some personal animosity there perhaps? 'Well, that's something you can never accuse me of,' she says, to change the subject, 'painting too much.'

'Indeed I can't,' says Magdalen.

'In fact if I don't do more work soon I'll either have to sell the house or take in lodgers.'

'Richard not coming back then?'

'I don't want him back.'

'Maybe if you gave up teaching,' Magdalen says.

'Then I'd go bankrupt.'

'That's what I mean. Nothing like it to concentrate the mind.'

'Oh well,' Helen says vaguely. 'We'll see.'

'Of course you know Jerome Ellis would love to commission you again. Every time I see him he asks after you most fondly. Still wants that Greek mural in his bedroom and there's no one else in the world who can do it but you.'

'God help me,' Helen says, 'it may yet come to that.'

*

51

She goes to the studio and rummages through the drawer where she keeps odd mementos from long ago: Sally's first baby shoes, her divorce decree, Richard's love letters when they first met, a photograph of Carey as a student, and yes, underneath it all, an article clipped from an ancient magazine, all yellow-faded now, about the adjacent studios and idyllic marriage of artist Jordan Griffiths and photographer Hannah Levinson. Under a caption of 'DOUBLE VISION' their faces smile out at her, Jordan looking absurdly young and happy, Hannah serene and thoughtful, rather as Anne Frank might have looked, if she had been permitted to grow up.

PART TWO

Inge is happy. She thinks of all the lonely Christmases she has spent waiting for Richard and getting drunk in front of the television while the boys were out at parties. Now she can hardly wait for them to go. She prepares the Christmas feast joyfully and watches them all eat it, but her own appetite is small: she is already too full of happiness.

She gazes at the candlelit faces of her three men, Richard and the boys, across the table as they eat her food; she remembers all the years she was afraid this would never happen again. Of course it's not perfect yet: Karl is still edgy with his father, she notices, hostile and displaced from his role as man of the house, while Peter tends to be clinging, wanting extra attention as if to reassure himself that Richard won't disappear again. But she understands all that: Michael has taught her things don't have to be perfect. Good enough will do. It's been a revelation to her. She has learnt so much from him. That was why she had to tell him her news first, ahead of everyone, even Richard. She knew he'd be on her side.

'Congratulations,' he said. 'I didn't realise you were trying.'

She actually blushed. 'Neither did Richard.'

'Ah.'

It's the therapeutic 'ah' that she has become used to. Sometimes she even practises it when she's alone, like a child trying on a parent's clothes, saying 'ah' the way he does as if at a great discovery but also quietly, in a satisfied way at having a suspicion confirmed.

'I'm so grateful,' she said. 'It's like a miracle. If you hadn't helped us . . . '

'You helped yourselves,' he said. 'You both worked very hard. And now? How will he react, do you think?'

'I don't know.' She didn't want to focus on that; didn't want anything to spoil her happy feeling. 'I know he may be angry but I don't want to think about that now. And after all, maybe he won't be. It could go either way. I just want to be happy now.'

He nodded. 'So that's our task for today, to focus on being happy.'

'Yes. I feel I've never done that before.'

'It's a new feeling then?'

'Yes.' She saw him smile slightly, indulgently, as if she were a child learning to walk, and unexpected tears welled up and spilled over. She went on talking easily through them. 'It's very strange. When we were first married I was happy but there was always a shadow because I was pregnant when Richard married me and I was never sure if he really wanted to. And when he came back to me I was happy because I'd got what I wanted and the cow was all alone. But there was still a shadow because he wouldn't make love to me. And then we came to you and you helped us and he did make love to me and now I'm pregnant. And I'm so happy I don't want to think of any more shadows, like if he's angry when I tell him. I just want to stay with the happy feeling.'

'So let's do that, it's important for you. Can you tell me more about it? What's it like?'

She smiled. She knew he was only doing his job, but no one had been so eager to hear her thoughts and feelings ever before in her life and it was a new sensation, a big treat. 'It's very physical,' she said. 'I feel so well, so warm, so peaceful. I feel there's something smoothing out all the rough edges inside me. I feel I'm being healed. I feel very calm and very excited at the same time. I don't even feel angry with Helen any more, I feel sorry for her. I want to stop calling her the cow. I even think maybe I should go round and see her or write and tell her I'm sorry for the other time I went and screamed at her. She must be very lonely and she had a bad time with her daughter.'

'So being happy makes you feel very well and you want to be nice to people.'

'Yes.'

'And what's the difference this time? There's a shadow but you're happy; when before there was a shadow, it spoiled your happiness.'

She thought about it. 'I suppose I'm cheating. I'm not thinking about the shadow.'

'And why do you call that cheating?'

'Because it is.'

'Is there anything else you could call it?'

'I told you I wanted to concentrate on the happy feeling.'

He said equably, 'Now you sound angry with me.'

'Yes, I am a little. Why d'you want me to talk about the shadow? I said I didn't want to.' It was a great luxury to be cross and able to admit it without fear. He wasn't going to reject her; he would just think it was interesting. She was safe.

'I want to know why you call it cheating to ignore the shadow for a while. Cheating is dishonest, is that how you think of yourself?'

'No. Well, I suppose a bit. Getting pregnant without telling my husband, that's cheating, isn't it?'

'Perhaps, but that isn't what we are talking about. We're on happiness today, remember? What could you call it other than cheating when you ignore the shadow, and why can you do it now when you couldn't before?'

'That's two questions,' she said. 'That's not fair.'

They both laughed.

'Well,' she said, 'I suppose I'm not looking ahead to trouble the way I used to. I just want to be happy now.'

'So what are you doing?'

'Oh Michael,' she said, 'you're asking me riddles.'

'Come on,' he said. 'You know it's better if you work it out for yourself.'

She thought about it. 'I suppose I'm living in the present.' She was rewarded by his smile, and he sank back a little in his chair as if relieved.

'So can you feel that for a while? Feel happy and know you're living in the present.'

'I've forgotten the other question,' she said.

'Inge,' he said, 'concentrate. You're so nearly there.'

She was suddenly reminded of reaching orgasm, which though usually easy could sometimes be a long hard struggle, a tiring journey, and a final exhausting triumph. 'I always spoil everything,' she said. 'That's what I said to Felix. By worrying about the future. By analysing too much. I make people leave me by being afraid they will. And now I'm not doing it any more.'

'And why's that?'

'Because I'm living in the present.'

'And?'

Brilliant as neon, it flashed into her head. 'I'm not thinking about Richard. Well, I am, but not all the time. I'm not letting him spoil anything.'

'And isn't that cause for celebration?' he said. 'That you don't always have to depend on Richard for happiness. Whatever happens in the future, you're happy now, and no one can spoil it for you. Doesn't that give you more control over your own life? Just think, you might even make a habit of this.'

She started to laugh. 'Yes, you're right,' she said. 'It's a lovely feeling. But very strange.'

Michael glanced at his watch. 'Well, it's almost time. Perhaps we should think about stopping in a moment.'

'It always jars on me when you say that,' she said. 'It's such a jolt.'

'Yes, it is difficult, isn't it? Is there a way we could handle it differently?'

Now, alone with Richard, she tries to keep Michael's tone of quiet acceptance and approval in her head to give her courage. It is a testing moment and she wonders if her happiness will survive it. 'Richard,' she says, 'can we talk now? There's something I have to tell you. Please listen and please don't be cross. I'm going to have a baby.'

He hears the terrifying words, and behind them the echo of twenty years ago, when she was first pregnant, and in a haze of pity and lust he married her. That child died and he should have run away then, he now realises, but instead he stayed and gave her Karl and Peter, as if to make amends. Karl, who now resents him, and Peter, who clings. He has betrayed them all, by going away and coming back. From the best of motives he has probably done more harm than Felix, who has only ever pleased himself. The irony hurts. If she is pregnant again, it is as if he has had to marry her twice, when the fact is he never wanted to marry her at all. And he feels like a fool to have such an old deception practised on him.

'I'm sorry,' she says humbly and yet somehow smugly, watching his face. 'I knew you'd be angry but I was hoping you might be just a little bit pleased as well.'

He feels such a surge of violence, wanting to hit her, that he quite shocks himself. 'I'd like to have been consulted,' he says, inadequate words for the rage inside him. He is terrified of his own anger. He hasn't felt as angry as this since he slashed Helen's painting, since he tried to murder Felix. All these months when he thought he was making progress and now he finds he has gone right back to where he was nine months ago. Nothing has been achieved and he is trapped in a worse mess than before. She has done this dreadfully dishonest thing that will chain him to her for ever. It is only now, realising that he can't run away, that he also realises that was what he was planning to do. His subconscious was just waiting to get Christmas over before saying to Inge, Look here, I'm sorry, we've tried our best but this simply isn't working, is it? Something like that. He'd even

59

thought she might agree with him, given time. He'd been planning to run away again, only this time with her permission for ever. He'd been planning to run away and beg Helen to forgive him and take him back. Now he sees the lovely ghost of Helen receding into the distance, the person he truly loves and can never have again.

'But you had a coil,' he says stupidly. 'You've always had a coil. Since Peter was born.'

'I had it taken out when you came back.'

So simple then. She doesn't even look guilty. She has a meek expression on her face, as if trying to ward off violence, but her eyes are calm and steady. She is pleased with herself. She knows she is in a strong position.

'God, Inge,' he says, 'you might have told me.'

'How could I?' she says. 'you might have said no.'

Was this how Felix felt when Sally deceived him? He doesn't want to think of Felix, make excuses for him. But the fellow feeling is there, sudden and strong.

'So that's why we had to go to that slimy therapist,' he says. 'So you could do this to me.'

And yet. And yet. A child of his own again. The image rises up as sheer delight. Not quite worth the nightmare of being married to Inge. But almost. Which of course she knows. She knows him so well. She is facing him with all the confidence of a woman whose husband wants children, whose husband doesn't agree with abortion. She knows she is safe.

'I wanted you to love me,' she says. 'I wanted you inside me again. I needed that, Richard, I needed it so much. How could I live with you and sleep beside you if we never made love? What's the point of coming back if we're going to be like that? But I'm nearly forty-one. If I'm ever going to have another child, it has to be now.'

'And you couldn't tell me that? Ask me? Give me a choice? Christ, I don't feel like a father, just a sperm donor.' He thinks of Helen when she talked Sally into having an abortion. Ignoring him. Going totally against his wishes. Now Inge's doing the same thing. He's the means to an end or an obstacle in the way. Not a person at all. Not someone with an opinion, with a right to be consulted. All his past is coming back to haunt him.

'You would have said no, wouldn't you?' she says.

'Yes, of course. It's too soon – we're not getting on well enough – God, Inge, it ought to be a joint decision. Maybe later.' But he knows he means never and he feels dishonest.

'But there wasn't any time,' she says. 'You might have left me again. I could feel you pulling away.'

'Surely,' he says, 'that's the worst reason to have a child. Isn't it?'

'I couldn't bear you to leave me again,' she says. 'And now you can't. You won't, will you?'

'No,' he says, staring at her in horror, seeing the long future ahead of them.

'I know she wouldn't have a child with you,' she says. 'Felix told me.' She means Helen. She has stopped calling her the cow but she can't quite manage her name. He wishes she wouldn't mention her at all, or Felix. He feels exposed. 'And I know you miss your step-daughter. Maybe we'll be lucky and have a girl. You'd like that, wouldn't you?'

He doesn't answer.

'And the boys are nearly grown up. They can babysit for us. We'll be able to go out whenever we like. It'll be much easier this time.'

She is so eager for him to agree, to make the best of it. Still he says nothing, punishing her with silence, the only weapon he has left.

'It might bring us closer together,' she says, still watching his face.

'But that isn't what children are for, Inge. Don't you know that yet? The boys didn't bring us closer together, did they, so why should a new baby?' How fragile it sounds. And he gets a sudden image of the newborn. The awful vulnerability that he will have to protect when he can't even protect himself.

61

'Well, I don't care. I was desperate.' A sudden burst of anger. 'You should have noticed. In the past, when you were really touching me, really looking at my body, you'd have noticed I wasn't bleeding every month. I couldn't have tricked you in the old days, could I?'

He ignores that. It's true but it only proves how far apart they are, how wrong it is to be having a child at all. He looks round the room at the farce of Christmas, the remains of the food she prepared so lovingly, the silly decorations, the holly and the mistletoe, where she made him kiss her before dinner, and the tree with its dangerous candles. He gets up to blow them out. He wishes he could burn down the house.

Helen goes to the studio on Christmas morning. She doesn't really expect to get any work done, though she is always hopeful; mainly she is trying to pretend this Christmas, the first one without Richard, isn't happening, and to forget last Christmas, when Sally was with Carey and they were alone together. Before he found out about the abortion. Before he tried to kill Felix. When everything was still relatively all right. She has a lot of avoiding to do in her head and she doesn't want any friends or neighbours to take pity on her and help her do it, or see her fail. The very word Christmas makes her feel allergic: she sees it in the papers, hears it on the radio. People keep wishing her a happy one, as if such a thing were possible. There is no escape from the word and it induces such an intense feeling of illness and rage that she is surprised when she looks in the mirror not to see herself covered in a rash.

This year Sally is roasting a duck, to defy tradition, and they are going to eat it quite late, about three. By then the light will have gone and Helen can't even pretend to work. So she will be quite entitled to watch television and get drunk, while Sally, having done her duty, goes out and enjoys herself with her friends. Helen might even enjoy herself too. It sounds like masturbation, she thinks, something she has done quite a lot of lately. Perhaps a good sign, that she is returning to life; there was a time when she was too tired and depressed to bother. But she doesn't like the way that feelings of anger and loneliness get mixed up with the pleasure. She would almost prefer to stay dead. A new way to spend Christmas, anyway, alone in front of the television drunkenly masturbating. Something to aim for, to give her a sense of purpose, although it's more likely she will fall asleep before she has the energy to start.

The studio is so normal it colludes with her pretence that this is just an ordinary day. At the same time she likes the feeling that the rest of the world is out there somewhere forcing itself to celebrate. The weather is chill and dank, a raw day but without wind, not really cold. It's the sort of weather she associates with Christmas, so it seems more appropriate than snow, which belongs on fanciful cards or in newspaper photographs of seasonal disasters or in the works of Dickens. The ghost of Christmas past. No. She switches off the memories and takes a good look at the work she has been doing lately. She attempts to assess it but decides against trying to do any more. Her excuse is that if she fails she will feel desperate and if she succeeds she will be too engrossed to go home on time and appreciate Sally's duck. Instead she primes a canvas and tidies up some of the accumulated clutter. This sort of occupation usually has a calming effect on her mind. She is using the studio as a kind of sedative.

But underneath all this enforced peace is a very special tension. She is waiting for something: a gesture from Richard. A phone call, a visit? She hasn't sent him a card, although in a way she does wish him well; she simply couldn't bring herself to write Inge's address. That's another problem with Christmas: it forces you to make decisions about situations that could otherwise be quietly left to drift. He has sent her a card, though, with the

word love on it as well as his name. This card made
her very angry. She wonders what the word love can
possibly mean in the context of their separate lives:
obviously not what it means to her. She has spent some
time staring at it and imagining his hand on the paper
writing it, then sealing the envelope and posting it secretly at work so as not to annoy Inge. He has turned
Helen into a mistress again, but a celibate one, the
worst of all possible worlds, she thinks. They have gone
back ten years and put everything into reverse. It gives
her, if no longer acute pain, a very strange feeling of
unreality. She pictures Inge gloating over her Christmas
triumph: her reunited family, her tree, her decorations,
her table loaded with heavy German food. Perhaps, to
complete the reversal, Richard will eventually make an
excuse to Inge and creep out to visit Helen on Boxing
Day. Is that what she is waiting for? She feels if he
doesn't make some gesture beyond the meaningless
word love on a card, then all is finally lost, and she
despises herself for still nourishing even the smallest
hope.

Jordan on the other hand has not sent her a card. That
is no surprise; he was never the sort of person who did,
even during their brief affair. Much too busy and careless
of other people's feelings, she tells herself, slamming
rubbish savagely into a black refuse bag. She is almost
sorry she went to his show: it stirred up memories of the
past that were safer buried. She met Jordan first when
she had just left Carey; to meet him again when Richard
has just left her seems an odd parallel, unlucky. She
doesn't want to be reminded of the vulnerable person she
once was and may be again. How many times must she
put her life in order only to have it destroyed? She takes a
break from sorting rubbish and sits in the old armchair,
staring at her unfinished work. She suddenly feels very
tired.

When the phone rings she is sure it is Richard. She
makes herself wait until it has rung several times before

64

she answers it. And Jordan says, 'Helen? You're very industrious.'

'Oh,' she says, 'hullo, Jordan, yes I am.' Her heart is beating very fast with surprise and excitement. Was this what she was waiting for, and not Richard at all? Was this what the recent upsurge of masturbation has been about? Surely not? Wouldn't she have told herself? How could she be so deceptive?

'I rang you at home,' Jordan says, 'and your daughter said you were here.'

'Oh, yes,' Helen says. 'She's roasting a duck.' Already the conversation sounds quite mad to her: she is saying the first thing that comes into her head. There is very little of her brain available to compose sentences because most of it is fully occupied reacting to the enormity of a Christmas Day phone call from Jordan. It's rather similar to being drunk. Only a fraction of her is functioning properly, like skeleton staff on a Bank Holiday. 'She's doing the whole Christmas thing this year,' she says. 'Letting me off the hook.' She wonders if she sounds cheerful and casual enough.

'Isn't it nice,' Jordan says, 'when they're big enough to do that? I've got my entire brood here waiting on me.'

'Lucky you,' she says, feeling she needs an interpreter to tell her if she is making sense. The words come out at random from some emergency store; they could mean anything.

'Plus some of their lovers and children,' Jordan adds. 'It's quite crowded.'

'Yes,' she says, 'I imagine it must be.'

Then there is a quite awkward pause. Clearly neither of them knows what to say. Perhaps he is as shell-shocked as she is, she thinks, but as he made the call, at least he had advance warning. Seconds pass that feel like minutes. She can hear him breathing and that seems very intimate. She wants to be back in bed with him fifteen years ago. She wants to hold his large heavy body again; she wants him to go down on her and let her come several times till it hurts and she has to stop; she wants to have his cock in her mouth and then inside her for a long time; she wants to hear him cry out when he comes; she wants to lie there in his arms and fall asleep. She suddenly wants all that very much. It would make her feel human again. She remembers that they always had trouble making conversation but no trouble at all making love.

'So I just thought I'd ring you,' he says finally, 'and wish you a happy Christmas.'

'I'm glad you did.' And why didn't you ask me out, Jordan? she screams inside. How about an old-fashioned date? Dinner even? Or just sex, I'm not proud. Something. Anything. Or what is the point of ringing me? Is this phone call and five minutes' chat at your show all we're going to have in this second incarnation?

'Well,' he says, 'we must get together some time.'

'Yes,' she says, heart leaping with hope, and then with a burst of courage: 'Let's make it soon.'

Another aching pause and then he says, 'I'm glad you came to the show.' He sounds heavy and remote now, as if he wants to get off the phone. She wonders what time of year Hannah died. Is Christmas a bad time for him, full of memories? Perhaps he needs more encouragement.

'It was very impressive,' she says. And it was also three months ago. God, Jordan, she thinks, you know I like your work but right now it's your body I want. How can two grown-up people, old friends, ex-lovers, be so inept at getting together? I don't want to have to invite you; I'd feel so much better if you asked me. She opens her mouth to say, 'Why don't you come round for a drink tomorrow?' That sounds normal and friendly, not pushy and desperate. Doesn't it? She hopes she won't add something ludicrous about mince pies or seeing how much Sally has grown. She can't be sure what the emergency switchboard in her brain may throw in.

Instead she hears him say, 'Well, have a good Christmas. I'll ring you,' and he actually hangs up. She can't believe it. How could she have been so slow and stupid as to miss her chance? And what is the point of his ringing her to say he'll ring her? She wants to kill him. Instead she laughs at the farcical misery of it all.

When she gets home for the much publicised duck Sally says hopefully, 'A man rang for you,' and Helen imagines her thinking, Someone to get you off my back perhaps? 'I told him you were at the studio. Was that all right?'

Sally is dressed all in black, enlivened only by a pair of diamanté earrings. She looks pale and sulky, but robust. Felix thinks her hair is just about back to a romantic length now, nine months after she had it cut, but when he tells her it looks wonderful she says, 'You never liked it short, did you?' and he knows it is not going to be a good day.

For Christmas he has given her a black and red Hermès scarf, which she has draped round her neck during lunch, with exclamations of delight, making him anxious that bits of it would fall in the food. She has given him a cassette of Mozart's Requiem to play in the car, and he wonders if this was carelessly chosen or if it is in some way prophetic. He feels uneasy as he watches her eat. Her appetite is impressive as ever, but it is not directed at him. Perversely he wants her more, as he watches her, whereas when she arrived and they greeted each other with their usual hugs and kisses, he had hardly wanted her at all.

'God, I hate Christmas,' she says. 'Mum's in a foul mood and she went to the studio yesterday same as usual and left me to do lunch. Some man rang up for her while she was out. I wonder if she's got a lover. I hope to God she has, it might cheer her up a bit.'

Felix is excited by the idea of Helen with a lover. Sometimes when he is making love to Sally he pretends she is Helen, always with good results. He has noticed that he needs fantasy more and more often these days and he wonders if Sally does too or if it's his age.

'I booked a room for us,' he says. The hotel restaurant is full of flushed and bloated Boxing Day guests and he is looking forward to lying naked and peaceful beside Sally in the afternoon twilight.

She looks at him very directly. 'Sorry, Felix, I don't feel like sex today. Maybe they'll give you a refund.'

'That's hardly the point,' he says irritably.

She shrugs. 'Oh well, sorry.'

'We could just lie down in it. Have a cuddle. Ruffle the sheets and see what happens.' Surely he isn't pleading with her? He watches the winter light from the window fall on her face, contrasting it with the pink-shaded hotel lamps. He can see the person she was and the person she is now, both confusingly present at the same time. He thinks of the girl in his book. She is still so young and yet the bloom has gone. Is that his fault? 'Come on, darling,' he says, smiling. 'I'm sure we could find something to do.'

'Don't keep on about it,' she says. 'I don't like hotel rooms any more.'

'Then why did you let me book one?' Now he wants her more than ever. It is several weeks since they have made love and the smell of her has got to him.

'How was I to know how I'd feel? I'm in a funny mood. I hate Christmas. I'd sooner go for a walk by the river.'

'In this weather?'

'It's not really cold.'

'It's bloody freezing.'

She pushes away her coffee cup. 'Well, you needn't come. I can go by myself.'

'Don't be silly, darling,' he says pleasantly, making the best of it. 'Of course I'll come. Do me good. I don't get enough exercise.' He puts his hand over hers on the table. 'Just tell me what's the matter?'

She shakes her head. 'Nothing. Bloody Christmas.

Mum's getting on my nerves, she's so depressed, and I'm fed up with looking after her. And I've got to go to my father for New Year, imagine seeing it in and knowing all those children are going to wake up at dawn.'

Suddenly, shocking himself, he desperately wants it to be the way it was. 'Come back to the flat,' he says. 'It's warmer than the river and much nicer than a hotel room. We can relax there.'

'I don't like your flat any more,' she says. 'I told you that back in the summer. It's full of horrible memories.'

'It might not be,' he says. 'You haven't been there for a very long time.'

'It reminds me of you telling me to have an abortion and Richard trying to kill you. I'd rather see you at college, in my room.'

'Sally,' he says gently, 'darling, you're going to have to put all that behind you sooner or later.'

'So you keep telling me. I don't know how you can work there.'

'Well,' he says, 'I don't have much choice.'

'You do, you could sell it and buy somewhere else.'

Defeated, he signals the waiter and pays the surprisingly large bill.

'How's the book going, anyway?' she asks in a more conciliatory tone.

'Final edit. Anther week with luck.'

'Well done. When can I read it?'

'Soon.' Always a tricky moment, that. He wonders how much she will identify. Will she be flattered or furious? Will she even see how much of it is fiction and not really about her at all?

They get up and go out. He puts his arm round her and they end up walking by the river after all in the grey afternoon light. He is afraid that although neither of them has used the word, they may have actually been saying goodbye.

*

When the doorbell rings on Boxing Day, Helen is sure it must be Richard. Who else would just turn up without warning? She is conscious of looking her worst as she goes to answer the door, having spent the morning viciously cleaning the house. She couldn't face the studio again so soon after her abortive phone call from Jordan. Part of her is hoping that later in the day she may ring him with the casual invitation she should have issued yesterday, and part of her knows she won't. These two parts are warring uncomfortably inside her. She wonders if this fantasy about Jordan will make her look at Richard with new eyes.

But it's Elizabeth on her doorstep, Elizabeth armed with a huge unwelcomed poinsettia as a passport to Helen's house. 'Surprise,' she says forlornly, looking unsure of her welcome as well she might after such a long silence and all the phone calls unreturned. 'I just thought . . . well, you know, season of goodwill and all that.' Her smile looks nervous and false.

Helen accepts the plant but feels as if Elizabeth has served a summons on her. Is she not entitled to say thank you and close the door? She did exactly that once during the summer when Elizabeth arrived with flowers. But now, of course, it's Christmas.

'Come in,' she says grudgingly. 'Have a drink.'

Elizabeth takes off her coat and settles into an armchair much too fast. She looks set for a long stay, Helen thinks; she has lost weight and is actually looking rather better than she sounds, smartly dressed and carefully made up, more like someone going for an interview than visiting an old friend. 'Where's Sally?' she asks, as Helen pours two glasses of wine.

'Out,' Helen says. She thinks she detects relief in Elizabeth's body language: her shoulders look more relaxed somehow. Sudden panic sweeps over Helen. Surely they are not going to have the confrontation they have managed to avoid so far, not now, so long after the event? She feels totally trapped in her own home and that, on

70

top of the disappointment over Richard and Jordan, makes her very angry.

'I know I should have phoned,' Elizabeth says, and Helen, abandoning all pretence of manners, says, 'Yes, you should.'

'But I thought you might make an excuse and I was right.' Again the placating smile.

'Well, I'm very fragile these days,' Helen says defensively. 'I can really only cope with working and living. I don't have any energy left over for people, I'm afraid. Sorry, Elizabeth, it's nothing personal. I just feel wiped out and I've nothing in reserve.'

Already she is shocked to hear herself talking so much. Does she need Elizabeth as a friend after all or is she so desperate that she will talk to anyone who can force their way into her home? No wonder Jordan isn't asking me out if I'm giving off distress signals like that, she thinks.

'And a lot has happened between us, hasn't it?' Elizabeth says. 'I'm not surprised you don't want to see me. But I kept thinking . . . this time last year we were all together and I couldn't bear not to see you. I thought if I left it long enough and then just turned up it might be all right.'

'Well, you're here now,' Helen says ungraciously. She finds so much honesty embarrassing. And she still feels an underlying threat.

'I would like us to be friends,' Elizabeth says, as if it's unlikely, 'but even if we can't be, there's something I have to ask you. I should have asked you before but I didn't have the courage. It's about Sally and Felix.' She pauses. 'They did have an affair, didn't they?'

Silence in Helen's living-room as Elizabeth waits for an answer.

'Shouldn't you be asking Felix that?' Helen says, poker-faced.

'Yes, but he'll lie,' Elizabeth says simply.

'God, Elizabeth, I resent this,' Helen says.

'I know, I'm sorry, but I need the truth. I thought I

71

didn't but I do. Please tell me the truth. I can't bear to live like this any more, with everyone protecting me and deceiving me and treating me like a stupid child. I do know really, it's the only possible thing, I mean that's why Richard hit him, isn't it? I've tried believing everything else and I can't manage it any longer.' And then, to Helen's horror, she starts to cry. Now I've got to be sorry for her, Helen thinks furiously. She pours two more drinks; she feels she and Elizabeth are going through wartime or enduring a siege, so that it hardly matters if they are enemies or friends. The legendary spirit of the blitz had taken over as they crouch behind sandbags sharing their rations, two people in trouble. God, if I were a man, she thinks, how I should hate women's tears.

She doesn't bother to find Kleenex for Elizabeth. She watches her grope in her bag for a handkerchief. Elizabeth looks as if she is luxuriating in her grief, as if she has come here specially to have it in Helen's living-room.

'Yes, they did have an affair,' she says. 'Satisfied?'

Elizabeth makes a sort of wailing sob and blows her nose. 'But that doesn't explain why Richard left you,' she says with extraordinary persistence. 'There's something else, I know there is. It's even worse, isn't it?'

Helen is feeling quite sick now, as if she has no privacy left, as if Elizabeth is trying to drag out pieces of her inside. Perhaps it is her own abortion fifteen years ago that she is remembering and not Sally's at all, but she very much doesn't want to use the word. She feels angry and violated. She suddenly understands why Felix treats Elizabeth badly, although this is not the moment she would choose to see Felix's point of view about anything. She would like to treat Elizabeth badly herself. Elizabeth seems to bring out the worst in her. 'Okay,' she says, 'since you're so keen to know, Sally got pregnant and I made her get rid of it without telling Richard. When he found out he wouldn't forgive me. Is that enough for you?'

Elizabeth, quite calm now, puts away her handkerchief. 'Oh Helen,' she says, 'I'm so sorry.' She sounds like a mother apologising for her badly behaved child, Helen thinks, as if Felix is a toddler who has run amok and damaged the furniture. But perhaps to be fair she is in a mood to find anything Elizabeth says offensive. 'I'm so sorry.'

'Well,' Helen says briskly, 'there we are. But you must have known. What else could it be?'

Elizabeth shakes her head. 'I tried so hard not to see it,' she says. 'So hard.' It occurs to Helen that Elizabeth may actually want sympathy and this adds to her feeling of rage. 'God, how awful, what a mess,' Elizabeth says.

'Yes, it was pretty bad.' The words seem quite inadequate for what she and Sally actually endured.

'When was it exactly?'

'Last year, just before she went to Sussex. Look, Elizabeth, I really don't want to talk about it any more. It was an absolute nightmare but it's over.'

'I'm sorry,' Elizabeth says again. 'I hope Felix paid.'

'With money, yes.'

'Oh, poor you, poor Sally. It must have been dreadful. But I don't understand how Richard found out.'

'God, Elizabeth, how much more d'you want? Inge told him. She found a letter from Sally in Felix's flat. Must have been a big thrill for her. Must have really made her day.' Helen pours herself another drink without offering Elizabeth one. Wartime camaraderie has vanished and she is hoping Elizabeth will leave soon. But she goes on sitting there, holding her empty glass and looking sad.

'So Felix had an affair with Inge too,' she says. 'It just gets worse and worse.'

'I don't quite see,' says Helen sharply, 'how that's worse than Sally having an abortion.' Now she has actually said the word and she feels it reverberating between them. But Elizabeth, of course, is only thinking of herself.

'No, of course not, I didn't mean that, it's just one

73

more thing I've got to take into account . . . I suppose I knew really but . . .' Elizabeth's voice trails away.

'Well, I don't want to talk about it any more,' Helen says. 'I never did, it makes me feel quite ill.'

'Yes, of course, I'm sorry.'

'And I really don't see why you have to bring it up now. It's over a year ago and you're still together, what the hell is the point of asking me all these questions now?' She hears herself becoming strident.

'I couldn't face it at the time, I panicked,' Elizabeth says. 'Felix nearly died, after all, how could I interrogate him as soon as he got home? And then he was doing the book . . . well, I didn't want to upset that—'

'Oh, God forbid,' says Helen, heavily ironic. 'My daughter could have died too but what a shame if one of Felix's books got upset by his private life. So why now? Why turn up here on Boxing Day, as if Christmas isn't bad enough already, and put me through all this?'

'Because I think it's still going on.' Elizabeth looks up and very directly at Helen, as if challenging her. 'Or it's started again. And I want you to tell me the truth. I can't face another year like this. I suppose I thought if it had happened, at least it was over and maybe we could put it behind us. But if it's still going on . . .'

'Well, it was in the summer,' Helen says, suddenly almost relieved to have no more pretence. 'Sally pretty well admitted it when I asked her. I was appalled, of course, but there was nothing I could do. I don't know how things are right now.' She closes her eyes for a moment: the conversation has exhausted her.

'I knew it,' Elizabeth says softly, and then: 'Oh, Helen, why didn't you tell me a year ago?'

'Why should I interfere in your marriage? I was having enough trouble with my own. If you didn't want to know, that was up to you. Anyway, the whole thing made me feel sick, I didn't want to talk about it. What good would it have done to come running to you? A sort of revenge, to make you unhappy as well? Or more like

74

asking someone to call off their dog. It was easier to say nothing and just not see you very much.' She wonders if that sounds very insulting.

'I'd better go,' Elizabeth says, standing up. 'Thank you for being honest with me at last. I'm sorry I stayed so long.'

'If I wasn't so tired,' Helen says, 'I'd have been more polite.' And they smile faintly at each other, in some kind of sad recognition of the friendship they used to have.

Elizabeth drives home very slowly and carefully, as if she has been involved in an accident. Felix is still not back and she wonders now if he is with Sally, who was also out today. He had said he was going to work through the holiday to get final revisions of the book done by the end of the year, but that of course could be meaningless as well as true.

She is past caring; she is glad to be alone. She removes her shoes and has a brandy, then undresses and takes a hot bath before sinking into her dressing-gown. She is treating herself like an invalid. 'Well, I asked for it, and I got it,' she says to herself. 'Now I know everything.' She is slightly embarrassed to hear her voice aloud in the empty house, more so to recall that she has just made an exhibition of herself in front of Helen. Still, who better than a painter to witness that? The thought actually makes her laugh. She has a headache now and she takes two aspirins with her second drink, sitting by the window and looking out at the wintry river. She reckons she has just a few days in which to make a decision: she can't face another year like this. If she could, she would not have interrogated Helen at all. Part of her knew what she would hear, but another part, she is shocked to discover, was actually hoping to be told she was wrong.

It feels like such a huge deception, such a saga of misery, so much worse than any affair he has had before.

75

Sally's age makes it worse, and the link with Richard and Helen, almost like abusing a member of the family. The abortion makes it worse, the betrayal of Richard's friendship, and the end of Helen's marriage. She feels responsible, as if her loving tolerance of Felix has enabled him to create such wreckage and escape unscathed. Is it now up to her to punish him and if so, how can she do it without also punishing herself?

She thinks it isn't punishment she wants to achieve so much as peace. Somewhere in the part of her that knew the truth but chose to overlook it, she believed that he had learnt his lesson. That Richard's violence and her own unspoken forgiveness would impress him so deeply that he would never do anything quite so bad again. She was wrong. The fact that it is still going on makes her feel he is laughing at her, that the enormity of his crime has completely passed him by. She has lived all this time with someone who speaks a different language, whose value system is as alien as if he came from another world. Sitting there at the window, with her third drink in her hand, she watches the river and reflects that she is going to have to do something as painful as cutting off a limb without anaesthetic, and the thought makes her shake with fright.

But she can't do it yet. When Felix returns several hours later and finds her still sitting in the dark, she says nothing.

'What's the matter, darling,' he asks cheerily, 'Christmas blues?'

And she says, 'Something like that.'

'Never mind,' he says, 'it's nearly over. God, what a day. I hate this stage. You read the bloody thing again and again and each time it looks different.'

He kisses her and pours them both drinks. He looks so normal: friendly and affectionate. Innocent. She thinks about how much she will be giving up. It is almost as if she has never loved him more, which alarms her. And yet it is also as if a dead person has come into the room.

*

Helen finds herself strangely affected by Elizabeth's visit. After years of pitying and despising her for putting up with Felix, she sees what an enormous effort of courage it must have been for Elizabeth to face the truth and she admires her for it. She has no idea what Elizabeth will do with the information, but it seems to have turned her into an active person, going home to take charge of her life in some way, perhaps for the first time. Elizabeth has made Helen feel passive by comparison. Here I sit, Helen thinks, waiting for Richard to come back to me when I'm not even sure I would take him. At least Inge knew she wanted him and she got him. Perhaps he is even happier with her; perhaps he needs that kind of devotion after all. Maybe it's like warm sunshine after putting up with my moods. He won't have to cook meals or compete with a career for attention; he won't have to feel guilty about his children or divided about money. Maybe Inge really is good for him after all.

It seems a revolutionary thought, almost funny. And why am I sitting here waiting for Richard, she asks herself, when I am lusting after Jordan? I could at least cheer myself up with some sex. No wonder Sally despises me; I can see it in her eyes. She wants me to have more guts. I've turned into a spineless wimp and it's taken Elizabeth to make me see it. There seems to be some irony in that, worthy of hollow laughter, she thinks. If Elizabeth can take action, then surely so can I.

Time to make something happen. She gets out her address book and looks up Jordan's number. She goes to pour a drink to give herself courage, but reflects that she is already drinking too much, and stops. She will make this call quite cold. After all, there is no shame in ringing a man who rang her yesterday. There is no shame in contacting an ex-lover and inviting him round. There is even no shame in throwing herself at him if necessary. He has seen it all before. If she is going to take risks, better it should be with Jordan, who is almost like an old friend, than with a stranger. And how would I ever meet a stranger, she asks herself, when I never go anywhere? And besides, I actually want Jordan.

That is the frightening part, she discovers. Actually wanting someone again. Putting herself at risk once more. Well, it's only sex, she tells herself, dialling, and Jordan will understand that. He won't mind. He may even be flattered.

A woman's voice says, 'Hullo?' She sounds at home.

Oh God, Helen thinks, his latest mistress, of course, he only rang yesterday to be polite, no wonder he didn't ask me out. But she forces herself to be resolute. 'Oh, hullo,' she says, trying to strike the right casual, confident tone. 'Is Jordan there?'

'Yes, who's calling?' says the woman.

'Helen,' says Helen, her heart thumping. She feels about five years old. She realises that if losing Richard has not broken her heart it has certainly dented her self-confidence.

'Just a minute,' says the woman. She goes away and Helen hears her shouting, 'Dad? Telephone. It's Helen.'

Helen waits. She feels relief. She feels a smile beginning to spread over her face. Presently Jordan comes on the line and says, 'Hullo.'

'Hullo, Jordan,' Helen says. She has no idea what to say next.

There's a pause while they both just breathe. Then Jordan says, 'Not working today?'

Helen says rapidly, 'No, I'm sick of it all, work and Christmas and the whole damn thing, so I rang to invite you to dinner on New Year's Eve.' As soon as she hears the words she realises that is what she most wants, to start the year with Jordan, but she has loaded the dice against herself. Almost everyone in the world will be already booked up and that includes Jordan.

He hesitates. 'Well, that sounds good but I'm meant to be going to a party.'

'Of course. Never mind.' Heart dropping like stone to bottom of well. Gut-wrenching disappointment. Worst

78

fears confirmed. I must go to the doctor tomorrow, she thinks, get some pills for this. I'm in a dreadful state. Much worse than I thought.

'Would you like to come with me?' Jordan says.

She's astonished. 'Yes.' But she wouldn't. She hates parties and people hate her at them. She's no good at small talk and she makes enemies instead of friends. She gives offence easily and has to leave early in a bad mood. The way she remembers it, Jordan used to have a similar problem.

'Or I could get out of it and come to you instead,' Jordan says suddenly. 'Would that be better?'

'Oh yes,' she says, heart singing. 'That would be much better. I'm no good at parties.'

'Neither am I,' says Jordan. 'Eight o'clock-ish?'

'Perfect.'

She hangs up, smiling. Ask and ye shall receive, she thinks smugly. She has got what she wanted and she has five whole days to look forward to it with perfect equanimity. She has been rewarded for her daring. How simple life can be if you have a little courage, she thinks.

Elizabeth chooses New Year's Eve, or perhaps it chooses her. She can't do it any sooner, but if she waits any longer she is afraid she may not do it at all. They are getting ready for a party, long ago accepted when it seemed easier than being alone with the occasion, but which they now don't want to attend. Felix comes into the room saying plaintively, 'Do we really have to go?' and Elizabeth hears herself saying, 'No, I don't think we can, I think we'll have to talk instead.'

She is watching his face very carefully and hating herself for doing so. She sees instantly, almost subliminally, something in his eyes showing he knows exactly what she means, and then the look is gone, so quickly that she could almost believe she imagined it. It is replaced by an expression of innocent enquiry. 'Oh really, what about?' he says.

'Sally and the abortion,' she says simply.

There is utter silence in the room.

Felix says, frowning, 'Oh darling, what *is* this?'

'Please don't lie to me,' she says. 'Please spare me that. I went to see Helen on Boxing Day. But I think I knew anyway. And I've been checking the mileage on your car. I've sunk pretty low really, though not as low as you, of course. You've been to Brighton a lot in term time, haven't you? Must be a relief now she's back in town. I know it's still going on, Felix. And I can't take it any more. That's all we have to talk about.'

She is surprised how quiet and calm her voice sounds. Inside her chest there is a sensation of thudding, pounding adrenalin that nearly deafens her. She can see him thinking fast, almost as if there is a glass screen in his face behind which she glimpses the whirring parts of his brain, as in a surrealist painting. She has suddenly developed a kind of X-ray vision and she finds it unnerving.

'I'm so sorry,' he says. 'But it's over. We've said goodbye. Darling, I can't bear to see you hurt like this. I never meant it to happen and I never wanted you to know. Can you ever forgive me?'

She can see this is meant to be a rhetorical question. She says, 'No. I don't think I can.'

He looks very shocked. She wonders if that means he believes her or if it's another assumed mask. He doesn't speak. His face is very blank now, wiped clean of expression. She can see him evaluating the situation, somewhere behind his eyes. She doesn't like her new clear-sightedness but it's useful.

'Well, that's it,' she says eventually. 'There we are.'

He says, 'Darling, I'm sorry, I'm sorry. What can I say? It's the worst thing I've ever done but it's over. Must have been a mid-life crisis.' He waves his hands about distractedly. 'How can I ever make it up to you?'

Denial wouldn't help him, but the more he grovels, the

more powerful and detached she feels. It is a new sensation and she wonders how far she can push it. She is surprised by this sudden deep hunger for vengeance. She doesn't like what she is learning about herself.

'That's the trouble,' she says. 'I don't think you can.' The words frighten her, and he begins to look worried too, for the first time, as if picking up her fear. She notices her old familiar instinct to comfort him but she controls it. He moves towards her, as if to touch her, and she says, 'No, don't.' He stops and they look at each other uncertainly.

He says, 'Lizzie?' with a note of real panic in his voice. 'I love you. Only you. Only ever you.'

'Whatever that means,' she says. She feels exhilarated by her own cruelty: she is amazing herself. She realises she would like to injure him: she has terrible images in her mind of cutting him into pieces with a knife. There is blood everywhere in her brain.

She says, 'I don't think I can live with you any more. I think we'll have to separate.' She can see from the shock on his face that he believes her and that makes her realise she means it. She is terrified.

'But I can't . . .' he says, and stops. She feels him thinking the words 'live without you' and even now, from habit, rejecting the cliché. Suddenly in their grievous state they both laugh. Then his face crumples up and he starts to cry. She takes him in her arms and then holds him, dry-eyed herself, and rocks him like a child to comfort him.

Jordan arrives promptly at eight. This is a surprise, although she has been ready since seven thirty, just in case: she does not remember him as a punctual person. He has brought a bottle of chilled vintage champagne, which is also unexpected, and presents it to her solemnly, saying, 'Happy New Year'.

She says, 'Thank you, Jordan. How wonderful.' She has after a lot of indecision put on her best black dress with silver earrings from Mexico and some rather uncomfortable shoes which make her legs look quite enticing. She is wearing a lot of her favourite scent. She has even put on glamorous underwear in case she gets lucky. She so seldom wears clothes like these that they seem like fancy dress. She feels like a desperate middle-aged woman and a silly teenager at the same time. It is rather a nice feeling: out of control, for a change. And she is glad she has dressed up because she can see that his clothes are very expensive: a camel overcoat over a black cashmere sweater and velvet trousers with suede boots. She has never seen him so formally dressed. Astonishment overrides her nerves and she says without thinking, 'I'd forgotten how rich you are these days.'

He smiles. Already he is filling the room: he has a bigger presence than she remembers, too. Surely all her memories can't be wrong?

'Have I overdone it?' he says. 'I wanted to get it right.' The Welsh undertones are strong in his voice tonight, whereas at his show and on the phone they have been overlaid by his years in New York.

She says, 'No, it's lovely. I really appreciate it. And you look so smart.' She doesn't know how else to put it: good enough to eat is the phrase that occurs to her, but that might be too full of innuendo.

He laughs. 'Oh, I got to be a sort of dandy in the States. Isn't that ridiculous? Only they seemed to like it. And they were paying me so much I thought I should give them value for money.'

She says, 'You look wonderful, you always did. I just never remember you being well dressed.'

'No, I was a derelict in the old days, wasn't I?' he says in a self-satisfied tone.

She is immensely pleased that he calls their shared time the old days. It sounds precious and cherished. Already their conversation is flowing more easily than on the phone. They seem able to pick up signals from the sight of each other. He opens the champagne, saying, 'Let's have this now, shall we? After all, we might drop dead before midnight,' and she watches his hand, very strong as it twists the cork out of the bottle. She thinks of the other things she has seen it do. Then they chink their glasses together. 'Well, happy New Year,' he says again.

She would like him to say something romantic or most of all to touch her, but instead he wanders around looking at the few early paintings of hers that she still has hanging in her living-room. There is the usual silence in which they looked at each other's work in the past. They had learnt early on that constructive criticism often led to ill-feeling, although if they were in a jokey mood they could get away with awarding marks out of ten.

'Oh yes,' he says presently. 'I remember some of these. Some of my favourites from way back. How nice to see them again.'

'We were both derelicts in the old days,' Helen says. 'Only I still am.' She isn't sure if she means badly dressed or poor or both.

'You haven't compromised,' he says.

'Neither have you. But I haven't got lucky either.' She wonders if she sounds nervous. Perhaps she really is envious. She is shocked: how dreadful to envy Jordan his success. He deserves it. Only she deserves it too. She hopes she is not going to turn out to be mean-spirited, especially with a man she desires.

'I like your house,' he says. 'Now I can stop thinking of you living in your studio. It's nice to have a new space to think of you in.'

'Oh yes, of course,' she says. 'You've never seen the house.' She hates thinking she has existed in his memory as this impoverished person camping with her child in a draughty work place surrounded by paraffin heaters. But at least he will have remembered her as young. And she likes the way he talks, as if he is thinking of her often. She is pleasantly surprised.

83

'Did you buy it with your husband?' he asks. It's the first time he's mentioned Richard, as if he wasn't sure he existed.

'No, I bought it for me and Sally. Richard joined us later. Wasn't he lucky? I sweated blood to get this house.' She thinks she sounds bitter and it is not attractive. She remembers afternoons with Jordan when after working all morning she would go to his studio and they would make love on the floor or if it was cold between far-from-clean blankets on a very hard single bed. On the other afternoons he would visit her studio. She remembers them as being scrupulous about alternating their visits, as if equality was very important. Perhaps it is the loss of that painstaking equality that is troubling her now, rather than a lack of generosity about his success. They are equal no longer. Or is it simple nostalgia for past happiness? How idyllic it seems in memory: to work all morning, make love in the afternoon, then collect Sally from school. To have her three roles as painter, lover and mother so clearly defined, each filling their allotted space. She wonders if they were in order of priority too, but that is not a question she wants to answer. What a well-ordered life she led then, it now appears, but at the time she remembers thinking of it as chaotic because Jordan was married and in the evening she would see him passing her studio to go home to his wife. Sometimes he would call in with a present for Sally, a toy he had made or a piece of fruit left over from his lunch, and Helen would ache with longing for him, his presence starting a reminiscent echo like a pulse beating in her vagina. The more she got of him, the more she wanted, but she did not like to think of herself as a mistress, an other woman, a committer of adultery. It seemed to make nonsense of her parting from Carey. She kept thinking of Jordan's wife in the same position that she herself had occupied so recently, the humiliating position of the one deceived. And for that, a mere matter of principle, she had painfully let Jordan go. Whatever her purpose, she had not achieved

84

it, and her clear conscience had not comforted her much. She had deprived herself of pleasure and she had not saved the marriage with her sacrifice. Jordan had left her as instructed, but he had left his wife too, and gone to New York, where he met and married Hannah. That could have been me, she had thought, until she met Richard. By then loneliness had eroded her high-minded resolve and she had let him leave his wife for her. And the result was the same: she had ended up alone. Now, looking at Jordan, she is thinking again, It could have been me in New York with you. How different our lives might have been, Sally's and mine. No Richard, no Inge, no Felix. Just work and sex and the end of poverty. She had not thought of Jordan in a romantic light at the time: she only knew that they fitted. They could separate to work and meet to make love, and they gave each other space.

'Roast lamb,' she says. 'I hope that's all right.'

They pass a miserable evening. He can't understand her decision, now that he has admitted his fault and begged her forgiveness. He doesn't see why the decision can't be reversed. 'It's like a sentence of death,' he says. 'What are you trying to do, kill me? D'you want me to die, Lizzie?'

She hopes it is not something as banal as trying to teach him a lesson; the level of pain she feels seems way beyond that and mere spite will not soothe it. She says, 'I feel something has to change. We've never separated before but I've put up with all your affairs, whether I knew or not, for sixteen years, and this is the worst one ever. They were our friends, almost our family, and you can do this to them, to me. An abortion's a terrible thing for a young girl. And you've wrecked a marriage. And we've never talked about any of it, we've just carried on as if nothing happened, and now you've gone back for more as if you know I'll put up with anything because I always have. Surely you can see, Felix, something has got to change. I've got to do something to make you understand how I feel. I can't live like this any more, with you not caring how much you hurt me. I can't absorb all this pain indefinitely. There has to be some cut-off point, like limitation of damage, something you won't do because it hurts me, some sacrifice you can make, so I don't do all the giving and you all the taking. Can't you see that?'

Somewhere during this long speech she sees the hands of the clock moving through midnight and suddenly it is another year.

Jordan looks comfortably at home in her kitchen. He eats a lot. He praises her cooking. They discuss work, the art world, London and New York, Magdalen, gossip about old friends, compare notes on their children. They don't talk about Richard or Hannah. In fact they don't say anything of importance but as time goes on Helen thinks it matters less what they do or don't say. They are relaxing with each other, perhaps because they are old friends, perhaps because they have finished his bottle of champagne and are starting on her bottle of claret. He says, 'This is so much better than going to a party.'

'Well, I think so.' Helen smiles. She is beginning to feel euphoric. The luxury of having Jordan for New Year's Eve is really getting to her. 'I'm hopeless at them, I've given up. I can't stand the noise and what passes for conversation. People hate me anyway, I'm so anti-social.'

'So am I. But I've been pretending lately. Since Hannah died.' He says the word defiantly, as if to prove he can. 'Getting out and about. Being high-profile. All that rubbish. Singing for my supper.'

'Well, you don't have to do that here.'

'Don't I?' He looks at her very directly. 'Are you sure you're not expecting more than I can deliver?'

'I don't know – am I?' She feels embarrassed yet relieved at the directness.

'I'm no good to man or beast at the moment,' he says. 'Just so long as you know that.'

'Well, I'm not either of those. I'm just glad you're here. I'd be having a gruesome evening otherwise.' She feels disappointment tug at her; she feels apprehensive. There is something ominous about being warned off. It's as if she has suddenly stubbed her toe on something solid and sharp. Simple grief, perhaps. It hurts and it pulls her up short.

'Me too,' he says.

They still haven't touched. No handshake, no kiss on the cheek. They never went in for social touching. It is as if they are still circling round each other, sniffing.

'Is your husband around?' he asks suddenly.

'You mean, is he going to burst in? No, we separated last spring.' She glances at the clock. 'Last year, I'll be able to say in a couple of hours. It sounds tidy, put like that. But it was very messy.'

'I'm sorry,' he says. 'Or maybe not? Should I be sorry?'

'No, it's all for the best. I'm just beginning to realise that. He's gone back to his first wife actually. I really have a magic touch with men, don't I?'

Jordan laughs and after a moment she joins in. 'Well,' she says, getting up to clear away the plates, 'chocolate mousse be all right?'

'My God,' he says, 'for a woman who hates cooking, you've really pulled out all the stops.'

'I know,' she says. 'Flattering, isn't it?'

As she passes him he suddenly gets up and puts his arms round her. She hugs him so tightly she quite frightens herself. They stand there in silence holding each other for some time. It is such a relief. They don't kiss. She can feel their hearts beating. She breathes in his smell and goes back fifteen years.

'You've had a bad time,' he says, not a question.

'So have you.'

More time passes. She says, 'Will you stay?'

'I may not be any good to you.'

'You don't have to be good,' she says. 'You just have to be here.'

They go upstairs with their arms still round each other and into her bedroom where they undress and get into bed without drawing the curtains or putting on the light. There is moonlight and a streetlamp. His body is heavier than she remembers. They hold each other naked in bed and she starts to cry. She cries for a long time and he goes on holding her. Eventually she stops crying and gets some tissues from the bedside table to blow her nose. She says, 'Oh. I didn't know I was going to do that.' She feels exhausted, drained but peaceful.

'It's good for you,' he says calmly.

They lie there in silence for a while. Then there are a few sounds of cheerful, drunken people shouting in the street, cars passing, bottles breaking. Then silence again. She feels safe and realises she hasn't felt safe for many years.

He says, 'D'you mind if we don't see in the new year? I'd rather not know the time,' and she turns the bedside clock to face the wall.

He says, 'I haven't made love to anyone for a year. I don't know if I can make love to you although I'd like to.'

'It doesn't matter,' she says, meaning it.

He says after a pause, 'I had an affair while Hannah was dying. I'd never been unfaithful to her all the time we were married, never wanted to be, but I needed someone then. Hannah took eighteen months to die. She had three operations and chemotherapy and all her hair fell out. She shrank before my eyes. She got so light, she was like a dead bird at the end. And I had this affair. I used to have this woman every day at the studio and then I'd go back to Hannah, back to the hospital or back home, wherever she was, and do what I could, just be with her. And I did the series of drawings I told you about. People thought it was weird but she liked me drawing her right up to the end. I'm not sure if she knew I was having an affair. And then she died and I immediately broke off the affair and never saw the woman again. And I'm not sure who I treated worse, Hannah or the woman.'

Helen says, 'What was her name?'

'She didn't have a name.'

He is shaking. Helen says, 'It's all right, Jordan, really it is.'

He says, 'It doesn't feel all right.'

'You had to get through it somehow. When was it? Last Christmas?'

He says, 'It was tonight. A year ago tonight. It's now. We're right up against it now and I don't want to know the time.'

She says, 'It's all right, we won't look.' She cuddles him like a child, holding him protectively in her arms and stroking his head. Presently, they sleep.

Towards dawn they wake and kiss for the first time. She feels his cock pressing against her leg, not very hard but hard enough. He strokes her breast and slides his hand between her legs in a tentative way as if checking to see if she wants to be aroused. She shakes her head slightly and helps him ease his cock inside her. He sighs and they move gently, tenderly together in a sort of trance, half awake, half asleep, until he comes with what sounds like a cry of relief. It is not the fantasy sex she has imagined or remembered, but it is what they both need. She is not thinking of pleasure, more of coming home after a long journey, of filling an empty place.

Felix says humbly, 'I'll do whatever you say. But you don't have to make me leave. Don't send me away,

Lizzie. I won't be able to manage. You really are my life. I thought you knew that.'

She says, 'But I don't like the way you show it.'

He says, 'I know I'm a selfish person, maybe even a bad person, but I love you. I really do love you. As much as I can love anyone.'

'Felix, that's just a word. It doesn't mean anything. It just oils the wheels. That's how you get your own way with everyone.' She hadn't realised how hard she could be.

He says, astonished, 'You sound as if you hate me.'

'I'm very tired.'

They lie tensely side by side in the darkness in their big bed. They hold hands.

He says, 'Lizzie? Can I stay? Tell me I can stay.'

'No.' She is even beginning to feel sorry for him instead of herself. 'We have to have a break.'

'But why? I've learnt my lesson. God knows, you've frightened me to death, if that's what you wanted.'

She says, 'I just can't live like this any more. I want something to change. We've got to have time apart, time to think.'

He hears the finality in her voice. After a while he says, 'How long?'

'I don't know.' She notices they are both assuming it can't be for ever and she wonders if they are right.

He says hopefully, 'A week?'

She says, 'No. At least three months,' and hears him gasp as if in pain. 'Let's try to sleep now,' she says. A clock strikes three.

They wake early after a wretched night. Felix feels as if he has not slept at all, though he presumes he must have done at some point, however briefly. He knows Elizabeth has because he heard her snoring occasionally, something she rarely does, unless of course he has usually fallen asleep first and so seldom noticed. It seemed like especially heartless behaviour: he was shocked that she could actually sleep after causing him such pain. He didn't even like to give her the vicious dig in the ribs he felt she deserved, in case she woke up and said more dreadful things to him, or banished him to the spare room, or left him alone in the big bed. It is a new sensation to be afraid of her.

Through the night in a haze of exhaustion he told himself that in the morning he would get her to change her mind, but now it is morning and she is still implacable. The night has been like a bad dream that is still going on even now it is daylight. He has sometimes dreamed he was dreaming before, a dream within a dream, so that when he woke with relief from one nightmare the other was still going on and he was not yet awake. It was like running down an endless corridor where one room opened into another for evermore, and it always left him weak and shaken, which is how he feels now.

They sit in the kitchen in their dressing-gowns drinking coffee. Elizabeth looks terrible, much older than her age, her skin papery, her eyes puffy and deeply shadowed. She looks wrecked. He feels as if he has never loved her more.

He says, 'Lizzie? Can't you forgive me now? Don't send me away. I really have learnt my lesson.'

She shakes her head with a curious calmness, almost automatic, as if matters were quite beyond her control. 'I'm sorry, Felix, but something has to change.'

'But it will,' he says. 'It has already.'

'No,' she says. 'I don't think so. If I let you stay now, it will all go on just the same, the way it did before.'

His eyes feel gritty and swollen with lack of sleep. He remembers crying in her arms the night before and how even that didn't move her. He feels the ground is opening beneath his feet.

He says, 'You really want to punish me, don't you?'

She repeats, 'I want something to change, that's all.'
After a pause he says, 'But where am I meant to go?'
She shrugs. 'I don't know. You've got the flat.'
'And if I don't move out?' he says, playing his last card.
'Then I will.'
He obviously can't let that happen. That wouldn't prove his love for her at all.

They sit in the kitchen again, Jordan looking ridiculously large in a dressing-gown so ancient that Richard didn't bother to take it with him. Helen makes coffee. Jordan eats the chocolate mousse from last night.

'Just the thing for breakfast,' he says.

'Happy New Year,' Helen says seriously.

They take aspirin with their coffee. They don't quite have hangovers but they don't quite feel all right either. It's like being students again, Helen thinks, although of course they never were students together: a sort of ramshackle feeling about the day.

Jordan says, 'What happened with Richard?'

'Oh.' She wonders if he's really interested or just being polite, if she owes him the whole miserable tale because of the things he told her last night, to balance up their confidence, to make them equal. 'Long story,' she says. 'I probably never should have married him in the first place.' She's surprised to hear herself say that but it suddenly feels right; it seems to be the conclusion she has reached and nothing to do with Felix or Sally at all. It's quite a shock. I thought I was a different sort of person and it turns out I wasn't.'

Jordan says, 'Yes, that *is* a long story.'

'Oh, I expect I'll tell you all about it some time.' What she really means is, if you give me another chance.

'Do you miss him?'

'Not at the moment.'

They smile at each other.

'Why did he go back to his first wife? I can't imagine doing that. Not that either of my ex-wives would have had me back, of course.'

'Well, she's a very forceful German woman and she just never gave up till she got him. I played into her hands, I suppose. I behaved as if it was still just Sally and me on our own.'

'That's how I always thought of you,' he says.

'Yes, of course. That's how I was when you knew me. And it's how I am again, except now she's at Sussex. Funny really, fifteen years on and I'm back in the same place as if I've gone round in a circle. Just older. It's as if I haven't made any progress at all.'

'You've got the house,' he points out.

'Yes, I've got the house.' She can sense him edging away from her, preparing to leave, and she feels panic. 'I hope we're going to keep in touch,' she says steadily. She's afraid he may be already regretting their sudden intimacy.

'I expect we will,' he says, as if it were beyond his control. 'I'm just not very good with people at the moment. If I ever was.'

'I'm not people, Jordan,' she says.

'I know. Just . . . if you can think of me as covered in bandages it may help.'

'Me too,' she says.

'Well,' he says, stretching, 'time I was getting some clothes on.'

She longs to say, Stay with me, we need each other, let's spend the day together as well as the night, but she doesn't. Instead she watches him go upstairs and when he comes back he is dressed for departure and she feels an ache of loneliness beginning. But then he puts his arms round her. They have a big hug and it is suddenly all right again.

'Well,' he says, looking down at her.

'Yes, quite,' she says. They smile.

He says, 'The thing is, I just don't have very much left to give anyone at the moment.'

'I know. But I seem to want it anyway. Just so long as you don't give me any of that sixties' crap about not getting involved.'

'I won't.' He kisses the top of her head. 'See you soon.'

'Take care.'

She watches him leave. She goes back upstairs, gets into their sheets that still smell of him and without even blaming herself spends the rest of the day in bed. If I were in hospital, she thinks, they'd say I'm doing as well as can be expected.

PART THREE

It's quite a shock when Richard rings the next day. 'Helen, can I see you?' he says. He sounds urgent.

She's completely overturned by his voice, as if he had risen from the dead. Her mind is still occupied by Jordan and New Year's Eve, and she is stupefied from excess sleep after spending all day and night in bed. So she feels alert but stunned at the same time, like someone on guard with cotton wool in her ears, or swimming underwater, with the real world muffled and a long way off. 'Richard?' she says stupidly. He seems remote to her. She can't think why he is telephoning.

'Please let me come round,' he says, as if she were arguing with him. 'I need to talk to you.'

'What about?' she says. It can only be reconciliation or divorce, she thinks, for what other options are there? And she doesn't particularly want to discuss either right now, if ever. She feels unfairly caught, at a disadvantage in her dressing-gown: another half hour and she would have left for the studio.

'Can I tell you when I see you?' he says. 'It's hard to do on the phone.'

'Well, I suppose so,' she says doubtfully. The habits of marriage are hard to break and she is still predisposed to say yes to him. But it feels very odd: it is months since they've spoken and all the old anger is rumbling inside her, overlaid with new feelings about Jordan. 'When d'you want to come?'

'Could I come now?' he says. 'I'm at the library and it's hard to make another excuse for later.'

'Oh, for God's sake,' she says. He sounds like a little boy playing truant, and she nearly tells him so.

'I'll be there in half an hour,' he says and hangs up.

Before she can say no, presumably. She gets dressed and makes fresh coffee. He has messed up her nice clean promising day, like a child scribbling on a blank canvas.

He arrives in forty-five minutes and apologises for the Northern line. She is shocked to see how changed he is: he looks tired and ill and he has lost weight.

She says, 'God, you look awful. Isn't she feeding you? I thought at least she could manage that.' She frowns at the sound of her own words, the shrewish tone. We really shouldn't meet, she thinks, if I'm going to be like this.

He says, 'Oh, please don't,' and she says, 'No, I'm sorry.' She pours him some of the coffee she has just made and gives it to him. They sit at the kitchen table where they have so often sat before, where he still looks at home, like a husband. But it's also where Jordan so recently sat and she has the double image in her mind. He says, 'Oh Helen, why did we ever break up? I can't believe the mess I'm in. Inge's just told me she's pregnant and I feel so trapped.'

She's shocked, not just by the news but also by the obvious fact that he is expecting sympathy. She can tell from the way he looks at her, as he often did after a bad day at work, expecting her to listen and make it all magically better by saying the right thing. And often she had. But now she just says, 'I don't think that's any of my business.' She's angry that he wants sympathy from her for a mess of his own making. She thinks quite viciously that it serves him right. She feels disgusted and jealous and she hates him for making her feel like that.

'I had to tell you, that's all,' he says hopelessly. 'She told me on Christmas Eve, it was such a terrible shock. I didn't want this to happen, I mean I was hoping we could get back together one day, you and I.'

'Oh really?' she says, astonished. 'You didn't bother to tell me that. Look, Richard, you left me last April, we didn't talk about it, you came and took your things like a burglar, it's months since we've seen each other or even spoken. Why d'you think you can turn up here and tell me Inge's pregnant but you were hoping we could get back together? Why d'you expect me to be all sympathetic? For God's sake.'

He says, 'Yes, I can see you're very angry, quite rightly.'

'Fuck you,' she screams at him, amazing herself. 'I'm not one of your fucking clients, don't give me all that understanding shit.'

He looks quite surprised. He obviously couldn't see that she was as angry as that. She feels a lot better for her explosion and she pours herself more coffee without offering him any. A small revenge, but it's a start.

'I should never have gone back to her,' he says, as if to himself.

'Well, you wanted to punish me, didn't you?'

'And I've only punished myself. Yes, it serves me right. Only now there's another child to consider.'

'Well, you could have avoided that,' she says sharply.

Then a long silence, and she wishes he would leave. She keeps seeing Inge swollen with pregnancy. She thinks what a triumph it must be. She imagines the jubilation. And she suddenly wonders if she will ever see Jordan again. She looks at Richard across the table and thinks how far apart they are.

He says, 'I was wrong, I'm sorry. I should never have left you, whatever you did about Sally. I need you, I love you. I can't bear to live like this.'

She thinks how recently she would have given anything to hear those words.

He says, 'Look, I've had time to think – I know I've made a dreadful mistake. When I went back to Inge I was angry with you and there didn't seem anywhere else to go. And I wanted to do right by her and the boys, you know, give it another chance. But if this hadn't happened I think I'd have left again anyway, sooner or later.'

'It doesn't just happen, Richard,' she says. 'It doesn't fall from the sky.'

'I know. I'm sorry.'

He looks so defeated that in spite of herself she almost feels sorry for him. A sudden sharp twinge of pity, quickly suppressed.

'But we hardly ever, in fact,' he says, looking embarrassed. 'I mean I really didn't want to, we had to go to a therapist and —'

'Shut up,' she says, 'please. I don't want to hear about any of that.'

'Anyway, it means I can't leave her,' he says. 'Not now.'

'So why are you here? D'you want a quick divorce or something? Is that it?'

'No.' He looks shocked. 'That's the last thing I want. I want to see you, be with you. I don't know how to get through this if I can't see you.'

'Oh, Richard,' she says, feeling already heavy with the burden he is trying to share. 'What a mess.'

'If I could just visit you sometimes,' he says, pleading. 'It's the only way I can bear life with Inge.'

'Visit me?' she says. 'How d'you mean? Like when we met? As if none of this had happened? Just wipe out the last ten years?' The idea makes her feel crazy, as if they have gone back in time, especially after seeing Jordan again: various circles of her past life are returning and orbiting each other, so that she can't live in the present at all. 'You mean – for a chat? Or a bit on the side? Is that what you mean?'

He says, 'I don't know what I mean. I'm desperate, I just want you back on any terms at all. Whatever you say.'

'While you live with Inge.'

'Well, I can't leave her now.'

'Nobody's asking you to leave her. I'm just amazed you think you can walk in here and ask me to prop you up while you live with her. And I'm supposed to be thrilled because you'd rather be with me. God, Richard.'

'I'm sorry,' he says. 'I've put it badly. I've been lying

awake worrying about it but I'm no good at words today. I just know I feel awful and I need you.'

She's sick of being needed. It seems as if everyone comes to her and drains her energy, then goes away replenished, giving her nothing. Sally, Elizabeth, even Jordan. And now Richard. Why is she expected to be so strong that she can go on running on empty? Why is she supposed to be able to work and survive without any help?

'Maybe it won't be as bad as you think,' she says. 'You've always wanted another child and it may calm her down.'

'But I wanted one with you.'

His sentimental tone enrages her. 'What's the point of telling me that again now? I didn't want one when we were together, did I? Look, Richard, I was very lonely when you left me. I've had to make a huge effort to get adjusted to all this. You've just gone from me to her, but I've had to learn how to live alone again. Well, I'm used to it now. I don't want to be upset again, trying to help you with your problems when we're not together. Why should I? You're not trying to help me, are you?'

'You won't let me,' he says.

'God, you're not listening. When I needed help you weren't there, were you? And you're only here now because *you* need help.'

'I'm saying I'm sorry,' he says, as if it were an enormous gift. 'I've made a mistake. I love you.'

'But you've got Inge pregnant. That's a pretty big mistake. That's a *fact*. Love's just a word. It means whatever you want it to mean.'

'That's not fair,' he says. 'She tricked me.'

'God, Richard, she did that twenty years ago. Don't you know what she's like by now?'

'Yes,' he says, 'I suppose I deserve that. But I was trying to play fair with her.'

'And now you don't have to? Is that what you mean? And I'm supposed to be thrilled?'

'I don't know what to say any more,' he says. 'You're so angry with me. I suppose it's all my fault but . . .' His voice trails away.

'You hardly need me to be sorry for you,' Helen says, feeling spiteful. 'You're so bloody sorry for yourself.'

He looks surprised, as though she has hit him. Immediately she feels guilty, and furious that he can still have that effect on her.

'Oh, look,' she says. 'I shouldn't have said that. I know you're having a bad time with Inge. But it wasn't perfect with me either. Don't you remember? Honestly, when you think back, there was an awful lot wrong with our marriage. We expected so much of each other and we were so disappointed when we didn't get it. Don't you think?'

'No,' he says. 'Not till the very end. I thought it was wonderful.'

'Well, so did I at the time, but now looking back I think we were both compromising far too much.'

He shakes his head. 'What d'you mean?'

'Well, we didn't see each other as we really are till the end, did we?' She is thinking of what she said to Jordan about not being a different sort of person after all. 'And then we didn't like what we saw. We put each other on pedestals and then we blamed each other for falling off.'

He says simply, 'But I love you,' as if that can make everything all right.

She feels oppressed; she longs for him to go. And yet there is still a tug at her heart. What is it? His years of helping her bring up Sally, perhaps? Simple gratitude or just time spent together that she can't wipe out. Time when he stopped her from being lonely. Time when she thought she had made sense of her life.

She says, 'Look, I'm not saying we can't be friends. We can keep in touch, of course. You can ring me when you feel like a chat.' She means it: she can't quite let go. And yet at the same time she wishes he'd walk away from her for ever. It would be cleaner. It would be a quick cut, a painful relief.

He says, 'Well, I'd better go. It's a long time to be at the library.'

'Yes.' She gets up to see him to the door. She feels very tired. He seems to have been with her for hours, but she sees from the clock that only forty minutes have passed.

'I thought I might see Sally,' he says.

'She's having a few days with Carey.'

'Oh, of course. How is she?'

'All right. Fine.'

This gets them to the front door. A dreadful moment: she can see from his movements and the look on his face that he might be going to hug her and she doesn't want to be touched. She moves away from him. He says abruptly, with sharp suspicion, 'Have you met someone else?'

She is furious to be asked but she doesn't want to lie, although he deserves a lie, and the truth is too intimate to share with him. 'A new man, you mean?' she says, fudging the question. 'No, but I wouldn't tell you if I had. I don't think you've got any right to ask me that.'

He goes away without replying. His retreating back looks defeated and weary and she closes the door quickly after him.

All the way back in the tube he tries to contain his disappointment. She had a right to be angry, after all. Perhaps now she's expressed her anger she will think about what he said. Perhaps they will talk again and it can all be different. Foolish to imagine it could be resolved in one meeting, he tells himself.

But the thought of her with someone else torments him. A shadowy figure he can't put a face to, touching her, holding her, making love to her. He can't bear it. He thinks of her carefully worded answer and he senses, if not a lie, a prevarication. Is it his knowledge of her, after all the shared years, or his probation experience, an instinct that used to tell him when clients were not quite truthful? Someone from her past then? Carey, perhaps? Could she be consoling herself with Carey? Could Carey be taking advantage of the situation to insinuate himself back into her life through the link with Sally?

He nearly misses his stop and has to elbow his way out at the last moment. When he gets home Inge looks at him accusingly.

'Where have you been?'

'At the library – I told you.'

'You were so long I came to look for you and you weren't there.' Her voice is shaky.

'I went for a walk to clear my head.'

'I wanted you to help me with the shopping.'

'Well, we can do that after lunch.'

'And we could have had a walk together.'

'We can still do that.'

But he can tell she knows he has lied to her, just as he knows Helen lied to him. He smiles at her reassuringly, at her hurt sad face.

Felix hates living alone. He hasn't done it since he was twenty-five and he didn't like it even then. It makes him feel as if he doesn't exist. At first he is simply in shock, moving into the flat with a couple of suitcases and hourly expecting Elizabeth to phone him to say she's made a terrible mistake and beg him to come home. But she doesn't. He fiddles miserably with the final pages of the book, revising them until they seem to be all right, as far as he can tell. His judgment seems to be gone and the book itself has become irrelevant, though previously it was his dearest child. This has never happened before and it terrifies him. He doesn't like to think what would have happened if Elizabeth had dropped this bomb on him before the book was finished. Even so, he puts off sending it to his publishers. If they don't like it he will feel suicidal, whereas normally it would never occur to him there could be anything wrong with the book because Elizabeth would have spent many hours telling him in great detail how wonderful it was. He wonders if there is any chance that she might still do that if he asks her to read it, but he supposes not and he lacks the courage to try.

A week passes like this, during which he phones her twice. She sounds sad but composed. 'I did ask you not to phone me,' she says.

'That's too much to ask,' he says. 'You know it is.'

'Well, I can't talk now, I've got someone here.'

'Will you ring me back?'

A pause. 'No. It's better not.'

He leaves it a few days, smarting with the insult, then tries again.

'Felix, please don't do this,' she says.

'But I have to talk to you.'

'No. It doesn't help.'

He can't afford a hotel but he hates the flat now. It doesn't seem like a refuge any more: it is haunted by memories of Sally and Richard and Inge, the same memories that didn't trouble him before, that used to seem merely interesting and dramatic. He feels unreal in it now, as if he is living in a stage set. It was never meant to be home. He only ever intended it as a place for work and sex, and now it's not being used for either. As a delicious useful secret, it was glamorous; as his only refuge it is merely sordid. It only ever made sense in the context of going home to Elizabeth, and now he can't do that it is like one half of a seesaw.

It is also much too small: he finds it almost impossible to live in such a confined space. The bathroom and kitchen are tiny and he hates cooking anyway, so he eats out or has meals sent in. The bed is better suited to love-making than sleep and very soon gives him backache. He thinks with longing of his house, with its large rooms and its river view, his vast bed and his stereo system. He feels like an exile. He doesn't want to think of himself as lonely because it is such a dirty work, evoking pity or contempt, something that afflicts other less fortunate people, like bad breath or VD. But he realises how few friends he has, how work and affairs have occupied all his time, how he has depended on Elizabeth for his social life. Now is the time he needs Richard most of all. But Richard has never responded to his friendly notes offering a truce.

Grief and panic soon turn to rage. He is very angry with Elizabeth. She must know that she is calling up all his insecurity from the time his mother abandoned him when he was a little boy. He always begged her not to leave him and she promised she never would. Whereas he never promised to be faithful, and she accepted that. Her betrayal seems to him far more serious than his. He wouldn't say she is making a fuss about nothing, but his punishment seems out of all proportion to his crime.

He is still in this mood when he drives down to see Sally a week later: furious with Elizabeth and in need of consolation. He has also sent the book to his editor, and this now feels like an act of nervous aggression. But Sally looks surprised to see him and not entirely overjoyed. 'It's been ages,' she says. 'Why didn't you write?'

'I didn't feel much like writing,' he says. 'I get enough of that earning a living. You know that. If you were on the phone I'd phone you.'

'You've always written before,' she says. 'It feels funny, having you just turn up. I might have been out, or busy.'

'Or in bed with someone else,' he says. 'Is that what you mean?'

'That's not the point,' she says. 'I feel taken for granted if you don't let me know you're coming.'

She takes the flowers he has brought her and puts them in the wash-basin, which she then half fills with cold water. He wonders if she really has got someone else and how he would feel if he caught them together: excited or demeaned? Or would she simply lock the door and not answer when he knocked? There is so much he doesn't know about her. She seems combative today, as if she had been on some assertiveness training course, and it's not attractive. Perhaps he never knew her very well. But she is looking and smelling good and he wants her. He would like to blot out all his anxieties by making love to her, submerge himself in her body and forget about Elizabeth and the book and his mother, forget everything that has ever caused him pain. He would like to feel safe and desirable again. It doesn't seem much to ask. But when he touches her she pulls away.

'I'm hungry,' she says. 'Can't we eat first?'

So he takes her out to lunch and spends money on her, to purge his offence. He buys expensive food and wine that he doesn't want, and exerts himself to be witty and charming while anxiety thumps in his brain like a persistent headache. By the time they get back to her room he is exhausted and whatever erotic urge he had has gone. But now she pulls him close to her; she feels relaxed and forgiving, slightly drunk. 'Well,' she says, kissing him, 'are you going to fuck me now?'

His instinct tells him to retreat with honour and live to fight another day. Pride urges him on. They fall on the bed in a tense silence that seems to have very little to do with pleasure. She comes quickly and easily with his tongue or his hand on her clitoris; she comes several times and he feels envy. He gives her even more attention than usual in the hope of exciting himself or postponing the moment of defeat, but he knows with a dreadful doomed certainty that his cock is not going to obey him, that it is impervious to their hands and her mouth, though these all work with desperate efficiency and determination, like an emergency team trying to revive a cardiac arrest. He tries every fantasy that has ever succeeded for him, riffling through his filing system like someone slamming tapes in and out of a video recorder, but not even the dirtiest favourite will do the trick. He doesn't feel relaxed enough to talk her through one of them; he would rather stop before he is totally humiliated, bending and flopping against her, a travesty of his former self. If they could cuddle for a while, he thinks; if he could sleep for a while, perhaps. It wouldn't matter so much if it was someone else, on another day. He could even have made a joke of it. But it is Sally, and their relationship has been shifting for a long time. He feels dreadfully exposed with her: she is too young to understand that this can happen to anyone, though in fact it has seldom happened to him. This was meant to be an act of vengeance, a fuck of defiance, a V-sign directed at Elizabeth. And, probably for that very reason, it is not going to happen.

'I'm sorry, darling,' he says, stopping. 'I'm just not in the mood.'

'Don't you fancy me any more?' A small, resentful voice. He is angry with her for not being old enough to understand. No doubt all the boys of her acquaintance have permanent hard-ons. An older woman would have made excuses for him, pretended it didn't matter, blamed the wine, or assured him she was satisfied by all the pleasure he had already given her. Or she might have thought of some way of exciting him enough. Or they could have joked, cuddled, slept, and next time the phoenix would have risen from the ashes. Sally does none of these things. Sally wants blood.

'Don't be silly, of course I fancy you,' he says. 'I wouldn't be here if I didn't. These things happen. I'm very depressed, it's hardly surprising.' He hadn't meant to say that.

'Why are you depressed?'

He hesitates. 'Elizabeth and I have separated for a few weeks.' It frightens him to hear the words out loud: it makes it seem real. She is the first person he has told. 'I'm living at the flat. It's all taken a bit of getting used to, that's all.'

Sally sits up and pulls on a dressing-gown that was lying on the floor. She gets off the bed and goes to open a can of Coke that was standing on the window sill. It splashes her as it opens and she says, 'Oh, shit. Why have you separated?'

'It's only temporary,' he says. He feels suddenly cold now and starts to get dressed.

'Yes, you said. What happened?'

'She went to see Helen and got all the details out of her.'

Sally shrugs. 'I thought she must have known already. God, she met me coming out of your room in hospital, didn't she?'

'Well, we never talked about it before.'

Sally turns round with the tin of Coke in her hand. 'You're really upset, aren't you?'

'Well, of course. We had a horrible scene. And it's no joke trying to live at the flat.'

'And that's why we can't make love?'

He notices that she isn't counting all the clitoral orgasms she's had, though she wouldn't like to do without them; she is still making him feel he's failed because he hasn't come up with a duty fuck. 'Well, it doesn't help,' he says.

Sally drains the can of Coke and throws it into the full waste-paper basket, but it bounces off all the screwed-up paper and lands on the floor. 'I didn't realise Elizabeth was so important,' she says in a small cold voice.

*

They try to discuss it but they are uneasy with each other. They both need a proper drink now but he didn't bring a bottle, only flowers, so they go to the student bar where he has to tolerate noise and smoke and disco music that gives him a headache. He has two double Scotches rather quickly and hopes he doesn't get stopped on the way home. Then he remembers that he has no home.

Sally says, 'I thought Elizabeth was used to you having affairs. Why has she thrown you out because of me? After all, I wasn't that important, was I? You didn't leave her for me, did you? And I was really obedient, I had my abortion good as gold when you said I should, you and Mum.'

He can see that she is going for the jugular, choosing this moment for dreadful recriminations. The cruelty of the young. She has no mercy. Hit a man when he's down and all that. Put the boot in. And he doesn't like being described as thrown out. He gets a sudden image of himself hurtling through the air and landing on the ground. He can almost feel the gravel grazing his face.

'You were too young and too close to home. And she was upset about the pregnancy,' he says. 'And she found out we were still in touch.'

'So I am sort of special after all. At least I've upset Elizabeth. I'm sorry, I've always liked her. D'you think I should write and apologise?'

'Don't be ridiculous,' he says. 'Things are quite bad enough already.'

'Yes, they certainly are. I didn't realise we were so dependent on her goodwill.'

So much anger still. 'Oh Sally,' he says wearily, 'why do both of you have to do this to me now, when it all happened over a year ago?'

'I suppose we've both bottled it up for far too long,' she says.

They sit and look at each other in the noisy bar, and he wonders if it really is all over and he has inadvertently told Elizabeth the truth. But still they don't quite say good-bye.

Elizabeth wakes each morning to remember that Felix is no longer there. The bed seems hugely empty, and she has to reabsorb the enormity of what she has done. But once she has adjusted to the shock, a sensation of peace takes over. At least there will be no more pain. She has another day of calm ahead of her, when nothing can happen to disturb her equilibrium.

She sees herself as convalescent, giving her emotions a breathing space for the first time since she married Felix sixteen years ago, in much the same way that she might have lain in bed with a broken leg suspended in plaster. She is resting her heart.

She knows that Felix feels outraged and wounded by her decision, but she is determined not to give way. Three months apart, she has told him, and then they will meet to review the situation. Ideally, she would like him not to phone her and she has asked him not to, but he does. His voice moves her profoundly but she is also enraged at the way he still ignores her wishes. She tried to keep the conversation brief, again very much like an invalid who is too tired to talk. She can't quite bring herself to hang up on him, so she leaves the answering machine on as much as possible and she never rings him back. As time passes, she hears the sound of his voice change from pleading into anger and then coldness, until his calls become less frequent and finally stop. She is scared but she has to persevere, or what she has endured so far will be all for nothing. She is surprised by the strength of her own resolve.

She knows she is trying to achieve one of two things but she isn't sure which: either to accept that their marriage is over and she prefers to live apart from him, or to convince him that they can only survive together on different terms. She doesn't think of it as crudely as trying to teach him a lesson, although other people might; she thinks it is far more complicated than that, and she would not have had the courage to do anything so casually vindictive. She feels she is trying this experiment because she has no choice, because she is emotionally exhausted, because there is nothing else she can do.

She is lonely but calm. She has lived alone for many years before she met Felix, so it is not a skill she has to learn, rather something she remembers from her youth, like riding a bicycle, an ability people say you never lose. She tries to keep busy, though, so as not to have time to think, and she tries not to drink too much. She is beginning to realise how much she and Felix drank, and it scares her. She puts in more hours at the office, taking on a heavier workload, and going to more publishing parties to improve her image as well as her social life. It is a strangely exposed feeling, knowing she is there without Felix to go home to, alone in her professional capacity with an open-ended evening.

The parties are the same as ever, noisy and crowded, full of people smoking and drinking and exchanging gossip. Some of them she likes, most of them she can tolerate, a few of them she actually hates. She is beginning to feel herself on a party treadmill, as if she has signed on at a club to work out with weights for the good of her health. Perhaps this would be worth doing, she thinks; maybe she should take it seriously. Then one evening at one of these parties she finds herself in a corner beside someone's filing-cabinet next to a gaunt, dark-eyed young man who seems ill at ease, almost visibly skulking, as if he has no right to be there. She recognises him at once.

'You're David Johnson, aren't you?' she says, wanting to cheer him up with some attention, remembering how shy she had felt at parties when she was young. 'I'm Elizabeth Cramer, I'm an editor at Bloomfield Press. I loved your book. It's a great achievement, winning a prize like that with a first novel.'

He smiles faintly and swallows his glass of red wine rather fast. 'Those prizes are all very well,' he says, 'but they put so much pressure on you. People expect bloody miracles afterwards.'

She says kindly, 'Are you worrying about your second novel? I'd try to relax if I were you. Rest on your laurels for a bit. That's what the money's for, you know, to buy you time.'

'If only it were,' he says, seizing another glass of wine from a passing waiter. 'I'm afraid most of it is going to my wife and kids. We're getting divorced.'

Elizabeth is still surprised at the speed with which men tell her their troubles. It has been happening all her life but she hasn't got used to it. If she lets them, and she often does, out of a blend of sympathy, curiosity and inertia, they will talk about themselves for hours, then tell her she is a very interesting woman.

'It's ironic,' David Johnson says. 'She's stuck by me all the difficult years, when we didn't have any money. She's a teacher and I used to work in a pub so we could make ends meet and I'd still have time to write. We've been together fifteen years.'

'Good heavens,' Elizabeth says, 'you don't look old enough.' She doesn't mean to be flirtatious or patronising; she is genuinely surprised. She knows in fact from his book jacket that he is thirty-five, but if she hadn't known she would have guessed about twenty-eight. He has untidy dark floppy hair, heavy and straight, like an old-fashioned hippy, and a narrow, hollow-cheeked face; he is dressed all in black, with a turtle-necked sweater under his jacket, and he has bony protruding wrists, as if his sleeves are too short for his arms. Only his eyes are old, dark and intense, eyes that have seen a lot of trouble, she thinks. Then he smiles and he looks completely different, full of charm and ease. She finds herself noticing that he has a very beautiful mouth.

'I imagine it's always a shock when you break up with

someone after so long,' he says. 'Don't you feel that too in your situation?'

Elizabeth is startled. She thinks he is taking advantage of her kindness with a presumptuous intimacy and she feels her social smile freezing. 'News certainly travels fast in this business,' she says rather coldly. 'And it's only a trial separation.'

'I hope I haven't offended you,' he says, looking concerned.

Elizabeth says, 'Not at all. Excuse me,' and moves away. Her heart is suddenly racing and she is alarmed to realise how vulnerable she is. He hadn't even mentioned Felix's name.

A few days later flowers arrive at her office with a note from David Johnson: 'Forgive me for being tactless. Please have dinner with me.' The flowers are lilies, ornate and heavily scented, but so white and elegantly poised they remind her of swans. They are obviously very expensive too, a big romantic gesture. He has lashed out some of his prize money, the bit that hasn't gone to his wife and children. What to do? Courtesy dictates a reply, but should it be thank you, yes, or thank you, no? She really isn't sure what she wants. She has used up several weeks of her time apart from Felix and used it negatively in resisting his phone calls, which have now ceased. She feels a little bereft at having nothing to push against. She is beginning to miss him. She is beginning to wonder what he is doing with all his extra freedom and whether she was wise to give him so much of it. She feels that she and Felix are at war and involved in a dangerous game of counter-espionage. She feels exhausted from being so brave.

She rings David Johnson on the number he has given her, aware that she could instead have written a polite note declining his invitation. Does this mean that she wants to say yes or merely keep her options open? She feels split in two, and one half is not in the confidence of the other. It's alarming, when she has always been so steady and reliable. Is she perhaps becoming frivolous, so late in life?

As soon as she says his name he says, 'Elizabeth?' She's amazed that anyone could recognise her voice so quickly after one meeting.

'I want to thank you for the wonderful lilies,' she says. She hears herself being charming.

'D'you like them?' He sounds relieved. 'They're my favourites but I thought you might like them too.'

'I love them,' she says.

'A bit like *Swan Lake*,' he says, 'I always think.'

That is such a shock that she is silent and he says again, 'Elizabeth?'

She says, 'Yes, I thought that.'

'Does that mean you'll have dinner with me?'

A dreadful moment of choice. She thinks, What am I doing? I love Felix, why am I flirting with this young man who has a wife and children and problems of his own, and worst of all is yet another writer, with all the neurosis that goes with the job? Is it just to make Felix jealous? Am I just using this person? I don't find him particularly interesting or attractive. And how will Felix ever know unless I tell him? But her other self says disgustedly, It's only dinner, for God's sake, and you're not a virgin or a nun. How did sex get into this? she asks the other self.

'I'd love to,' she says, as if she'd known all along. They discuss where and when and she writes it all in her diary, marvelling at this efficient social person who is doing all the brisk chat as easily as if it happened all the time, when in reality it is sixteen years since she has had a meal with anyone who wasn't a friend, a colleague or one of her authors. Apart from Felix, of course. Since she has had a date, in fact. That is what it used to be called, when she was young. The very word makes her smile, it seems so incongruous and oddly American. But what else can she call it? And here she is, at fifty-two, arranging to have one. It seems like an anachronism. Perhaps that's why it's called a date, she thinks, because it's dated. She feels slightly hysterical at the thought but there is no one to share it.

'The trouble is,' David Johnson says over dinner, 'that Kate wanted me to go on Lithium, but I find it inhibits all creativity, and my doctor agrees with me that I'm not really manic depressive just because I've had episodes of depression and episodes of mania. I mean I couldn't have written the book otherwise, could I? There is a price to be paid for that. But it's only isolated outbreaks, not a regular pattern, so it's absurd to treat it with drugs all the time, especially something as powerful as Lithium. I think it's a real comment on our society that we're so keen to prescribe mood-altering drugs like Lithium that level you out, and even keener to forbid drugs like cocaine and heroin that give you highs and lows. Huxley was right: we obviously want everyone nicely cheerful and subdued on Soma tablets. Anyway, luckily my doctor saw my point of view, but Kate accused me of having him in my pocket and wanted me to get a second opinion. In other words she wanted me to shop around until I found a doctor who agreed with her. It didn't seem like a very good way to run a marriage. But I would have hung on indefinitely because I really do believe that marriage is for life and we've been together since we were students, quite apart from the fact that I was very involved with the children, having been at home with them a lot when they were small and Kate was teaching, and I do think children need a father as well as a mother, I mean a father who's really involved. But I was fairly shocked that Kate wanted me subdued in this way, it was almost as if she'd like me castrated or given a pre-frontal lobotomy or put in a straight jacket so I'd be more convenient to live with. Not that I was ill-treating her or anything even when I was at my absolute worst. And the most extraordinary thing was that she came up with all this after the book was published and I'd won the prize and there was some extra money for the very first time so things were really easier. I mean I'd repaid her faith in me and all her patience and hard work and then just when she could relax and enjoy it all she said she wanted a divorce. I've never understood that but when I ask her about it she can't explain, she says she just reached breaking point, but I have a theory that if I hadn't been successful she'd still be with me, encouraging me to go on, and it's just the money she doesn't like, in fact if she was a man and I was a woman it would make perfect sense, it would be the old thing about envy and competition, the classic way marriages break up because it's too threatening when the woman gets more successful than the man. Only in our case it's supposed to be the right way round and you'd think that she'd be delighted that the pressure's finally off and she can relax a bit, I mean what's it all been for otherwise? I thought that was what it was about and what we were both working for and making all those sacrifices for, but now it's as if she wants to punish me for succeeding by taking my children away from me unless I take the sort of drugs she wants me to take which mean I won't be able to write any more. It's a pretty stark choice. Forgive me, I'm talking too much. Now tell me about you.'

'There's not very much to tell,' Elizabeth says. She points at the food on her plate. 'This is delicious.'

He drives her home. She did offer to get a cab but he said he wouldn't hear of it, a quaint phrase, she thinks. She has made the mistake of letting him call for her at home because it seemed more polite, more traditional, more like an old-fashioned date in fact, and they have travelled to the restaurant in his car. He has drunk very little, so she feels quite safe, but she has drunk quite a lot while she was doing all the listening because it seemed to help her pay attention. She thinks, Well, he needed to talk and it didn't hurt me to listen. I certainly didn't want to talk about Felix and if he hadn't told me his troubles we would only have talked about politics or publishing. There's still no such thing as a free dinner and maybe that's the price of dates these days. It used to be sex, welcome or not, and now it's listening. You open your ears instead of your legs. Or both, perhaps. Does she want to go to bed with David Johnson? She still thinks of him like that, quite formally by both names: he is still the person on his book jacket.

Listening seems a lot more effort than sex and much less fun. Towards the end she felt as if the words she couldn't absorb were bouncing off her head like hailstones splashing off a full water tank. But she has always found sex easy and pleasant, long before she met Felix, which helped her understand why he wanted to have so much of it with so many people. It didn't make infidelity any less painful to tolerate, but at least it wasn't an esoteric interest like train-spotting or stamp-collecting where she couldn't see the appeal. Felix never talked like that on a date, she remembers. Felix used to make me laugh and ask me questions. Felix used to listen. Felix was actually interested in finding out about me.

David Johnson plays a tape of Miles Davis on his car stereo and hums along with it now and then. She has never heard anyone do that with jazz before and wonders if she dare ask him to stop. She decides against it: she doesn't want to offend him and if he stops humming he may well start talking about Kate again and she can bear the humming better, at least for the short journey to Putney. Besides, she needs the time to decide if she is going to ask him in. Part of her wants to say goodnight and never see him again; another part very much wants to be unfaithful to Felix as soon as possible to see if she is capable of it. Decisions. She has never been good at them, clearly, or she would have confronted Felix earlier. She has always been better at waiting and seeing. How exhausting decisions are, especially after all the listening. She feels very tired and very old and not at all seductive. Listening has made her feel like a psychiatrist and undressing would be professional misconduct. Still, it has got to be done some time during her three-month sabbatical from Felix and the sooner, she presumes, the better, in case she wants to do it a lot. But it also feels rather more like making an appointment with the dentist for a check-up, to find out if she needs a course of treatment or just a quick scale and polish.

David Johnson parks outside her house. Miles Davis has stopped and so has the humming. Elizabeth feels more confused than ever. David Johnson is better-looking in the darkness of the car than he was in the restaurant. A nearby street lamp seems to flatter him more than candlelight. He has an urban, contemporary face with hollows and hard bony edges. He says, 'I'm sorry I talked so much, but it's partly your fault for being such a wonderful listener.'

Elizabeth says teasingly, 'I know, I've had a lot of practice.'

'Well.' He taps his fingers on the steering wheel. 'I hope you'll let me make up for it next time. I really do want to get to know you better. Is there going to be a next time, Elizabeth?'

The indecision is worse than ever. She is so evenly divided she thinks she might as well toss a coin. 'Why not?' she says lightly, aware that it doesn't sound very flattering.

'Good.' He turns to her then and she thinks this is the moment: he is about to kiss her and that will be a good test. How will the beautiful mouth feel on hers? If she can bear to kiss him, she can bear to go to bed with him; if she can't bear to kiss him, sex might still be all right but it may be difficult to avoid more kisses. She knows herself well, or rather remembers herself from way back, when she was still a free, independent person. Her two lives, before and after Felix. She still thinks kissing is the most intimate part of a relationship, perhaps because it is so close to the brain, and it is a pity it has to come first.

But David Johnson only brushed her cheek with his lips as anyone might at a party, a social kiss, even a goodnight kiss, and in the context of the evening she finds it oddly tantalising. Without giving herself time to think she says, 'Shall I invite you in for coffee?'

He shakes his head. 'Don't tempt me. I always work from midnight till four. Those are my best hours.'

'Well,' she says, rebuffed, and now divided between relief and anger, 'I'll say goodnight then and thank you for my lovely dinner.' She feels like a little girl reciting a speech her mother has taught her to be polite.

'I'll phone you,' he says, the way men do, whether they mean it or not, as if women are not allowed to pick up the phone, as if it was entirely a male decision as to what happens next. She gets out of his car and goes into her house as he drives away.

It is very quiet and empty. She pours herself a brandy and sits down to consider the evening. She feels restless. She gets up and puts on a CD of Strauss's Four Last Songs. She realises she wants to ring Felix but knows she won't. It is war between them and there is no room for weakness: that is not the way battles are won. Loneliness sweeps in like a tide. She thinks what a long way she has to go.

David Johnson takes her to the Festival Hall to hear the Verdi Requiem.

'So you're not just a Miles Davis man,' she says.

'I like jazz in the car. It doesn't do violence to the sound. The Verdi Requiem is what I'd like to hear on my deathbed. I usually try to go to a performance two or three times a year to have it fresh in my mind in case I die young – and not in a car crash, of course.'

She doesn't know if she's supposed to laugh, but he looks and sounds perfectly serious. 'Wouldn't it be enough to keep playing the CD at home?' she asks.

'Not at all.' He looks shocked. 'Where's your sense of occasion?'

'I was thinking more of a sense of urgency. You could play it any time of the day or night. In case of sudden illness.'

'I do that as well. I love the grim terror of it as well as the final hope. I always think Fauré chickened out by not having a Dies Irae.'

'I always thought it was rather sweet and optimistic of Fauré,' she says, meaning it. 'There seems to be quite enough wrath in this life already.'

'A requiem seems to bring out the best in composers, though,' he says. 'Have you noticed that? I don't think I've found a duff one yet.'

'No.' She runs through the list in her head. 'I think you're right.'

'So, what's your deathbed music?'

'Oh – not a requiem. Strauss, I think. The Four Last Songs. Probably the last one.'

'"Im Abendrot"? "Can this perhaps be death?" Yes, very soothing.'

'I think peaceful rather than soothing,' she says firmly.

'Yes, you're right. Wrong word. That was careless of me and rather patronising. Sorry. What a lucky old man he was, to write such music so near the end.'

So they've exchanged credentials. Taken a few turns round the floor, shown off their medium-level expertise. They're both acceptably cultured but not too grand or obscure. Now what? How do they get from music to bed? She doesn't have time for a leisurely friendship, however desirable that might be: she is already halfway through her trial separation and she can hear the clock ticking. Is he ready to make love to her so she can find out if she can respond to anyone other than Felix after sixteen years? It's something she's never tried but it might give her some power in the marriage, she thinks. She has had the deathbed music conversation long ago with Felix, who she remembers chose the end of *Götterdämmerung*. When she said it was an amazing choice because it represented the destruction of the world, Felix said if he was dying that's exactly what it would be. If they died together, they agreed, as they had once wanted to, at the very beginning, when they were first in love, there would be an almighty collision of sound, or someone would have to relinquish their choice. She thought she would probably be that someone. Why does everything remind her of Felix?

David Johnson takes her out for dinner and talks about his children. She realises she is flattered to be seen out with an attractive man who is even younger than Felix. Seventeen years seems a lot more than eleven. She imagines people are looking at her with envy, unless perhaps they think he is her son. He does look younger than his age and they both have dark hair. She must try to lose more weight, she thinks: that might make her look younger and impress Felix on his return.

'I actually think it's worse for Annabel than Thomas,' David Johnson says. 'I think girls need a father more than boys, especially during puberty. She's thirteen now, she was twelve when we split up and it couldn't have happened at a worse age. I'm afraid it will affect her relationships with men all her life. Whereas Thomas is only ten and I think he needs Kate more than me at this point. I have them both every other weekend, but it can't be the same as everyday life. You get that sense of special occasion which may be just what you want in a love affair but is actually the last thing you need with kids. And no matter how hard I try to explain to them I love them and I've only gone because Kate and I can't live together any more, the fact remains I've moved out so it looks as if I've left them, although it's only so they can go on feeling secure in the same house. But I can't be sure they understand that, and I've no way of knowing what Kate tells them about me when I'm not there. If I tell them the absolute truth, which is that I wanted to stay but Kate threw me out, it looks as if I'm trying to turn them against their mother, so I have to pretend it was something we agreed on, which really goes against the grain. There's no way I would ever have chosen to leave them or Kate.'

Elizabeth feels it is all very familiar, as if she is reading an article in the *Guardian* or listening to a talk on *Woman's Hour*.

'You don't have children, do you?' he suddenly says.

'No.' It's a shock that he knows so much about her.

'I've often read interviews with your husband and there was never any mention of children.'

'No,' she says again, feeling exposed and defensive.

'Did you not want any or was it not possible?'

'I don't want to talk about it.'

'I'm sorry,' he says. 'I didn't mean to offend you.'

Suddenly it is not pleasant to be out with a good-looking younger man. Nothing makes up for having her sore places probed like this. She's amazed he can be so tactless. He is so brutal and direct, he is like a child himself, asking some mutilated person how she got her injuries.

'I'm sorry,' he says again. 'But I've told you so much about me and you've told me almost nothing about you.'

So easy to say, That's because you've hardly given me a chance; you won't shut up long enough. But it wouldn't be altogether true. She doesn't want to confide and it's been much easier to let him talk and condemn him for doing so.

'It's too painful,' she says truthfully.

'I only thought it might help.'

He drives her home with Bessie Smith on the car stereo, and this time he kisses her goodnight on the lips. She likes the feel of his mouth; in fact she is surprised how much she likes it. She would like a lot more of it. But that is all. One kiss. No other touching. They sit in his car outside her house like an old-fashioned courting couple. She feels young.

This time he says, 'Goodnight, Elizabeth. Will you ring me?'

And she says, 'Yes, I will.'

And she does. The very next day. To thank him for dinner.

'Shall I take you to the opera?' he says.

'That would be lovely.'

Nothing is said about Felix.

Helen is surprised when Elizabeth rings her up about a month later. She is trying to pretend she is not disappointed that Jordan hasn't rung, that Elizabeth is not in fact Jordan ringing her now. She despises herself for having these adolescent hopes about the phone.

Elizabeth's voice is full of excitement beneath a controlled surface. 'I wanted to thank you for telling me the truth and putting up with me that awful day,' she says. 'I'm actually having a three-month break from Felix to try and sort things out. I thought you might like to know that.'

'You amaze me,' Helen says. She really is amazed. She had imagined a row but never a separation. She didn't think Elizabeth had the guts.

'I amaze myself,' Elizabeth says. 'Of course I'm hoping when we get back together it may be better, well, different anyway.'

'You're sure you're going to have him back then,' says Helen, sorry that Elizabeth's courage doesn't extend to divorce. She would like to see Felix humiliated, lonely and penniless, since a slow painful death doesn't appear to be a realistic option.

'I can't imagine life without him,' Elizabeth says, almost fondly, as if she has already forgiven him for everything. 'I just want him to behave better. But meanwhile' – and Helen can hear the thrill in her voice – 'I'm actually going out with someone else, isn't that a joke?'

'Well, why not?' says Helen, determined not to be impressed or worse still, envious.

'Well, he's only thirty-five, separated from his wife and children, and he's borderline manic depressive.'

'Sounds perfect,' says Helen stoically.

'And he's another writer. It's David Johnson actually.' She waits for Helen to react. 'Well, he did win the Tessimon prize for his first novel and he seems very nice. I mean very civilised, even if he does talk about himself rather a lot, well, they all do that at first, don't they? It's probably nerves.'

'So you're having a good time,' Helen says. 'That's splendid.'

'It's a very strange feeling to be actually dating someone at my age. It sounds very silly but I don't know what else to call it.' She gives an apologetic little laugh.

'Well, why not?' Helen says again. 'Make the most of it.'

There is a pause.

'Anyway, how are you?' Elizabeth asks in a solicitous voice, as if Helen were ill. Underneath, Helen imagines she can hear exasperation that Elizabeth's news hasn't achieved greater impact.

'Fine,' she says irritably. She hugs Jordan to herself. She doesn't want to share his existence; she'd rather be seen as a social failure. The idea of exchanging girlish confidences with Elizabeth revolts her. Besides, she doesn't know if she'll ever see Jordan again. She finds the uncertainty very painful and she resents the pain. She is appalled that after their shared past Jordan should use her just for a one-night stand to comfort himself when they are both in such a vulnerable state. And she wonders if she asked for it. And she wishes she hadn't bothered to cook. A month of silence is quite insulting.

'Any news from Richard?' Elizabeth asks.

How remote Richard seems now. It's a strange feeling to have this man she has lived with for eight years transformed into someone she doesn't want. It seems quite easy to talk about him to Elizabeth.

'Yes, he called round three weeks ago. He's got Inge pregnant and he's in a panic.'

'My God,' Elizabeth says.

Perhaps Jordan is just very busy, Helen thinks. Or away. Or too depressed to ring up. Perhaps there is a very good reason that will mean she doesn't have to hate him.

'What a shock.' Elizabeth sounds very concerned.

'Yes, Richard seemed quite shocked. Apparently Inge didn't talk it over with him first.'

'But where does this leave you?'

It feels like an odd question. But then Elizabeth is out of date.

'Exactly where I was before, I imagine.'

'You're being very good about it,' Elizabeth says, sounding puzzled.

'I think it's rather funny,' Helen says, surprising herself.

'Funny?'

'Yes. Richard always wanted me to have a baby. He hated Sally having an abortion. And now Inge's pregnant and he doesn't like it but he's stuck with it. Don't you think that's funny?'

'Well, it's certainly ironic.'

'Oh, all right, ironic then.' Suddenly she is desperate for Elizabeth to get off the phone.

'I'm sorry,' Elizabeth says. 'Are you going to divorce him?'

Helen sighs. 'I've no idea. He hasn't asked me to. It doesn't seem to matter one way or the other. It's just a word. Sometimes I feel as if he's always been married to Inge and I was just someone he lived with for a while. It seems to make more sense that way.'

'Oh dear,' says Elizabeth in a maddeningly sympathetic voice.

'It really doesn't matter,' Helen says.

She is almost asleep when the phone rings. It's after midnight. Her instant thought is Sally, trouble; she snatches the phone. 'Yes?'

'Helen? Did I wake you?'

'Oh – Jordan.' So many emotions flood through her: panic into relief into rage into pleasure, so fast she scarcely has time to breathe.

'Is it too late?' he says.

'For what?' she says.

'I'm visiting friends near you and I wondered if I could call in.'

Silence while she thinks. She ought to be angry and she is, but she's also thrilled.

'You'll have to put the money on the dressing-table first,' she says.

He laughs. 'All right, I deserve that. In ten minutes?'

'And I don't take cheques,' she says.

She lies there for a moment after he hangs up, letting her heart stop racing, checking how she feels. I'm definitely cracking up, she thinks. I've been holding myself together for too long and pressing too hard: now I'm in fragments.

Then she gets out of bed and takes off the ancient

T-shirt she sleeps in now she's alone, puts on a bathrobe, brushes her hair, sprays herself with scent. She finds she is suddenly thinking of Richard sleeping beside the pregnant Inge, not thinking of Jordan at all. She told Elizabeth it was funny, which is true, but it hurts as well, she's surprised how much. It's confusing. Is that how it is for them too? Does Richard get images of her as he lies in bed with Inge, does Jordan see Hannah slowly dying even as he picks up the phone? Are we all so badly damaged we can never love whole-heartedly again? she wonders as she prepares herself.

Opening the door to a stranger smelling of whisky who puts out the light and takes hold of her by the throat. Being held so she can't cry out while he removes her dressing-gown. Being forced down naked on to the carpet of her own hall in darkness while his hands touch her everywhere. Being violated in her own home. Hearing him tell her in detail what he is going to do to her and how much she will enjoy it and how she will beg him to do it again. Making her repeat the words after him. The weight of him. The smell of his sweat. Feeling him heavy on top of her as he talks in a low monotonous almost casual voice about the detail of what is going to happen to her and how many times and what it will feel like. Hardly believing what is already happening now. The sound of him unzipping. Her face crushed against the carpet as he penetrates her. Feeling him huge inside her. Hearing the sounds he makes. Hearing the sounds she makes. Losing herself, giving up, going under. The rhythm taking over, getting inside her head, like music, like dancing, like violence, like heartbeat, like death.

'Well, it makes a change,' Jordan says. He shifts his weight. 'Are you okay?'

'I'd have cleaned the carpet if I'd known. And it's thirty quid extra for the dirty talk.'

He puts his arm round her and kisses her neck. They giggle like children. 'When in doubt, try an old favourite,' he says. 'God, I could use a drink, I'm knackered.'

They get up with a big effort and stagger into the living-room. Her face in the mirror is younger, softer, blurred with pleasure, a transformed face, a face she remembers from long ago. She pours them both whisky while he takes off all his clothes, very old jeans and cracked boots with an ancient leather jacket over a faded shirt, the sort of clothes she remembers him in, not his New Year's Eve finery. He puts on her bathrobe, which looks ridiculous, as if he's in drag. They both laugh.

He says, 'God, I love to look at you naked. You've got such a functional body. Nothing's just for decoration. I think you're the most naked naked woman I've ever seen.'

She kisses him. 'Pity it took you a month to remember that.'

'It can't be a month. Can it?' He looks genuinely astonished. She nods. He shakes his head. 'I've got no sense of time, don't you remember?'

She gives up on that. Why spoil it all? 'I'm getting cold,' she says. 'The central heating's gone off.'

'Shall we go to bed then?'

She could say, 'And you shouldn't ring after midnight, after a month's silence, and expect a welcome. You're using me to cheer yourself up. You're taking me for granted again after fifteen years and it's just not fair. You know I'm in a vulnerable state.' And of course he will argue that she could have said no.

She says, 'Oh, d'you want to stay?'

'Can I?' He sounds completely neutral.

'Yes, of course.'

He leaves his clothes lying in a heap on her living-room floor and they go upstairs with their arms round each other. He looks at home in her house. He looks as if he belongs there.

In bed he slips his hand between her legs and probes inside her for the juices they have both left behind, using them slick on his fingers to stroke her and slide her into another climax. 'Come on,' he says coaxingly in his most beguiling voice, at its most Welsh again now, as his fingers move, 'you're so wet, you can manage one more, I know you can, you didn't have quite enough just now, did you, and even if you did you can always manage one more, I remember, you don't think I'd forget a thing like that. Come on now, Helen, just a little one, it's easy, a little one won't hurt, it'll settle you for the night, help you to sleep, just you relax now and let me do all the work.' And presently she finds to her surprise that he is right and it happens, fluid and effortless, gliding her into pleasure again where she thought there wasn't room for any more.

'Well, I owed you one from last time,' he says, touching her lips with his fingers so she can taste herself and him. He isn't hard again and she doesn't bother trying to make him; she wraps her leg across his body and rests her head on his shoulder. He puts his arm round her. They seem to be like a couple of friendly animals trying to get comfortable, arranging themselves for the night.

'Shame we can't sleep like this,' she says.

'I know, we'll have to turn over eventually. Get some oxygen.' He assumes an exaggerated American accent. 'Get some personal space. It's only in movies people can sleep like this for Christssake.'

'And wake up wearing lip gloss. It's nice to be having

our second night. We only ever had afternoons in the old days.'

He yawns. 'I always meant to take you away for a dirty weekend but I didn't, did I?'

'No, you certainly didn't.'

'I didn't have the cash. Would you have come?'

'Probably not. I had a conscience in those days.'

'If it didn't stop you screwing in the studio, why should it stop you screwing in comfort in a hotel?'

'Humping in a hotel. Fucking in a flat. I don't know, I suppose I'd have felt I was stealing from Laura and the children.'

'She was glad to see the back of me. I was a big disappointment. She thought it was going to be glamorous being the second Mrs Painter. Don't ever marry one of your students, Helen, they get very angry when you don't turn out to be God.'

He's falling asleep. She can tell from the sound of his voice, slowing down, blurring at the edges of the words. Well, he's entitled, she thinks; he's worked hard giving me all that pleasure. But something about the conversation disturbs her. His casual tone. His assumption she might marry again someone other than him. She's shocked to be suddenly in so deep, as if, idly paddling in the shallows, she had suddenly missed her footing and plunged into a hole she didn't know was there, up to her neck, maybe even over her head, in cold dark water. Three meetings, a couple of phone calls, a few hours' conversation, two lots of sex and she appears to be more involved than she was before. At any rate she is having fantasies of permanence, like a silly teenager. Like Sally, in fact. She's scared. It was probably just a meaningless affair to him fifteen years ago; how much more so now when he is mourning Hannah? He still reminds her of Carey, which is why she gave him up in the first place. He is still the person who left two wives and five children. What is she doing, imagining a future with him?

He kisses her shoulder and turns over with a heavy

movement, settling down to sleep. She puts her arm round him and cuddles him, her face against his back. She loves the smell of his skin. I'm on the rebound, she thinks, and immediately pictures herself leaping over Richard and bouncing into Jordan's arms. The image makes her smile. She goes on holding him as he sleeps. She puts off turning over as long as she can.

In the morning they wake early and she climbs on top of him before he is fully awake, hoping to fuck her way into his heart. It is lovely to watch his face, at first drowsy and crumpled with sleep, then growing ever more defined and focused by pleasure, like a photograph emerging in developer. She rides him lovingly, not thinking of herself this time, only wanting to give, but at the end she is surprised by the power of his climax and she too comes faintly on the strength of it, almost too late, like an echo, as if catching the last of a wave. She collapses on top of him and says presently in a casual voice, 'Morning,' and they both laugh. They lie there for about ten minutes while he strokes her hair and she is lulled by his heartbeat slowly returning to normal beneath her ear. Then he says, 'Well, time to get up,' and she has to slide off him. He goes into the bathroom and she listens to the sound of the shower and pictures him washing her off his skin.

She makes coffee. She has put on jeans and a jersey; she doesn't like to be in her bathrobe once he is dressed. It seems to put her at a disadvantage. He says he doesn't want any breakfast, then has a few plums from the fruit bowl.

'Trying to lose some weight,' he says. 'I got on the scales the other day, gave myself quite a shock. I must have put on all the weight Hannah lost.'

She is startled by his casual use of Hannah's name. She herself is never sure when it's all right to mention Hannah, so she takes her cue from him. Then she wonders if he's using the name to warn her off, a simple way of telling her not to forget he's still in mourning and special allowances have to be made for him.

'You look fine to me,' she says. But the image stays with her, of him assimilating the weight of his dying wife, light as a dead bird at the end, he said, as some kind of morbid legacy, a way of becoming Hannah perhaps or carrying her around with him. Is it hopeful that he's starting to be ready to shed some of her now?

'Well, thanks for the night of passion,' he says in a jokey tone. 'I'll remember it.'

'How long for, another month?' The words snap out before the censor gets to them.

His shoulders sag. All the energy goes out of him. He looks irritated. 'Oh, Helen,' he says, 'I did warn you.'

'I know, about the bandages. What about my bandages?'

'I know,' he says. 'We're the walking wounded, both of us.'

Silence. It would be so easy now to let it drift, end on a sour note, see him walk out of the door and perhaps not come back. She's scared how much she wants him. She makes a big effort.

'I know being bereaved is different from being divorced.'

'I thought you weren't divorced yet.'

'No, but we will be.' She hadn't known she was thinking about that; now she hears herself say the decision has been made. 'Jordan, I'm so angry with Richard, I think my life took a wrong turning when I met him and I want to get back on track. I've had nine months of nothing and I'm sick of it.'

'So you're randy,' he says, not her favourite word. She supposes it's accurate but it seems to trivialise what she feels. Does he use it to put her down or protect himself from emotion? 'Well, so am I. Now and then. Like last night. I'd had a good evening with my friends and I wanted to see you. But other nights I just stay at home and get drunk and think about Hannah and I don't want to see anyone. It's that simple. I'm not sitting there thinking, "Now, how long shall I leave it before I ring Helen, how about a month, that'll show her."'

She manages to smile.

'Plus,' he says, 'I only got rid of the last of my brood a week ago, she thought I needed looking after. Plus I haven't done any serious work since before Hannah died and I'm trying to start again before I get in a financial mess. Plus I've only been renting a flat and a studio since I came back and next month I'm buying a place in Docklands and moving in . . .'

She covers her ears. 'All right, all right, you're at full stretch. I do understand.'

'And I warned you,' he goes on relentlessly. 'I said I'd be no good to you or anyone else. I told you that on New Year's Eve.'

'I know, I know. That's why I haven't rung you, I didn't want to be demanding.'

'What's the bloody good of that,' he says, 'if you're only going to nag me when I don't ring you?'

Suddenly, simultaneously, they both burst out laughing.

He says, 'Oh, come here, woman,' and she goes round the table and they hug each other. The hug seems to obliterate every problem. Till the next time, she thinks.

'You know,' he says. 'Not only do we fuck pretty well, we could have a bloody good row if we put our minds to it.'

They kiss.

'Forget bandages,' he says. 'Think crutches.'

David Johnson takes her to see *Duke Bluebeard's Castle*. At Covent Garden, in the best seats, where she has so often sat with Felix that she thinks of it as their special place. It is a shock to turn her head and see David Johnson beside her instead, although she is grateful, of course. He is spending a great deal of money on her and asking nothing in return. She can't help seeing herself as Bluebeard's wife, demanding to know too much of what goes on behind Felix's closed doors. No wonder it all ends in tears.

'She brought it on herself,' she says to David over dinner. She is just beginning, with an effort, to think of him by one name at last.

'I don't agree at all. He should have been more open with her. I never had any secrets from Kate.'

'Some people think secrets are essential to happiness,' she says.

'By some people d'you mean Felix?'

'Yes,' she says, embarrassed by his directness, by his intense dark eyes staring at her across the table. 'I suppose I do.'

'That's not my view of marriage. I think the openness is the whole beauty of it.'

She's struck by his use of the word beauty. She has never thought of marriage in that way. Something about it reminds her of Lawrence.

'I bet you're a D. H. Lawrence fan,' she says.

'Wasn't that obvious from my book?'

'No. You've got your own voice.'

'God, if I could write as well as Lawrence, I'd die happy.'

'Well, there's plenty of time,' she says, smiling. She is enjoying herself with him again.

'The poems,' he says with passion. 'The novels, yes, but especially the poems. He's ridiculously underrated. It's the English disease. They're embarrassed by all that feeling so they send him up.'

'You're right,' she says. 'It's self-defence.'

'I'd go to the barricades for him,' he says, as if he were a friend or a hero.

'Just so long as you don't have to grow the beard.' She wonders if she is flirting with him. It feels awkward and unfamiliar, like a muscle she has not used for years. But she likes it.

He says, 'You know why I talked about myself so much when we first met?'

'Because I was a good listener, you said.'

'It wasn't just that. Because you wouldn't talk. Because if I asked you about Felix you were angry and you clammed up and I didn't want to upset you, I wanted you to like me.'

'There are other things we can talk about apart from Felix,' she says, wondering as she says it if it is true. He fills her heart.

'Are there?' he says. 'You mean like small talk. Party chat. I've got no talent for it. That's why I was cowering behind the filing-cabinet when we met. You wouldn't catch David Herbert making small talk at a party either, I bet. Life is too short to talk about trivia.'

'What did you mean about the beauty of marriage?' she says.

'Oh, that opening up your soul that you get when it's really going well,' he says in a matter-of-fact tone, as if discussing something routine like cooking, nothing deep. 'I know it's fashionable these days to say you miss your children most when you split up, and I miss mine very much, but what I miss most of all is the intimacy I had with Kate. If I can't have that again with another woman I'd really rather not be alive.'

She hasn't heard a man talk like that before. It shakes her.

When he takes her home this time there is no music on the car stereo, just a rather tense silence in the car. He parks at the house and they kiss for several minutes. She feels very aroused and thinks surely tonight he will come

136

in and make love to her. She puts her arms round him to hug him and he feels wiry and young, very unlike Felix's muscular, slightly flabby body. She strokes his dark floppy hair. He put his hand on her knee and strokes the inside of her stockinged leg for a moment, sending tremors of desire through her. She is surprised how much she wants him. Then he takes the hand away.

'Well, back to work,' he says. 'Will you come to lunch on Sunday? I'm a good cook and I'd like you to see my place.'

She doesn't know if she is being teased or promised something. She says yes.

She wakes in the night. Four o'clock in the morning, a favourite danger time. She wakes with panic that something terrible has happened and Felix is dying or dead. She can't remember if she has been dreaming about this but it seems real. Her heart thumps with terror and she lies there shaking, sweating, taking deep breaths to calm herself. This doesn't work: it still feels like an emergency. She thinks of Jane Eyre and Rochester calling each other across space. What if Felix really needs her? Suddenly it seems like lunacy to be trying to force herself to have an affair with David Johnson as a revenge when she knows she really loves Felix and wants him back. How could she be so petty and stupid? Perhaps she has destroyed both their lives.

She picks up the phone and dials Felix's number, this number that used to be a secret, that has only recently been given to her. It rings once, then she hears Felix's beloved voice with a curt message: 'Felix Cramer here. If you leave a message I'll ring you back.'

This calms her sharply, like a slap, and she doesn't speak; she hangs up before the tone. Suddenly Felix doesn't seem dead or dying any more, but fast asleep or out enjoying himself. It makes no sense: if he were dead she would certainly get the answering machine, but her panic has gone at the sound of his voice.

'How long is your husband away for?' Felix asks. He is so relieved that all has gone well that he feels almost fond of Ella. Obviously the humiliating incident with Sally was a one-off and directly linked to Elizabeth's behaviour. Foolish of him to let it worry him. Better perhaps not to see Sally again, though, until after he's back with Elizabeth: a clear message from his subconscious, he thinks. But with Ella it was just like old times, no problem at all, and she seems positively grateful, the usual advantage with older women.

'Till Monday.' She strokes his thigh. 'D'you want to stay the weekend?'

This seems like a very good idea. Regular sex and meals and sleep in a comfortable bed would really set him up. Then next week he can go through his address book, ring a few more ex-girlfriends, say Christine, Linda and Ruth for a start. He should have done that before, not taken Elizabeth's revenge so much to heart that he let it depress him, and then expected Sally to cheer him up when he knew she was inclined to be spiteful these days. The trick is not to let anyone know he's temporarily alone: it changes his image and weakens his position. Once they know he's at a disadvantage they go in for the kill, all of them. Perhaps on second thoughts a weekend is too long to spend with anyone. Maybe a little holiday in the sun would be a good idea, on his own, to see if he can find someone new to refresh him. He deserves a treat for finishing the book and he's sick of living in the flat. A package holiday would be cheaper than staying in a decent English hotel, which is what he'll soon be desperate enough to do. Then he'll be nicely tanned and relaxed before he sees Elizabeth again. Only six weeks now and he's certainly not going to contact her ahead of time. It occurs to him how much he misses Richard, who would be the ideal person to talk to in this situation. How ironic he can't invite Richard to join him on holiday; he's willing to bet Richard is longing for a break from Inge by now.

'I'd love to,' he says to Ella. She's put on weight in the four years since he's seen her, which is a pity, but she still has magnificent tits and gives great head. 'But Elizabeth gets back on Sunday night, so I'd better go home in the afternoon.'

'That's all right.' She looks at him speculatively. 'You know, if you give me a bit of notice, I can always do lunch during the week. D'you still have the flat?'

He nods, remembering to look cheerful.

'Happy memories,' she says.

Inge is in the supermarket when the first pain strikes. She's been feeling less than well ever since she had the amniocentesis, but it was such a vague feeling that she told herself she was imagining it, and then it was submerged in the joy of knowing she is going to have a daughter. She thought that knowledge would make all the difference to Richard, but when she said to him, 'Aren't you pleased it's a girl?' he just said, 'Yes, of course I am, it's wonderful,' in a very flat, dutiful voice. She was hurt but she thought, Well, it's still hard for him to accept, but when our little girl arrives and he sees her, then it will be all right. He'll love her, I know he will, and then perhaps he'll start to love me again too. Pregnancy seems to cushion her against letting him upset her; she feels much calmer about everything, insulated by the baby. She remembers feeling the same during her other pregnancies.

She's had a much more intimate relationship with the baby since she knew its sex. It has changed from being a way of keeping Richard and become a real person she can love and talk to, another woman she will understand. She hopes she will be able to give her daughter a happier life than she has had. She talks to her when she is alone and plays her peaceful music when everyone else has gone out. She is touched by the way Karl and Peter take an interest in the baby, much more than Richard does in fact, asking her how she is feeling and making jokes about vetting their sister's boyfriends when she grows up.

It's a low griping pain, sharper than a period pain, and it takes her by surprise. She's halfway round the supermarket with a few things in her trolley for her birthday supper the next day. Richard had offered to take her out but she could tell he didn't really want to so she said no, let's do that after I've had the baby. She thinks he will be more pleased with her by then: it would be sad to spend her birthday evening in a restaurant finding they didn't have enough nice things to say to each other. At home there will be the boys to help out.

She panics, hanging on to her trolley with one hand and clutching her stomach with the other. The pain comes in waves like contractions and she remembers it instantly from the first baby she lost, the one that caused the marriage, although it is twenty years ago. She doesn't know what to do. That time it happened at home. There seem to be so many things she should be doing all at once: finding a lavatory, asking a shop assistant to call an ambulance and phone Richard at school, seeing if she can sit down in the manager's office. But she does none of these things. She is too terrified to move or speak. She can feel the trickle of blood, wet and sticky between her thighs, and she thinks it is getting heavier. She feels as if her insides are falling out. She clenches her knees together and lets go of the trolley, hugging her stomach and sinking down on to the floor of the supermarket. Safer not to move at all. She daren't do any of the things she should be doing; she can only concentrate on hanging on to the baby. If she sits there on the floor for long enough someone is bound to notice. And sure enough a young girl comes up to her presently and says, 'Excuse me, Madam, are you all right?'

Richard is in the middle of a lively though somewhat irrelevant discussion with 4B as to whether *The Merchant of Venice* should be banned by the Race Relations Board on the grounds of anti-Semitism when he sees the school secretary signalling to him through the glass panel in the door.

'Your wife's been taken ill,' she says in a low voice when he goes to her. 'They've just rung through. She wants you to go home. I've told Mrs Johnson and she's coming over.' And in a moment he sees Kate hurrying across from the main building and down the corridor. 'I'm so sorry, Richard,' she says. 'You get off now, it's all right, I can cover for you. I've got a free period.'

'Please save my baby,' Inge says to the ambulance men. 'Please save my baby.' It's all she can think of to say, over and over again, like a litany.

'We're doing all we can, love. You just relax now.'

She curls up under the blanket, hugging herself, bent double with the pain, pressing her knees together, feeling the blood getting thicker and more relentless. The last time she was in an ambulance was when she tried to kill herself by cutting her wrists after Richard told her he was leaving her for Helen.

Richard hurries to the car park, but the car won't start. It could be a flat battery but he thinks it's more likely the alternator. There's no time to do anything about it now and he hasn't enough cash on him for a cab. He hurries down the road to the tube station, looking out for a bus at the same time. He's worried, of course, but he's also aware of another emotion that he doesn't want to examine. He doesn't altogether want to get home quickly. He doesn't quite want to know what this summons may mean. He doesn't like the way an element of hope is creeping into his fear.

But when he gets home there is no sign of Inge and he suddenly wonders if the school secretary got the message wrong or if he misunderstood her. He stands in the kitchen wondering what to do. The house is very quiet and it strikes him how seldom he is alone in it. He wonders if he should telephone the hospital. Perhaps that is where Inge has gone. Perhaps that is where he was supposed to go, but the message got garbled while it was being passed along, as in the old children's game of Chinese whispers.

'I'm so sorry,' the doctor says when he gets there, 'but it's almost inevitable at this stage.'
   He does his best to present a face of grief. It is not too difficult with a stranger.

Inge is on a drip when he sees her. He hates to see that; to him it always seems to make things look more serious than they really are. She is crying and he can see the pain in her face. 'My little girl,' she says. 'Oh, Richard, I'm losing my little girl. I can't hang on to her. I tried so hard.' He holds her hand for a moment and feels quite defeated: they know each other so well that even *in extremis* she can read what he feels. He says, 'Do you

142

want me to stay?' and there is a terrible moment when it feels as if absolute truth flows between them. He sees a look of horror in her eyes. Then she shakes her head and turns her face to the wall.

He arrives early at school the next day, glad to have somewhere to go to escape his thoughts, but Kate is there ahead of him. He has never yet managed to arrive earlier than Kate, not that it matters, but it gives him the image of her as someone somehow superhuman.

Today she looks anxious. She says urgently, 'Oh, Richard, how's your wife?'

'Well, she's all right, but . . .' He sees Kate's face settling into sympathy and he feels a complete fraud, a monster, because relief is still far stronger than grief, because he is like a man who has found his cell door unlocked and can only slightly pity the fact that this is due to his gaoler's death. 'I'm afraid she lost the baby.'

'Oh, Richard, I'm so sorry. How awful. You shouldn't have come in, we could have managed.'

'No, it's all right, I'd rather be busy. I'm going to collect her this evening.'

'Well, if you need to leave early or anything . . .' Her kind, plain face is open and guileless. He can see her searching for the right thing to say. 'Please give your wife my best wishes. It's an awful thing to go through. It happened to me once so I do know how she feels.'

He brings her home the following evening after the D and C. It is her birthday and there are cards and presents waiting for her. She is very quiet and sad, but calm. He has already told the boys that she has lost the baby. They hug her and he sees how much they love her. It's as if he'd never properly realised that before. They love her so much more than they love him, if indeed they love him at all. Is it because of who she is or is it because she has always been there? Karl looks at him with hatred now and Peter won't meet his eyes. He's finally lost them both, he thinks.

'I'm so tired,' Inge keeps saying. 'I'm so tired.' She sounds surprised.

He makes scrambled eggs because she can't think of anything else she could manage to swallow and she has supper on a tray in front of the television. Then she goes to bed.

Karl goes out. Richard watches TV with Peter.

'Mum will be all right, won't she?'

'Yes, of course she will. She'll be fine.'

Peter goes to bed, rather earlier than usual, Richard thinks. He goes up to see if Inge wants anything, but she is asleep. He puts off going to bed as long as he can, telling himself he doesn't want to risk disturbing her, even wondering if he should sleep on the sofa for that very reason or would that be construed as rejection? Eventually he goes up again and finds her awake.

'How are you feeling?'

'All right. Tired. Sore.'

She looks very pale, her face fading into the pillow, as if she is being bleached out of existence. He feels so sorry for her. And he doesn't know where to hide his relief.

'Can I get you anything?'

'Could I have some more orange juice? I'm so thirsty.'

'Yes, of course. With ice?'

'Yes, please.'

He goes downstairs, glad to get away, nervous of going back, and returns. He gives her the drink.

'Thank you,' she says very formally. 'That's lovely.'

He watches her drain the glass.

'Would you like some more?'

'No, that's enough.'

Eventually the moment can't be put off any longer. He's tired too and there is school tomorrow. He will offer to come home at lunchtime, he decides, but he can't bear the thought of staying at home all day. He's terrified of being alone with her.

He has a bath and finally gets into bed beside her. He hates to think of all her body has had to go through to reach this conclusion. He presses her shoulder in a tentative gesture of sympathy.

'What a sad birthday for you. I'm sorry,' he feels bound to say.

There is a moment of silence. 'No, you're not,' she says. 'You're glad. You got your wish.'

David cooks well. Elizabeth doesn't think she's ever had such a good lunch in anyone's home before, without cooking it herself. It's clearly a feast in her honour and makes her feel cherished. Cheese soufflé that dissolves in her mouth; roast duck with crisp skin and apple sauce to counteract the sweetness, crunchy mange tout and waxy new potatoes in their skins; tangy home-made orange sorbet. She is beginning to wonder how his wife could bear to let him go. A mild case of manic depression seems a small price to pay for such food.

'Did you do the cooking at home?' she asks.

'Oh yes, all the time, Kate hates cooking. But not always as grandly as this, of course, this is specially for you. Still, my bangers and mash were pretty famous. I like cooking. I find it relaxing. I can think about work while I'm cooking.'

A man who likes Verdi and D. H. Lawrence and also cooks and has a beautiful mouth and is seventeen years younger than I am, she thinks. I ought to be very grateful and not thinking about Felix at all.

'I made all the curtains as well,' he continues. 'Kate hates sewing. Well, I couldn't actually write all day, of course, I hardly ever do more than four hours, but four or five hours manual labour after that, gardening, decorating, whatever, was ideal. It's the perfect way to iron out problems in the book without feeling you're idle or stuck.'

Perhaps that was what Felix was doing when he had affairs, Elizabeth thinks. Keeping busy. Sorting out the book.

'Well, that was a magnificent lunch,' she says.

'Coffee?'

'Oh – yes please.' She needs coffee; she feels rather drunk. She has brought a bottle of Sancerre and drunk most of it herself. David says he doesn't drink much at lunch-time and she wonders if he means ever or if he is planning to make love to her and saving himself for the event.

Over lunch she finally talked about Felix. Perhaps that was a declaration of trust, an admission that she is ready to make love. If she can talk about Felix, then sharing her imperfect body should be easy. Once she began talking she could hardly bear to stop. It was as if she had never talked about Felix before, as if all the hours with Helen and other women friends didn't count. She realised she had never before discussed Felix with a man other than her doctor, when she was very depressed about not having children.

She was surprised how well David listened. She hadn't expected that, knowing how much he talks, but apparently he can do both. She didn't want to maintain eye contact with him because the sympathy she saw was too much for her, so she looked all round the room, which is austerely furnished in black and white leather and tubular steel. She has admired the flat out of politeness but she isn't sure she likes it: it seems more like a showroom than a home. He then told her that he had employed someone to come in and do it all for him to a budget. 'I'm no good with things,' he said. 'People, books, music, yes, but things defeat me. If I were rich I'd live in a hotel.'

When she finally stopped talking about Felix he said, 'I

don't know how you managed to live like that all these years.'

Immediately she felt the need to defend Felix. Talking about him had brought him vividly into her mind, almost into the room, and increased her sense of loss. 'We were actually very happy a lot of the time. It's just that —'

'That he causes you terrible pain,' he said. 'It's a dreadful story. It makes me ashamed to be a man, the way I feel when I read about rape. I hope you don't think most men are like that. I've never been unfaithful to Kate in fifteen years.'

And are you about to start with me? she wonders, with a feeling of panic. She's not sure she can bear to be so significant; she had rather been hoping that he had had at least a couple of affairs in the past year so that she would just be one more. If she is using him to make Felix jealous she can hardly afford to be taken so seriously: it will make her feel guilty.

Now they are sitting on the sofa and she feels very tense. She feels nervous and silly and out of place, playing a rather distasteful game. She longs to say, Oh, come on, why don't we just get it over and done with, so we can relax, but she knows she can't. He puts down his coffee cup and turns to look at her; he says very gently, 'Well, Elizabeth, are we going to make love?'

'Yes, why not?' she says, thrown by the question. All sorts of even more flippant answers spring to mind and have to be suppressed.

He takes her face in his hands and looks at her very seriously. 'You realise I'm falling in love with you,' he says.

She can't think how to respond to that; it's so much more than she wanted to hear. But perhaps he doesn't mean it; perhaps it's just something he thinks it is nice to say. She plays safe and kisses him instead. She still likes the feel of his mouth. She puts her arms round him and she likes the feel of his body too. It is thin and boyish and eager. He feels very young in her arms and that is a

147

shock. Did Felix feel like that about Sally? She has to wipe out that thought very fast.

'Let's go to bed,' David says, as if everything is all right.

They go into the bedroom, another severely furnished black and white room, only smaller. She doesn't like to ask for an extra drink although she longs for one; she's afraid it will sound like asking for anaesthetic and he'll be offended. They have a long embrace and she feels his cock pressing against her rather impressively. She runs her hand over the bulge to show appreciation, feeling it would be ungrateful not to, but lacking the courage to unzip him, even when he puts his hand rather tentatively up her skirt. It is sixteen years since she has touched any man but Felix and she doesn't know how to start. The entire procedure feels like a very awkward manoeuvre, as if she were suddenly required to play chess and has forgotten the moves. She is afraid of making a fool of herself. But as his hand moves higher her body reacts even while her mind freezes. She feels like a teenager again, standing fully dressed in a strange bedroom being touched up. She's embarrassed to have this alien hand inside her most glamorous underwear, feeling how wet she is. She knows she could come eventually if he goes on moving his fingers and she lets herself relax and concentrate. But she doesn't want to: she panics and tenses instead and in a moment he takes his hand away. She notices he is very sensitive to her reactions. She wants to run away but she also wants to go on and have it done and over.

They help each other to undress, pausing to kiss. She feels dreadfully self-conscious, worried about how the sex will be and trying to hold in her stomach. He takes a condom from a drawer and slips it under the pillow. If he has been monogamous for fifteen years, does that mean he thinks she is a bad risk because of Felix's reputation, or is it simply an ordinary routine precaution? She doesn't ask; she is glad to be protected. It is like him to do the

148

right thing; it goes with the flowers, the dinners, the concert, the opera, all part of his general correctness. And it will help her to feel that it doesn't count. There will be nothing left behind to remind her of him, to prove he has been inside her. She will be able to pretend it didn't really happen.

Finally they are both naked. She was right about his cock, which is in fact rather similar to Felix's only not circumcised, but more impressive because it is attached to such a skinny body. She wonders if she should compliment him on it or if that would seem crude or give an impression of confidence which she certainly doesn't feel. She suddenly longs to go home and knows she can't, like a child at a party it is not enjoying. The whole procedure is as inevitable as labour now, which she has often dreamed about in the days when she longed to be pregnant. They have gone too far to retreat and their bodies will have to get them through it somehow.

'You're so beautiful,' David says. 'And these are so beautiful.' He kissed her breasts. Really he is being as nice as possible; it's a shame she can't let herself respond. It feels like the most difficult thing she has ever had to do.

They get into bed. She feels slightly better once she is under the duvet, warmer and less worried about her flabby stomach, more able to kiss and hug naturally. She wishes she hadn't eaten so much of the delicious lunch though. She feels ever so slightly sick now, either from nerves or greed, and she thinks how terrible it will be if she actually has to throw up. The ultimate humiliation, the ultimate insult. She concentrates very hard on convincing herself this is not going to happen. Felix keeps entering her mind although she tries to keep him out. She thinks she wants him to rescue her.

The nausea mercifully passes and with it some of her terror. She likes the smell of David and that is important. She strokes his floppy hair, the part of him which she finds easiest to touch. It is very dark and very shiny and

149

she realises why she likes it so much: it reminds her of the sixties and of being young, before she met Felix, when she slept around, when sex was easy and fun and a way of rebelling against her parents, not potentially lethal.

'Relax,' David says. He kisses her all over, but when he reaches her clitoris she doesn't want him to make her come that way although she loves it, because it seems to belong to Felix. When his tongue finds the right place she wriggles away, yet it feels like refusing a drink when she is dying of thirst. She wonders if he thinks she is being very difficult. She thinks that if she were David, she would have given up on her long ago. But he goes back to kissing other parts of her and she finally manages to stroke his cock, still waiting, still erect, standing patiently at attention until she gets around to it. She feels like a bad hostess who has neglected to ask a guest to sit down. She can't quite bring herself to take it in her mouth; that too seems to belong to Felix. Besides, it might just tip the balance with her uneasy stomach. He will have to make do with her hands, though no doubt he will be disappointed. She feels she is short-changing him in every possible way.

He makes all kinds of pleasured sounds then, as if she were doing something very clever, although she knows she isn't: she is giving a very routine performance indeed. Presently she says, 'Come inside.' She just wants it to be over. It seems grotesque to go on without either lust or love. This is not a suitable activity for two friends.

'D'you want me to?'

'Yes.' What is one more lie when the whole thing is a lie, a sham, a ghastly mistake? She is being punished for using him.

He puts on the condom very efficiently, while she thinks what an ugly necessity it is. She wonders what Felix is doing now. Perhaps the same thing. She feels the start of tears at the thought.

'I love you,' David says, sliding into her very gently.

It's a shock, both the words and the sensation. She's

150

tensing herself against him and he's a good fit, like Felix. She can remember lovers of her youth who were too small and how she felt nothing and had to pretend, because women were not supposed to care about size, all the books said so, and she didn't want to hurt anyone's feelings. David goes on moving and she doesn't know what to do; she senses she could come if she pays enough attention or even in spite of herself, at the sheer novelty of the situation. But she doesn't want to try and be disappointed, and she also doesn't want to try and succeed, as if she might then owe him something and threaten her whole existence by proving other men besides Felix can give her pleasure. Part of her wants to prove exactly that and part of her will do anything to avoid it. She feels she is watching her body perform from a long way off and it could be having a good time if only she could join in. She feels sad. They go on moving for a while as this tense battle goes on inside her, until she is so tired and confused she says, 'Come, please come.'

He says, 'Come with me.'

'I can't.'

'Are you sure?'

'Yes, please, please.' She is suddenly illogically furious at all this consideration. And he comes very quickly after that, so that she realises how close he must have been and how careful to hold back, but he does it very discreetly with soft moaning sounds rather than the loud cries she is used to, which is a relief in a way and yet makes her feel she has been cheated and missed the event, that it has gone on secretly without her and there must be a lot more under the surface that he is not sharing with her because she has shared so little with him. That makes him seem more independent and she feels great affection for him immediately afterwards, holding him tightly and stroking his wonderful hair, so thankful it is all over and they can go back to being friends and it serves Felix right.

He says sadly, 'You wouldn't let me give you pleasure.' And she thinks that is a nice gentle way of putting it.

She says automatically, 'You did.'

'Don't pretend with me, Elizabeth.'

'I'm sorry, I couldn't.'

'It's all right,' he says. 'Maybe next time.' He cuddles her for a while and she feels him shrinking out of her until he withdraws and disposes of the sodden remains that she doesn't want to think about, it seems so far away from friendship and the Verdi Requiem.

'You know,' he says matter-of-factly, 'we don't have to do this at all if you really don't want to. We could just hold hands and talk.'

She's amazed and embarrassed and relieved. 'Oh no,' she says, 'it's lovely, what d'you mean?' and he actually laughs.

'You sound like a child,' he says. 'In a minute you'll be saying "Thank you for having me." I ought to send you home with a balloon. Maybe that was the balloon I just took off.'

She laughs too. 'Well, why not? Why shouldn't I be polite and grateful?'

'Because you're beautiful and I'm lonely and I love you,' he says. 'These last few weeks have been the happiest I've had since Kate and I split up.' He kisses her. She feels very relaxed with him now. Presently he says in a very calm voice, 'It's all right. I know you're still in love with Felix. That lucky, worthless man.'

After that it all gets a lot easier. She feels a great sense of camaraderie with him, as if they have shared an ordeal, like pot-holing or mountain climbing, and survived. There is also a feeling of relief that they don't have to do it again just yet. She is reminded of going on an outward-bound weekend to encourage one of her authors, who was doing some research. Way beyond the call of duty, Felix said, but she went anyway, shared a dormitory, learnt orienteering, built a raft, climbed a thirty-foot rock and abseiled down. Going up, she shook so much while she groped for toe- and finger-holds that she nearly gave up. Only pride made her continue. But the view and the sense of achievement were a bigger reward than she expected and the magic of it stayed with her. Coming down, she did it all wrong out of sheer terror and bounced against the rock face several times. But she still felt brave as well as stupid. When she got home she had the most amazing purple bruises, which Felix said must be the result of a sado-masochistic orgy in the dorm. He urged her to confess so that he could enjoy the details. She laughed, but she had never forgotten that she had done something so unlikely and survived. Separating from Felix and going to bed with David seems to belong to the same order of courage. For the moment she can rest on her laurels.

They cuddle. He kisses her. She hugs him tight to make up for being so difficult about the sex. She wonders if he remembers what he said about love. She wonders if he meant it.

He says, 'I'm sorry I was rude about Felix. I just can't bear to think of you being unhappy.'

She smiles and doesn't answer. It is a big subject and she doesn't want to reopen it now.

He says, 'Let me give you a massage. I'm good at that and it might give you pleasure. Turn over.'

She turns obediently and presently she feels his hands moving over her back and shoulders and neck, unravelling knots she didn't know she had.

'Relax,' he says again. 'You're very tense.'

'It's wonderful,' she says. She feels cared for.

'I did a course, a long time ago. Kate used to get all sorts of pains and aches from school and it was the only thing that helped. Shall I get some oil and do it properly?'

'No, it will get all over my clothes. But thank you.'

'You could have a bath afterwards.'

'I'll have to be going soon.'

'Maybe next time,' he says.

*

The next day red roses arrive with a typed extract from a poem:

> 'The night was a failure
> but why not –? . . .
> I could not be free,
> not free myself from the past, those others –
> and our love was a confusion,
> there was a horror,
> you recoiled away from me . . .
> It is enough, you are near –'

Underneath David has written in his small spiky hand-writing: 'I hope DHL will forgive me for slicing it up rather, but I think he could be speaking for both of us, even though it was afternoon. Better times ahead, I promise. With my love, David.'

Elizabeth finds this both pretentious and touching. She takes out her copy of Lawrence to look up the poem but while she is searching for it she finds another one. The words seem to jump out at her:

> Good husbands make unhappy wives
> so do bad husbands, just as often;
> but the unhappiness of a wife with a good husband
> is much more devastating
> than the unhappiness of a wife with a bad husband.

It makes her pause. She wonders if what it says is true. It makes her speculate about David's relationship with Kate. She starts re-reading David's novel *Dark Sunshine*, about a man who like Othello murders his wife who unlike Desdemona really is unfaithful. The Lawrentian epigraph haunts her: 'I can feel myself unfolding in the dark sunshine of death.'

But mostly she thinks of Felix. Only a month now till they meet again. Till she can see him, talk to him, touch him.

*

154

'But I'm your greatest fan,' says the girl on the beach. 'Honestly. I've read all your books. Gosh, fancy meeting you here. Wait till I tell my friend. She'll be ever so excited.'

She does tell her friend and she is as excited as anyone could wish. They both look so sweet and young and inviting in their bikinis. They remind him of oysters in 'The Walrus and the Carpenter'.

'I do wish you hadn't killed him off, your detective,' the friend says. 'Poor old Tony Blythe. I really liked him.'

'Well, I suppose there's always a faint chance he might recover from that terrible blow on the head. But I think you'll like the man in my new book even better. He has a wonderful love affair with a beautiful young girl.'

They look at each other and giggle. By the end of the week he has had a very good time with both of them and he is ready to move on. Fortunately they are not staying in his hotel.

She settles into a pattern with David, meeting twice a week for dinner or lunch, a concert or a theatre. Afterwards they go to bed and he massages her neck and shoulders, back and arms and legs, until she is relaxed and he is excited. By tacit consent they seem to have abandoned any other sort of stimulation, which she finds a great relief. Massage becomes their standard form of foreplay. Then he enters her. She does not know how else to think of it. It is not mutual enough for love-making, not active enough for fucking. It is a curious hybrid activity, a formal acknowledgement that they are having an affair. There is a lot of hugging and kissing. David always comes and she never does. There are no reproaches or complaints or apologies. They don't talk about their arrangement. There is something peaceful and novel about her extreme passivity. It is like being comforted. She thinks that all she has to do is lie back and enjoy it, as the saying goes. She lets her mind drift away. It is rather like being on a sunbed: a lot of drowsy warmth in a confined space but no actual sensation. Nothing is expected of her but acquiescence.

And sometimes not even that. Sometimes they just sit and talk, about books, music, marriage. She thinks she likes those evenings best of all. She even begins to wonder if David is perhaps not very keen on sex and has merely been going through the motions to be polite. Or has she put him off by being so clearly in love with Felix? She wonders but she doesn't ask. It is a relief to have all this calm dating, proving beyond question over and over again that technically she is capable of infidelity and emotionally she is not. She is having her cake and eating it. They never quarrel. She watches the time pass. Every moment brings her closer to Felix.

'Well, the flat looks just the same,' says Linda. 'Time you got a new bed though, this one gives me backache. What a nice surprise, Felix. Why didn't you ring me before?'

Why indeed? She is looking splendid: younger and blonder and thinner than she used to be, and so cheerful. He does like cheerful women. 'You dropped me, don't you remember? You said you were in love. I was leaving a decent interval, you know how tactful I am. What happened?'

'Oh well, it all ended in tears as usual. Still, at least my husband didn't find out, thank God. How's Elizabeth?'

'Fine. We're just back from Tenerife.'

'Yes, I thought you looked very brown. Oh Felix, it *is* nice to see you again after all this time. We always had such fun, didn't we, and you never caused me any grief.'

'Lizzie?'

It is nearly the end of March and she had been wondering who would contact the other first. David has helped her pass the long dark cold winter pleasantly enough, but there has never been a more delicious spring. Every new shoot she notices seems to symbolise a fresh start, a second chance of happiness. There was never a better time for reconciliation, she thinks. All her pain and suffering seem to belong to last year, a lifetime away.

His voice is so magical to her that she can hardly speak: her lips are totally occupied by her smile.

'Hullo,' she says eventually. It is all she can do not to add, my darling, my love.

'Well,' he says, and she can hear him smiling too, 'so how are you?'

'Fine,' she says. 'I'm fine. How are you?'

'All right, I suppose,' he says. 'Surviving, just about. I've missed you.'

'Yes,' she says, 'I've missed you too.'

The hugeness of the understatement quite takes away her breath.

'Well,' he says again, 'am I allowed to come home now?'

She detects anger in his voice, coated with charm, like the pill in the spoonful of jam her mother used to give her when she was a child. She wants to say, 'Oh yes, please come, come now, this minute,' but she knows she must be cool, must negotiate, or the three months she has endured will be all for nothing.

'Why don't we meet and talk about it?' she says, shocked by her own daring.

There is a pause.

'All right,' he says. 'Let's have dinner at our favourite place. Eight o'clock next Wednesday suit you?'

'Yes,' she says. 'That's fine.' She wishes it were sooner.

'It's April the first,' he says. 'That seems appropriate, don't you think?'

*

Now she has to break it to David. What does she want to do about David? She doesn't know. What will he want to do about her?

'I'm going to see Felix next week,' she says when they meet again.

'Yes, I thought it was about time,' he says. 'So you're taking him back.' He sounds calm but angry.

'I don't know what's happening,' she says, 'but the three months are up so we're going to have dinner, talk things over. That was always the arrangement.'

'And then you'll take him back.'

She hesitates. 'Well, anything's possible. He may not want to come. Or when I see him I may not want him back.'

'Don't be silly,' he says, laughing nastily, 'you've been planning to have him back since before you sent him away. You just haven't had enough pain, have you?'

'But it may not be painful. He may have changed. We may both have changed.'

'People like him never change,' he says bitterly.

His sarcastic tone annoys her, but she feels she must be careful not to upset him. She may still need him and she is not used to dealing with mood swings. Felix has never been moody so she has not had much practice.

She says, 'Well, I don't know yet, but whatever happens I hope we can still be friends.'

He turns to her with the dark intense look that always frightens her just a little. 'Friends or lovers,' he says. 'We can be anything you like. I don't give up easily.' He strokes the inside of her wrist. 'Just think of me as a get-out-of-jail-free card. It might be useful to have me up your sleeve when you start bargaining. You are going to bargain, aren't you?'

'I don't know what I'm going to do yet.' But it sounds like a lie. She can already feel the touch of Felix's body.

'If you don't bargain you'll go right back to square one,' he says. 'Do not pass go, do not collect two hundred pounds.'

'You're being very understanding,' she says, feeling awkward.

'We all use each other,' he says, 'but that's all right. I don't mind. That's what people do. I don't want to let you go. I love you, Elizabeth. Perhaps if I'm patient you'll realise I can make you happier than Felix can.'

'He's being so nice to me,' Inge says to Michael. 'So kind. He does everything in the house. He waits on me. He cooks all my favourite things. Nothing is too much trouble. He even puts his arm round me at night.'

Then she starts to cry and sits weeping in her chair for several minutes, feeling the tears and the marriage flowing from her like another miscarried child.

'What's that about?' he says gently when she has nearly finished.

'It's over, isn't it?' she says. 'He really wants to leave. There's no way I can keep him now.'

'D'you want to keep him?'

She is so surprised. She looks at him in amazement, quite shaken out of her tears. It's such a shock to hear it spoken, but it matches with a feeling inside her, like something clicking almost silently into place.

'I don't know. I've always thought . . . it's been twenty years, Michael.'

'I know. It's a long time. How d'you feel about him right now?'

She thinks about it, testing her sore places. The part of her that always leapt up bright and strong for Richard no matter what he had done or failed to do doesn't respond. It's like stirring a dead fire or an empty pot, phoning an uninhabited house.

'I don't know. I think . . . I feel different. I think he's killed something. I never thought I could feel anything different. But I do. He really wanted my little girl to die.

And now I'm waiting for him to leave me. I'm sitting in the ruins waiting for him to drop the bomb on me.'

'It must have been rather like that in Hamburg when you were a baby. Only of course you won't remember.'

'I feel so helpless,' she says.

'What could you do to feel less helpless?'

In March Jordan invites her to his new place for the first time. It's a flat in a converted warehouse and the wall that overlooks the river is entirely glass. The bedroom, bathroom and kitchen are quite small but the living-room is vast and so is the studio. She's very impressed, even envious.

'Bit flash, isn't it?' he says. 'I always wanted a place like this, even in the old days, back in Penarth. I was never very subtle. Well, my work isn't very subtle, is it?'

'I stand on the Fifth Amendment,' she says, and they both laugh.

'Next time my lot come to stay,' he says, pouring her a drink in the living-room while she admires the view, 'they'll have to doss down in here. No more renting houses with bedrooms. None of that pampered rubbish. They'll have to bring sleeping bags and pretend it's fun.'

'Well, there's plenty of room for five in here,' she says. 'And you've got three sofas. You could have girls on the sofas and boys on the floor. Or am I being sexist?'

'Ah, but they bring all their hangers on,' he says. 'Ben's living with another doctor, so he brings her, and Tilly brings her husband and two kids.'

'My God,' she says, 'you're a grandfather.'

'Don't I look it? Mara and Susie come alone but Jake usually brings a girlfriend, a different one each time.'

'So he's a chip off the old block,' she can't resist saying. 'How *is* Mara these days?' She never met any of them but she always felt a special interest in Mara because she was the same age as Sally.

'Making wonderful sculptures of glass and wire. I think she's really original but nobody's buying her work. She won't let me help her with money so I bequeathed her my studio when I left.'

'That's quite a bequest,' she says.

'Well, she deserves it. And what else am I going to do with it? God knows what she lives on. She'll probably have to get a job.'

'Maybe she can teach,' Helen says. 'I don't mind teaching.'

'God, I hated it. I was useless. I seemed to spend all my time getting drunk with the students. And Mara's very like me, she doesn't know what the hell she's doing until she does it.'

They go into the studio and she is amazed at the degree of chaos he has managed to achieve in a few weeks' occupation. It's particularly remarkable compared to the stark orderliness of the flat. Or perhaps she's just forgotten how untidy he is.

'Not very homely yet, is it?' he says. 'It's too new. It'll be better when I've spilt a bit more paint on the floor.'

'It's quite a space,' she says covetously.

'Yes, that was the idea. I want to do more large-scale stuff. Be ironic, won't it, if I can't work here after all? Maybe it's too much of a challenge and I'll end up renting a place in Battersea again.'

'Well, that would be convenient,' she says boldly. 'It's a long drive out here.' She thinks the work in progress shows the same signs of strain Magdalen noted in the last paintings at his retrospective. She doesn't say anything. What could she say? And he may already know, or she may be wrong. Either way, it wouldn't help. The space is dominated by the series of portraits of Hannah: they are small and intimate, like the one at the show, but there are dozens of them. Standing in the studio is to be surrounded by charcoal drawings of someone in all the final stages of painful slow emaciating death.

'I've been told all this is pretty morbid,' he says, and she wonders by whom.

'Why not be morbid?' she says. 'Maybe you feel morbid.'

'Anyway, I find it comforting.'

He doesn't invite her to stay that night. Maybe it's too soon or maybe it's the talk of Hannah. He cooks spaghetti for her and after supper he says, 'I think I'd rather be alone tonight. I might even work. D'you mind?'

She minds desperately but she understands. 'Of course not,' she says. 'Just give me a hug and I'll go.'

'Oh, not yet,' he says. 'Later. But I'll hug you now anyway.'

'Oh good,' she says, 'an extra hug.'

'One more for luck,' he says.

The weeks pass. Richard goes on being nice to her. She goes on talking to Michael. She doesn't do anything as deliberate as planning it, but she can feel herself inching towards a decision by some devious route, as if snaking round to surprise herself. Or she feels she is in training, like an athlete building up her muscles for a great event. For the first time in her life she is going to have some control over what happens. It's a big change and it feels very odd.

One evening like any other when she is washing up and Richard is drying and they are alone in the house, she suddenly says to him, 'Richard, I don't want to wait any more, I think we should separate now.'

She doesn't even feel brave when she hears her own words; she seems to have gone beyond mere bravery and she is very calm and clear. She can't look at him, though, so she stares at the plate in her hands while she sees out of the corner of her eye that the tea-towel has stopped moving. She thinks she will always see the pattern on the plate differently after this.

He says, 'What d'you mean?' and his voice sounds tight in his throat.

'Maybe you were going to say it tomorrow or next week, I don't know, but it's better for me to say it first. I need to do that, I think. It's dead, Richard, isn't it? Our marriage is just as dead as my little girl. It's really finished this time.'

Then she does manage to turn and look at him and she sees relief in his face as well as guilt. Infinite relief. It's the face of a man who has been reprieved and she thinks, At last I've been able to give him something he wants.

'I'm so sorry,' he says. 'I really am. I did try my best but it wasn't good enough.'

'If you have to try as hard as that,' she says, 'maybe you shouldn't be trying at all. I've tried my best too but it doesn't work. We shouldn't have to try so hard, it's all wrong. I don't want to live on crumbs any more.'

As she talks she is surprised to feel not only pain but a curious sensation of lightness and freedom creeping over her, as if she is shedding a heavy load.

'I used to think anything was better than not having you, but I don't any more. You don't want me, you want to go back to her. Well, go, please go. You're going to go anyway, I'd rather send you, I don't want to wait. I've been offering you so much more than you want and you let me do it. But you couldn't give me enough in return, could you? It's not worth it any more, Richard, let's stop it now, please, before we hate each other, before we do the boys any more harm.'

'All those years,' she says to Michael. 'Ten years together and ten years apart. All that time. Two children. Two miscarriages. All that love and waiting and hoping and deception and therapy and hard work. I can't believe it's all over but it is. It's gone.'

'How do you feel about it now?'

'Sad. Empty. Very tired. Sort of . . . disbelieving, more than anything, I think. It's half my life and it's all gone. It's such a big thing. I don't know what it's like.' She stops to think. 'It's like a landslide. It's like having an earthquake in the back garden.' She shakes her head in disbelief.

'When you've taken all the time you need for grieving, you might like to think how much energy you'll have released for other things. Work, friends, lovers. Or just for yourself. You can have a whole new life if you want to. All the energy you put into the marriage could be just for you.'

'I'm exhausted,' she says. 'I can't think about that now.'

'Then don't. But you could put it on your list for later on.'

'We tried so hard,' she says. 'And we couldn't make it work.'

'Maybe you couldn't do it,' he says, 'because it was impossible.'

PART FOUR

On the morning of her reunion with Felix a bouquet of spring flowers arrives and she thinks, How wonderful, how typical of him, and tears open the envelope to read his message. But she finds another typed poem:

'Sea-weed sways and sways and swirls
as if swaying were its form of stillness;
and if it flushes against fierce rock
it slips over it as shadows do, without hurting itself.'

And underneath in David's writing: 'Don't let him hurt you again. Be like the sea-weed. Love, David.'

She resents the message but loves the poem, although by now she rather feels she is being pelted with D. H. Lawrence. And yet how touching, how thoughtful, she tells herself. She takes the flowers out of their cellophane and starts arranging them in water in her best vase. But the disappointment that they are not from Felix makes it hard to enjoy them. Perhaps they will at least make him jealous. It is not the sort of card she can leave on display, so she hopes he won't think she has bought them herself.

He sees her walking across the restaurant towards him in a black dress that flows with her movements, a Jean Muir that he bought her three years ago, and her anniversary pearls. Any other woman would have bought something new for the occasion, but she has chosen an old favourite. His heart lifts: he finds it very lovable of her. He is sure it means she wants to reassure him that all will be as it ever was; she wants to look familiar and comforting. But he thinks the shoes are new: the heels are a little higher than usual and she is walking carefully in them. That too is touching, that she wants to appear taller and thinner and show off her legs; he is very moved by the sight of her. And he is tremendously angry that she has punished him with three months' separation. It is as if he has held his anger in check, put it on ice, so that what was grief at first has been coldly suspended, biding its time; but now at the precious vision of her, looking so lovely and known, at the certainty that all will be well, it is safe to let it boil up into hot rage.

He stands up and smiles at her as the waiter leads her to his table; he says, 'Hullo, darling,' and they kiss on the cheek, as if they had only been parted for a day, very much a public kiss, but enough to make him desire her again as he smells the warmth of her skin and Mitsouko, another old favourite. It's going to be a really nostalgic evening, he thinks, the only way to start a new life.

'You're quite brown,' she says.

'Yes, I had a few days in Tenerife. I thought I might as well be miserable in the sun.'

'Lucky you,' she says. 'I've been working very hard.'

'Well, once I'd done the final edit I thought I deserved a holiday. I'll have proofs soon. D'you realise, this is the first book you won't have read in typescript?'

'Yes, I've really neglected my duty this time, haven't I?' she says lightly.

'Oh darling, don't tease me. I've served my sentence.'

'Let's eat first and talk about it later,' she says, with a social smile, as if it were a business meeting. He's reminded of lunching with film producers to discuss scripts for movies that would never happen.

There's an awkwardness between them, which he supposes is only to be expected, but he can see from her eyes that she still desires him, that she is tremendously excited to be with him again. The sooner he can get her back home and into bed, he thinks, the sooner life can return to normal. She must be desperate for it by now. He wonders what she can read in his eyes; he doesn't think she is picking up the anger or she would be looking rather more anxious. Instead she is smiling and flirting with him. She never has been very good at reading faces, he thinks, while he is particularly adept at disguising what he feels, practised at presenting emotions that will be profitable and filtering out the rest. So they order their food and wine; they make polite conversation while they eat and drink, almost as if they are pretending to be on a first date. He resents having to woo her again; it seems ridiculous with his own wife. But he tells himself it's amusing, just a game, and he puts on his best behaviour: charming and sexy, penitent yet forceful. There must be no more grovelling. He did quite enough of that on the night she sent him away and to no avail: he will never forgive her for that.

Over the coffee and brandy she finally says, 'Well, Felix, what are we going to do?'

'Get back together, I hope.' He uses his most beguiling smile. 'Surely you've punished me enough. You know I love you. Haven't you missed me at all?'

'Yes, very much.'

'Well, then. Why aren't we celebrating?'

She sighs and says, 'If only it could be that simple.'

He feels a chill of fear, as if he were facing his bank manager for a loan or an overdraft that was about to be refused. He feels a corresponding surge of anger too.

She says, 'I've thought about this a lot, and of course I still love you or I wouldn't be here. I love you very much. But we've got to have a new deal or it won't work.'

He's shocked that she's actually daring to bargain with him. 'Of course,' he says, smiling. 'Name your price.'

'Well, the old deal was you having affairs and me putting up with it. I don't expect you to be faithful, I know that's too much to ask, but I am asking you not to have anyone I know. That was the worst part. I don't think you can imagine how bad that feels.'

He keeps his voice level and pleasant. 'D'you mean if I was having an affair and you met her by chance, you'd expect me to break it off? Or is it just people you already know who are out of bounds? I want to be quite clear about this.' Really, it's ridiculous, he thinks, it's comic. How is he to know which women it's safe to let her meet? He can't always tell immediately the ones he's likely to screw; if he can't get those he wants most, he sometimes has to make do with a few borderline cases, especially in a lean year, and sooner or later she's bound to meet some of them, either before or after the event. For an intelligent woman she's really come up with a totally impractical idea, and he'd like to make her see the funny side of it: it would lighten the whole evening.

She says, 'I haven't thought it through like that. Both, I suppose. I just want to make sure I never meet anyone you're sleeping with, before or after. I want you to do that much for me. It's painful enough without knowing them.'

'Darling, I've never meant to cause you pain, but you knew what I was like when you married me. What you're saying now is that you have the right to break up any affair I have simply by meeting the woman.'

'Just keep them away from me, all right?' Her voice is low and edgy, surprisingly close to tears. He puts his hand over hers on the table and she hangs on to it tightly. 'Whoever they are. I can't stand it on my doorstep. Having to see them. People knowing before I do and pitying me.'

'We move in the same circles though,' he says, bemused by her logic. 'It might be simpler if I just try to be faithful. We've never tried that, have we?' He doesn't mean it but he thinks it might cheer her up and stop her pursuing a bargain that sounds like an absurd game of hide and seek.

'No, because it wouldn't work and I don't believe you mean it. This way we have a chance. Just keep your two lives very far apart.'

'Well, all right, darling,' he says. 'Whatever you say. I've never understood why you mind so much when you know I love you and nobody else has ever been important.'

'I want a solemn promise, Felix.'

'All right,' he says easily, keeping his face serious. He remembers when he was a little boy crossing his fingers when he lied. He has a sudden urge to do it now, under the table. But he is so angry at the way she is trying to control his behaviour that he thinks she deserves to be lied to anyway. Even the little boy would think the lie didn't count.

'If you break it,' she says, 'that's the end of us, you know. I mean it, Felix. I can't go through something like this again.'

'Neither can I. Don't threaten me, darling, I've promised. I don't like it when you threaten me. Now can we go home? I want to take you to bed and make love to you. I want to undress you very slowly and put —'

'There's another thing I've got to tell you,' she says, 'and you may not like it. I've been having an affair.'

He's very shocked. Well, surprised more than shocked, but so much so that he says flippantly, 'You've got such a lot to tell me, we should have started earlier.'

She doesn't smile. 'Don't you believe me?'

'Yes. I don't think you'd lie to me.'

'Well, you always said I could have as much freedom as you, only I didn't want to before. Now I do. I'm having an affair and I want to go on with it.'

He's interested in his own reactions: after the surprise comes a jealous pain that's quite severe, like a physical thing, but closely mixed with it is a terrific excitement. She has finally done something he has often fantasised about. Her body won't ever be quite the same to him again. He starts picturing the things this other man must have done to her, the things she must have done to him. Their bodies move on the flickering screen in his head. He doesn't speak.

She says, 'D'you want to know who it is?'

'Why not? I'm not making any conditions, am I?'

'David Johnson.'

That really is a body blow. 'Christ, not the one who wrote that godawful book?'

'I think it's quite good.'

'You can't. We laughed about it, don't you remember? How he got the plot from Shakespeare and the title from D. H. Lawrence and those were the only two good things in it. How he must have got that prize for finally learning to read, it certainly wasn't for writing.'

'You're really jealous, aren't you?' she says thoughtfully.

'I'm disgusted you couldn't do better than that. "I shall blossom like a dark pansy." I bet he will too.'

'You actually know the poem,' she says, sounding surprised.

'Of course I know the poem, I'm not fucking illiterate, am I? "Gladness of Death", isn't it? "Unfolding in the dark sunshine" and all that. He can't even come up with his own title.'

'You wear your scholarship so lightly,' she says.

'Jesus, I don't care how many lovers you have, but d'you have to choose such a bloody awful writer? There must be dozens of people who'd like to screw you and you choose someone like him to make me look an absolute laughing stock.'

'Ah,' she says, 'so that's it. Now you know how I feel.'

'I don't think anyone laughed about me and Sally. They all just thought I was a lucky shit and she was a victim and you were a saint. Wasn't that enough for you?'

'And what about Inge?'

'Oh, for God's sake. Two that you know in sixteen years.'

'Two in a year that I know and found out. Who knows about the rest? There has to be some balance in this marriage, Felix,' she says, 'or it can't go on.'

'So that's why you did it? It wasn't good clean lust, oh no, it couldn't be that, could it, that's much too simple, it has to be some revolting power game. I've never treated you like that, Lizzie.'

At the sound of her name her face crumples up and tears spill out. 'You didn't have to,' she says, sobbing, 'you've always had all the power.'

'Darling, oh darling, come on now, let's go home, mm?' He's suddenly aware of the silence, that the restaurant has emptied around them, and the lounging waiters are looking at their watches. 'It's after midnight, they're wanting to close. Let's not stay till they put the chairs on the tables and turn out the lights, eh?'

She smiles weakly and he pays the bill while she fixes her face. They stagger out into the street, exhausted with emotion, and fall at once into a close embrace, kissing desperately like teenagers with nowhere to go. She says with her arms round him, 'Oh Felix, I love you so much.'

'Well, I don't think we can use that restaurant again for a while,' he says, and she manages to laugh. 'Let's go home,' he says.

He takes her home and makes love to her, violently and tenderly, for much of the night. She feels he is purging her of David Johnson. Everything works naturally, effortlessly, without thought. Everything about him feels right. It is such a relief to be in bed with the right person, the right shape, the right touch, the right smell. She cries a little while they are making love. At one point he says lovingly, 'I'd like to fuck you to death for sending me away,' and she says, 'Oh, please try, what a lovely punishment.'

She had gone much further than she meant to in the restaurant, but he had looked so cocky it enraged her, so sure that she was desperate to have him back, as indeed she was. She hadn't meant to bargain; she would have had him back on any terms at all. But she had released

173

what she thought was just a little resentment, and years of accumulated rage had gushed out.

Felix wakes in the night while Elizabeth is sleeping and gets up to make friends with his house again. He understands now why animals want to spray their territory. He is glad to have it all to himself, moonlit and quiet. He pours himself a glass of water and stands at the window looking at the river. He finds it incredible that he was debarred from all this simply for screwing Sally. The dark, silent house comforts him and welcomes him home. Eventually he goes back to Elizabeth and gets into bed, warm with her smell. She wakes and embraces him. He feels sad. He knows he can't ever trust her again and it's a terrible feeling, like a death in the family.

Next day, while Felix is fetching things from the flat, Elizabeth goes to church. She feels an urgent need to give thanks, as if she has a hotline to God. She is so grateful to have Felix back, to know that he has gone out only to return in a few hours, and she can have all the luxury of looking forward to normal life again, day after day. She feels very blessed and it makes her wish she was religious. She walks down the road to the church, goes in and lights a candle. She's forgotten how to pray so she just says in a whisper, 'If you're there, thank you. And even if you're not.'

'I think we should do it casually,' Jordan says. 'Don't make a big deal of it. I'll just drop in one day and you introduce me. I'm an old friend back from New York.

Well, that's true, isn't it? She may even remember me, she must have been about four when I was around.'

'Maybe.' Helen is disappointed; she wants to make a big deal of it, trumpet her love to the sky. She doesn't like Jordan describing himself as a friend: she thinks a friend is someone you can ring at any time. And it's conceited of him to imagine Sally may remember him.

'Maybe she'll remember or maybe we should do it casually?'

'Well, both. I don't think she will remember, actually, but of course I want to be casual, you can't imagine I'm going to sit her down and announce I've got a new lover and she must meet him.'

They are having a late breakfast at the kitchen table. She loves the domestic image of Jordan, cramped in Richard's old shabby bathrobe, looking as if he belongs in her home. She will miss these mornings if she can't have them while Sally is home. Not that there have been so many of them.

'You'll probably want some time on your own with her first,' Jordan says, yawning, 'so let me know when to drop in.'

'If you stick to your natural rhythm,' Helen says, with horror that she can't stop the words escaping from her mouth, 'you could easily miss her altogether. She only gets a month for Easter.'

'If that's what you'd prefer,' he says instantly, very steely and controlled.

'No, of course it isn't, I'm sorry, I'm just nervous and we've only got a day to decide.'

And then the footsteps and the key in the front door.

'Or less,' Jordan says, very calm.

'Mum,' Sally calls from the hall. 'I got the early train.'

They hear the sound of luggage falling to the floor. Helen looks anxiously at Jordan, who looks amused.

'In here,' she calls back. Sally comes into the doorway of the kitchen and stops at the sight of Jordan, who says hullo, as if this kind of thing happens to him all the time.

'I've got a friend for you to meet,' Helen says to Sally, feeling embarrassed and foolish.

'So I see. Hullo.' Her face is quite expressionless.

'Jordan Griffiths. We've met before,' Jordan says easily, 'but you may not remember. I used to call in your mother's studio when you were about four.'

To Helen's surprise some flicker of recognition crosses Sally's face. 'Oh, you were the fruit man. I don't remember you actually, I mean if I passed you in the street, but I remember somebody tall bending down and giving me fruit.' And she smiles, just a little.

'I thought you weren't due back till tomorrow,' Helen says.

'Obviously,' says Sally, and she and Jordan both laugh, making Helen feel like an intruder in her own home. 'No, it was always today. I just didn't know which train. You must have got muddled up.'

Helen is appalled, not at the meeting, which seems to be going quite well and has at least got the whole thing over and done with, but at her own incompetence. She never gets dates wrong. She is sure it was meant to be tomorrow. Surely she didn't actually want it to happen this way? Did she?

'Are you enjoying Sussex?' Jordan asks.

'It's okay. Quite hard work actually.'

'D'you want some coffee?' Helen says.

'No, I had some on the train.'

'Well,' Jordan says, standing up, 'nice to see you again, but I should be going.'

'Not on my account,' Sally says, very formal. 'I'm going to unpack.'

'On my own account,' Jordan says. 'I've got work to do.'

'Oh, of course,' Sally says, 'you're another painter, aren't you?'

Jordan smiles, rather sadly, Helen thinks. 'Well, I used to be.'

*

He goes upstairs to dress. Sally goes upstairs to unpack. They go up one after the other, almost like a couple, which is disconcerting. Helen, left alone in the kitchen, makes fresh coffee for herself and feels shaken up, as if she were the child and Sally the parent, as if Sally had actually caught her in bed with Jordan. Worse, perhaps: there seems something rather more intimate about breakfast in your dressing-gown. It suggests a degree of friendliness that doesn't always go with sex.

Jordan comes back dressed and says, 'Well, the best-laid plans and all that. Robbie Burns knew a thing or two.' He kisses her goodbye. 'See you soon.'

'A likely story,' Helen says. She sees him to the door.

'She's a credit to you,' he says, departing.

Presently Sally comes back downstairs and into the kitchen. 'Sure you don't want coffee?' Helen says. 'I've made some fresh.'

'Oh, all right. It'll take away the taste of British Rail. Mum, why ever didn't you tell me? I felt such a fool.'

'Well, how d'you think I felt? You were due back tomorrow.'

'Today. Don't start that again. It's not my fault if you got it wrong. Why didn't you tell me about him before, I mean? He hasn't just turned up, has he? Or has he?'

'No, of course not.' She pours the coffee. 'I met him again last October. He'd just got back from the States and he had a retrospective. Magdalen took me. I've been seeing him since New Year.'

'Seeing him,' Sally says. 'Don't be so coy.'

'All right, sleeping with him,' Helen says, angry. 'It's not really your business, is it?'

'It is if I walk in and he's in Richard's dressing-gown. I felt so stupid. You could have warned me. You could have told me you'd got someone.'

'Well, I haven't really,' Helen says. She feels naked,

horribly exposed. She doesn't want to share her uncertainty with Sally but she can't claim more than she has. 'We just meet now and then. He's getting over a bereavement actually, his wife died of cancer fifteen months ago.'

'God, how awful.'

'So he's a bit erratic. He's got a daughter your age, and one a bit younger. She's at Oxford.'

'God, how awful to have your mother die of cancer.'

Helen is touched by this reaction. 'Well, it wasn't her mother. He's been married before.'

Sally drinks her coffee. 'I should've known. God, I'm stupid. Tell me the worst. How many times? How many children?'

'Twice before. Five children, all grown up. None with the dead wife.'

'Oh, Mum.'

'I know.'

'You're in love with him, aren't you? He's another one like my father and you're in love with him.'

'Is it that obvious?' Helen says.

'It is to me. Just the way you look at him. He probably doesn't know you as well as I do.'

That night she comes into Helen's room around midnight and sits on the end of her bed.

'Look, I won't be around much this vac. I'm going to see my father for Easter and I'm going to Amsterdam for a week with some friends.'

'Hardly worth unpacking,' Helen says.

'I mean I won't be here to cramp your style.'

'That's all right. I don't have much style to cramp.'

'He's okay. I don't mind him. Just don't let him hurt you, that's all.'

Helen finds she suddenly wants to cry.

'I think I'm a bit jealous,' Sally says, 'if you really want

178

to know. You're having more fun than I am.' She kisses Helen briefly and stands up. 'Nice to be home, all the same.'

'Nice to have you home,' Helen says.

Richard uses the Easter holidays to find somewhere to live. It has to be done and it's a good excuse to spend time away from Inge. She is being so generous that he finds it hard to look at her. She has even offered to help him search for a place, but he finds that too saintly to endure. Perhaps she only means that she is in a hurry to have him gone, now the decision has been made. He certainly wants to spend as much time as he can away from the house. He can't bear the expression in Peter's eyes. Although Inge helped him break the news, as she had promised she would, he could tell that both boys blamed him entirely; he plays the scene over and over again in his mind as he looks at one dingy furnished room after another. They didn't even let him get to the end of his prepared speech about him and Inge having talked it over and agreed it was better to separate. How he wouldn't be far away and they could visit whenever they liked and he hoped very much that they would, both of them. How sorry he was. How he had never meant this to happen, any of it. He had lain awake most of the night working out what to say and they didn't let him say half of it. 'But Dad, you promised,' Peter said, a terrible look of betrayal on his face that cut Richard to the heart.

'It's not your father's fault this time,' Inge said. 'I asked him to go. I don't want to live with him any more.'

'Don't blame you, Mum,' said Karl. 'Neither do I. He can piss off right now if he likes. Pity he ever came back. I knew he'd do something like this.' His voice was full of the grim pleasure of being right.

'But you can't leave Mum when she's been ill,' Peter said, blinking rapidly.

'It's all right, Peter,' Inge said. 'I'm better now and I don't want him to stay. We haven't had a row or anything. It's just better this way. We made a mistake, you see, and we're going to put it right. We shouldn't have got back together.'

'Well, I'm off out now,' Karl said. 'I'll see you later, Mum.' Then he turned to Richard, facing him very directly. 'Proud of yourself, are you?'

'I'm so sorry, I'm so sorry,' Richard kept repeating. But Karl was already gone, out of the room and out of the house, the front door slamming behind him, the motorbike revving up in the street. And Peter, chin quivering, was running upstairs to his room, where he bolted the door and played loud music. Later on in the evening Richard managed to talk to him and make it a little better, but Karl rang up and told Inge he was going to stay with his girlfriend until Richard moved out. 'Maybe it's all for the best,' Inge said wearily. She looked grey with fatigue and Richard put his arm round her. 'Oh Richard,' she said, 'what a mess. I'm so tired.'

He finds a bedsit not too far from school. It's all he can afford: he knows it's impossible to stretch to even a one-room flat. The landlady is a large Irish woman who reminds him of one of the Proles in 1984 as she toils up and downstairs with him behind her, but she is pleasant enough and the room is clean. It has two burners and a grill, a washbasin and a fridge. There is a shared kitchen and bathroom. He doesn't bother to sit on the bed: it can't be more uncomfortable than the sofa at home that he is sleeping on now.

He goes home and tells Inge he has found somewhere.

'That's good,' she says. 'Is it nice?'

'It's all right.'

They look at each other in silence and look away.

'Well,' he says, 'what do we do now?'

'I don't want to say goodbye to you, Richard. It's too difficult.'

'Yes, it is.' He feels the prickling of tears: he hadn't thought he would find the parting so painful. She is being so reasonable.

'Next week Peter is going on that school trip, you remember?' she says, fiddling with the cutlery on the table. 'I'm going to tell him you won't be here when he gets back. And I'm going to go out every day for three hours in the afternoon. I'll go to the library or the pictures. I don't want to know what day you're going. I just want to come back one afternoon and you're not . . .' She bites her lip.

'All right,' he says, 'if that's what you want, we'll do it like that. And we'll keep in touch, won't we?' Suddenly after all this delay it seems to be happening very fast.

'Yes, of course. But not yet. Give me some time. I don't want to see you for a while, I don't know how long. And then when I do it will all be different.'

'All right,' he says. 'I'll leave you my address and phone number and I'll wait to hear from you.'

'Shall we have a lot to drink tonight?' she says, with an attempt at a smile.

'That's a good idea,' he says. 'Let's do that.'

After a moment's silence she says in a small voice, 'Will you go back to her, d'you think?'

He hesitates, then decides there is no reason at this stage to lie. 'If she'll have me.'

'If you're going to continue in therapy without your husband,' Michael says to her one day, 'would you like us to speak German together?'

She is very surprised and pleased. She answers, 'Ja, das würde ich sehr gerne tun.'

He says, 'Dann lass en sie uns das machen. Ich dachte, es wäre entspannender für Sie. Es war meine Muttersprache aber ich benutze sie heutzutage nicht sehr oft. Ich würde mich über die Gelegenheit freuen.'

It is the first personal thing he has told her. After that they always speak German together. She is amazed at the difference it makes. Now at last she can say exactly what she means. She feels as if she has come home.

The loneliness of his room appals him. He feels like a displaced person or a middle-aged student, rootless, feckless, dispossessed, cramming his few belongings, his books and clothes and records, into a confined space. The walls are thin, the sound-proofing minimal. The communal telephone rings constantly, the bathroom is always occupied. Other people's cooking smells waft along the corridor, other people's noise and music from above and below and next door keep him awake as they shout, squabble, laugh, entertain, make love, slam doors, give parties, snore. A mixture of pills and exhaustion makes him finally sleep. He is grateful to have a demanding job that wears him out. He doesn't want time to think. Contemplating the wreckage of his life is more than he can bear. But it creeps in. Into the loneliness of the room. Into the space in his head. It is lying in wait to ambush him when he wakes up in the morning; it is crouching by his pillow last thing at night. All the damage he has done, to his children, to Inge, to Helen, to himself, and all with the best of intentions. Even now he can hardly believe it. How did it happen? How can he put it right?

He rings Helen. She sounds surprised to hear from him, as if they were distant friends or former neighbours who had moved apart, as if she had never expected to hear from him again. 'Oh, Richard, hullo,' she says. She doesn't sound pleased either. 'How are you?' she says, very formal and polite.

'I'd really like to see you.' The sound of her voice can still make his heart turn over, but he doesn't want to seem like a suppliant; he knows that will not make him more attractive, if indeed he is still attractive at all. He wants her to take pity on him if necessary, if pity is all he can have, but it would be wonderful if she had actually been missing him after all this time. He hopes desperately that perhaps she has. Does the coldness in her voice mean she is still angry?

'Well, I'm awfully busy,' she says.

'Could we meet just for a drink?'

She sighs. 'I'm teaching today.'

'Maybe I could call in about six.'

A long moment's silence. 'No, don't come to the house. I'll meet you in the pub near college – I can't remember its name, but you know the one. The one on the corner. Say – about twelve thirty. And I've only got half an hour.'

'I've left Inge,' he says quickly, so she can have time to think about it before they meet.

He hears a sharp intake of breath.

'I'll see you later, Richard.'

And she hangs up.

She walks into the pub at quarter to one, when he has already been waiting twenty minutes because he couldn't resist arriving early. It is so long since he's seen her that she is even more beautiful than he remembers and he feels a physical ache of loss all over again. She is wearing jeans and no make-up and a huge old shabby jersey that was always a favourite. She is looking very well, very rested, younger, with a sort of bloom to her skin.

'Sorry I'm late,' she says. 'People kept catching me just as I was leaving.'

'What can I get you?' He longs to touch her but he knows he mustn't.

'I'll just have tomato juice.'

He goes to the bar, waits, returns with her drink. All the time he is thinking of her and how much he wants her back. If he can have her back he will never ask for anything else for the rest of his life.

She says in a tone of polite curiosity, 'Well, so you've moved out. How did you manage that?'

'It's not how it looks. Inge lost the baby. She had a miscarriage back in February and we did a lot of talking and thinking about it and she actually suggested I should go. She's being very reasonable. She's really accepted it's final this time.'

Helen considers this, sipping her drink. He feels she is playing for time and it gives him hope.

'Must have been tough for the boys,' she finally says.

'Yes. Yes, it was. It is. They took it badly. I feel terrible about them.'

'Well,' she says, as if she doesn't quite believe how terrible he feels, 'I suppose apart from that it must be a great relief. Now you can really get on with your life.'

The expression disturbs him, although he's often heard it used and in fact had used it himself to clients on probation, and they had used it to him. Then it seemed to be quite a handy phrase to describe being active and positive and forward-looking, all desirable qualities. Now it suddenly has no meaning for him. In fact it sounds grotesque. He has no life to get on with if she won't have him back.

He says inadequately, 'I miss you very much.'

Her eyes close for a second. 'Please don't start that again.'

'I know you were still very angry with me last time I saw you and maybe I had no right trying to get you back then while I was still with Inge, but it's different now, can't you see that? I'm free. And I'm so sorry. I was wrong about you and Sally. You had a right to do what

184

you thought was best, she's your child. If you felt you couldn't talk to me about it, that must have been my fault, maybe I was too—'

'Oh Richard, please,' she says, cutting in sharply, 'it's ancient history.'

'I should never have left you, anyway,' he says, which is all that seems to matter now.

'Well, you did,' she says. 'You left me a year ago.'

'And I've regretted it every single day.'

She finishes her drink. 'Well, I'm sorry, but there we are.'

He is terrified she's going to leave and there is so much more he wants to say but he can't find the words. Her beauty and his terror seem to have paralysed his brain. No wonder she doesn't want me, he thinks; I can't say the right things so she doesn't understand how I feel. He has a dreadful sensation of panic, as in a dream when struggling to run and only succeeding in standing still.

'Please can we try again?' he says. 'I love you so much. I miss you terribly. I've made the worst mistake of my life leaving you.'

'Please don't, Richard,' she says. 'This is so embarrassing.'

There is a silence between them then and the pub noises suddenly flood in as if he hadn't heard them before.

He says, 'Is there someone else? Is that it?' remembering how he felt there might be when he saw her in January and how he pushed the thought away because it was too painful. Now he is already in so much pain it hardly seems to matter.

She says, 'I don't think you've got any right to ask me that, but yes, there is.'

He swallows hard. 'Do I know him?' He still thinks it might be Carey.

'No, you don't. But even if he wasn't around I wouldn't want to try again. You've got to accept that, Richard. I'm sorry, but it's hopeless, I don't think we ever saw each other the way we really are. You wanted me to be so perfect to make up to you for leaving home and I couldn't manage it. And I was so determined to fall in love with someone who wasn't like Carey and there you were. I think we both had to compromise far too much.'

'But that's marriage,' he says, aghast.

'I know, up to a point, but I don't think you even like the person I really am. Oh, I'm not explaining very well but I've thought about it a lot and I know it's no good. Felix and Sally and the abortion were just the last straw. I don't think things were right with us for a very long time.'

'I can't believe you mean that,' he says. 'I thought it was wonderful right up to the end.'

'Well, this isn't doing any good,' she says, standing up. 'We're only going to hurt each other more. Let's leave it, Richard, maybe I'm wrong about the past, I don't know, but it feels dead now, I do know that.'

'Please don't say that,' he says. 'Please please don't.'

'I'm going to go now,' she says. 'I really can't stand this any more. I do wish you well and all that.'

Felix embarks on a programme of celebration with Elizabeth, taking her to theatres, concerts, films, reworking all their familiar territory like an animal spraying trees with its scent. Social infidelity, he thinks, is largely an unexplored area but he feels it keenly. All the places she has gone with David, as if they were a couple. Being seen in public together. He has never flaunted his own affairs like that. It must mean she always intended to tell him, making secrecy unnecessary. More than a fling, then. Something deliberately planned, to bring him to heel.

After one extraordinary juxtaposition of Tchaikovsky and Mahler he says to her on their way out, 'They do make you wait for your climax, these Germans. Whereas good old multiple-orgasm Tchaikovsky is in there straight away, like a rat up a drainpipe.'

She laughs. Encouraged, he goes on: 'Remember how we always used to say Tchaikovsky rated a lower second? Now I'm not so sure.'

'Don't tell me you're getting sentimental in your old age.'

'Remind me how the grades went.'

'You haven't forgotten.' But she slips her hand into his as they stroll out of the Festival Hall and beside the river. The lights on the water are unchanged, timeless, reassuring. He could never live without her but he can never trust her again. Something precious has gone for ever and she doesn't even know. It's not the sex that has done it, it's the sending him away.

'Wagner and Mozart starred firsts. Beethoven, Brahms and Bach ordinary firsts. Verdi, Sibelius and Schubert upper second. Rachmaninov, Tchaikovsky and Puccini lower second.'

'But Dvorak, Grieg and Schumann got thirds.'

'Lucky to get them, some say. Had to pull strings.'

'What about Mahler?'

'The examiners are going to have another meeting.'

'Trouble is,' he says, 'I seem to prefer the chaps who got lower seconds.'

They go on playing the game all the way back to the parking lot, feeling childish, feeling nostalgic. In the dark of the car he kisses her as if they were teenagers, aware of the unseen presence of that other, the lover, the rival, as keenly as if he were sitting on the back seat watching them, waiting to be given a lift home. He loves her very much and he can't wait to punish her for betraying him. He drives home with one hand on her knee.

Richard gives Kate his new address on the first day of term. He waits till everyone else has gone home and she is putting her things together in the empty staff room. It's been a stressful day and she looks tired. She says, 'God, one day back and I don't feel I've ever been away, do you?'

He says, 'I know what you mean.' He feels quite embarrassed about telling her his news. The only time they have talked about anything personal was when Inge had her miscarriage and Kate was so sympathetic that he felt like a hypocrite.

'Well, I'm off.' Kate slings everything in a hold-all and makes for the door.

He says, 'Oh, by the way, I've moved, so I'd better give you this,' and hands her a piece of paper with his new address and phone number. 'Just in case you need to get hold of me any time.'

She looks surprised. 'I didn't know you were moving. Quite an upheaval, isn't it? I don't think I could face it again.'

He hesitates, but he must tell her or sooner or later she will ask about Inge. It will have to come out and he wants to get it over. But he's afraid she will disapprove of him for leaving his wife so soon after a miscarriage and it will spoil their working relationship.

'Well, actually, it's just a room. I've moved on my own.'

'Oh, Richard, I'm sorry.' Her face softens. 'What a shock. I don't know what to say.'

'Well, we've been having problems for a long time and over the holidays we just decided this would be the best thing.'

She looks thoughtful, watching him. 'Still, it's never easy is it? Especially with children. It happened to us eighteen months ago and I've only just got used to it.'

'Oh. I didn't realize.' He's surprised. In a year of working with her he's only heard her mention her husband a few times but never with any hint that they were divorced or separated. She hasn't spoken much about her children either, so he just assumed she was a naturally discreet person who guarded her privacy.

'No, well, it's not something I like talking about,' she says. 'You always think it can't happen to you, don't you? Until it does.'

'Yes, that's true,' he says. He doesn't like to tell her it's happened to him twice, and indeed there are times when he can't believe it himself: it's so far from what he intended.

'Oh well,' she says, 'I suppose it gives us something more in common with the kids we're teaching, poor little devils. Not too many happy families there either.'

'Hullo?'

He hesitates. It sounds like Helen but it ought to be Sally at this time of day. He hasn't rung the house since Richard left so he can't be sure. He attempts to disguise his voice with a Scots accent, always the one he finds easiest, for no particular reason, and has used many times on tiresome husbands who shouldn't have been there.

'Is that Helen Irving?' He'll have to pretend it's business if it is and then disconnect himself in mid-sentence. He really doesn't fancy a conversation with Helen after all this time: he has the feeling she could almost castrate him over the phone. He also doesn't want to foul up Sally's Easter vac.

'No, it's her daughter. Mum's at the studio.'

'Oh, Sally.' There is something endearing about her public persona, which he would never normally encounter. 'Your voices are so alike.'

'Felix.' She sounds surprised, disconcerted, not altogether pleased. 'It didn't sound like you.'

'No, I was trying to be devious.'

'Well, that shouldn't be difficult,' she says instantly.

He's annoyed with himself for walking right into that one. He must be getting careless. He laughs. 'Darling, don't tease me, I'm ringing to invite you to lunch.'

There is a pause, and then she says, 'After all this time,' in a small, cold voice.

'Well, I've been busy with the book and I've been away. I did send you postcards.'

'Yes,' she says. 'I got them.'

'I'll take you somewhere nice on the river. Shall I pick you up at the end of the street about one o'clock?'

'Today?' she says in a shocked tone, as if she had a social secretary.

'Yes, why not?'

'I'm busy today. It'll have to be tomorrow.'

He doesn't know whether to be amused or offended by this. She probably just wants time to wash her hair, he thinks. But he remembers a time when she would have been eager to see him at no matter how short notice.

'All right,' he says. 'Tomorrow.'

She doesn't reply and he's just about to say goodbye when she suddenly asks like a detective pouncing on a suspect, 'Are you back with Elizabeth?'

He hesitates only slightly, then says, 'Yes,' in what he hopes is a cheerful, casual tone.

'Ah.'

'Well, I told you it was only temporary.'

'Must be a great relief,' she says, with a nasty edge to her voice.

'It's certainly nicer than living at the flat.' He keeps his tone even and relaxed.

'I'll see you tomorrow,' she says.

It's a perfect spring day. He drives her down to a riverside hotel where he has booked a room in case she is in the right mood after lunch. It's hard to tell: she is pleasant but remote, which could mean she is playing hard to get or, equally, gearing up to say goodbye. He doesn't know her tastes in clothes or music any more, so he has bought her a string of pearls because he thinks it's about time she

190

has some. On the drive, while they chat about nothing in particular, he imagines her pleasure when he gives them to her and wonders if they will tip the balance in his favour. He's never had to offer a bribe before and he hopes it won't look like that now: either way they should be an ideal present, whether for reunion or farewell.

He still wants her, but he no longer knows if it's desire for her as she is now or nostalgia for the lost Sally or simply as a revenge on Elizabeth. He has such mixed feelings about her, he's given up hope of disentangling them. She looks older, thinner, more beautiful. She looks like a stranger. He still wants her and yet he knows she's more trouble than she's worth and he should have got out long ago. Or rather, he should never have gone back. But it was so tempting.

'Oh, Richard's left Inge again,' she says importantly.

'Really?' This is interesting. In fact it's the first interesting thing she's said. 'When?'

'Don't know. Recently, I think. I haven't seen him. Mum told me.'

Felix thinks over what this could mean to him. 'Is Helen going to have him back?'

'No, she's got someone else. It's exciting, isn't it?'

'Yes,' he says cautiously. 'Very. Who's she got?'

'An old painter she used to know when I was little. He's quite nice but he's had three wives and five children.'

Perhaps this is why he still desires her, he thinks. Because she reminds him of Helen and he will probably never see Helen again.

'D'you mean he's got no spare cash?'

'No, he's quite rich apparently. I mean he doesn't sound very reliable.'

'Well, that should make a change from Richard.'

'Oh, I don't know. Richard turned out pretty unreliable in the end, didn't he? Leaving Inge twice and leaving Mum and trying to kill you.'

'Don't exaggerate,' he says. 'A punch on the jaw is hardly attempted murder.'

'It is when he left you unconscious and didn't call an ambulance.'

'Well, I'm still here,' he says, irritated, 'alive and well. And it's not your problem about the old painter.'

'It is if he makes Mum unhappy. I want her settled. I want her off my hands.'

He laughs. 'You sound like Mrs Bennet trying to unload one of her daughters.'

'Maybe that's how I feel. But it's not very flattering of you to say so.'

'Why not? Mrs Bennet is a wonderful character. I'm very fond of Mrs Bennet.'

'She's a pain. I think Jane Austen is overrated.'

'Oh, Sally.'

'Oh, Sally, what?'

'That's like saying Mozart isn't musical.'

'He's overrated too.'

So they are already arguing as they arrive. She looks sullen. It will be too ironic if they end up not going to bed because of Mrs Bennet and Mozart.

He orders champagne, thinking, well, even if it doesn't help, he's never known a situation where it made matters worse. They study the menu and sip their drinks while sitting outside on the terrace in the soft spring sunshine. That always lifts his spirits.

'What perfect weather,' he says. 'Reminds me of Cambridge. Our lovely weekend.'

'That was July,' she says.

'Yes, I know. But it's just the same sort of feeling, sitting by the river on a fine day. And I don't know any poems about July. But everyone knows "Oh, to be in England now that April's here". There's always a sort of optimism about spring, don't you think?' He wants to lighten her mood. 'D'you realize we've known each other properly for two whole years. Or should it be improperly? In the Biblical sense, anyway.'

'Or "April is the cruellest month,"' she says predictably.

'Oh, Sally. Not that again.'

'Yes,' she says. 'That again. We could have a child a year old by now and you're rabbiting on about the weather. Don't anniversaries mean anything to you?'

'Only happy ones,' he says sadly.

'I don't understand you,' she says. 'You're obviously expecting me to enjoy being with you all over again and yet we've got all that behind us.'

It's the only place for it, he thinks, but it wouldn't help to say so. 'Can't you let it go?' he says. 'I'm sorry it happened but it was a long time ago.'

'And it was my fault. That's what you mean, isn't it?'

'Well, you were in charge,' he says reasonably. 'If I'd known you were taking a risk I'd have been more careful.'

'It's that simple, is it?'

'Well, those are the facts, aren't they? I'm sorry, my darling, I'd love to change the past but I can't.'

'Even you,' she says.

The waiter comes and takes their order.

'D'you know why I keep going on about it?' she says when they're alone again. 'Because I didn't have a choice. You and Mum just told me what to do and I did it.'

'You did have a choice,' he says. 'You could have told Richard.'

'Not really,' she says. 'I'd have had to have it adopted. Mum didn't want to bring it up. There was no point in telling him, not once I knew you wouldn't leave Elizabeth. I didn't want to make him angry with you for nothing. I'm not spiteful. But if we'd stayed together and had the baby he wouldn't have been so angry.'

'You wouldn't have liked life with me and a baby,' he says. 'You honestly wouldn't.'

'You mean you wouldn't,' she says. She sounds fierce. 'I'd like to have had a choice, that's all. And I'd like to have felt that someone was putting me first for a change.'

'By someone you mean me,' he says. 'Do you?'

'No one has ever put me first,' she says.

'I should have thought Helen has put you first for twenty years. Isn't that what mothers are supposed to do?' But not mine, he thinks.

'No. Her work. And now it's this man.' She pauses. 'I'm sorry, I'm ruining our lunch, aren't I? I don't know why I keep doing this. I can't seem to leave it alone. I keep thinking I've finished and I never have.'

'We'd better go inside,' he says. 'They must be nearly ready for us. And it's clouding over.'

They eat wonderful food in a half-empty dining-room overlooking the river. He watches drops of rain splashing into the water. April showers, he thinks, and the Disney tune sparkles up from his memory bank along with the cheerful cartoons. He thinks how much he hates gloom, how futile it is, when they're all going to die in a few years and should be concentrating on having a good time. Gather ye rosebuds. *Carpe diem.* Think positive. All these philosophies are the same really, he reflects, ancient and modern. Mankind hasn't really come up with anything original to counteract the one undeniable unbearable fact of death. He smiles at her encouragingly.

'And my father left and Richard left and you left,' she says.

'I didn't leave,' he says. 'I'm here now, aren't I?'

'Not really,' she says.

'In that case I'd better give you this,' he says. 'As proof of my presence.' And he hands her the slim parcel of pearls.

She stops eating and unwraps it slowly. 'My God,' she says. 'Are they real?'

'Well, they're cultured, not wild. They're not fake, if that's what you mean.'

'They're beautiful,' she says.

He puts them on for her and she admires herself in the mirror.

'You're very good at presents,' she says. 'You've given me so many lovely things.'

'Well, it gives me pleasure.'

'Is this to make up for last time?' she asks. 'It was so horrid last time.'

'I was limp,' he says bluntly, irritable at being reminded. 'It happens to everyone.'

'I didn't mean that,' she says. 'But you didn't want me. You were sad about Elizabeth.'

'We've been married a long time.' He can't think what else to say: it's like trying to tell a blind person about the sea.

'I suppose you've booked a room here, just in case,' she says.

'Yes. Why not? I'm an optimist.'

'What did you tell them?'

'That we were changing planes and couldn't bear to stay at Heathrow.'

'Will they believe you?'

'I shouldn't think so but it doesn't matter. It's just something to say.'

'Where's our luggage?'

'At the airport, of course.'

'I wish we could have had a proper holiday,' she says. 'With real luggage, gone somewhere hot. Or to Venice. We talked about that once, d'you remember?'

'Well, we still can.'

'No.' She shakes her head. 'Don't you see, Felix, I'm trying to say goodbye?'

'Yes,' he says, 'I rather thought you were.'

There are tears in her eyes. 'I don't know why it's so hard,' she says, 'when I'm so angry with you for not loving me enough. Well, for not loving me at all really.'

'Oh, come on,' he says, 'that's not true.'

'I know I've been horrible to you every time we've met for the last year. I know I've been unfair. It was my fault what happened. So why can't I say goodbye?'

'It's because we still fancy each other rotten,' he says gently.

'Oh,' she says, 'is that all it is?'

'Goodbye is quite hard to say anyway,' he explains. 'Even to someone you don't really like. It's a bit like dying. It's too final. You don't want to do it till you absolutely have to.'

'Well, I absolutely have to. I'm in love with my tutor and he doesn't have a wife.'

'I'm glad,' he says, 'if that's what you want.' He wonders if she is lying.

'Don't you even care? Aren't you even upset?'

'I'm very upset but that won't make you change your mind, will it?' He thinks how he will never get used to the eddy of feelings, loss and relief and anger, all swirling into each other and getting confused, how two people are never quite ready to part at exactly the same time.

She manages a wan smile. 'Do I have to give back the pearls?'

'No, of course not,' he says. 'Wear them with my love.'

'That word,' she says.

They drive back without speaking, leaving the room unused. In the car he puts on some music, Bach; he wants something measured to fill the aching silence, but she switches it off. When he stops at the end of her street he suddenly says, 'It's funny, but I could make love to you now.'

'Then do,' he says. 'Come back to the flat, or another hotel. Just to say goodbye properly. I could make it really special today. That will take all the pain out of it, I promise you. Let's end on a good note.'

'No,' she says. There are tears in her eyes again. 'I could but I'm not going to.'

She gets out of the car without kissing him and runs

196

towards her house. He doesn't watch her go; he drives off at once and is out of sight before she reaches the door.

When he gets home Elizabeth is reading the book.

'It's wonderful,' she says, looking up with a troubled face. 'I think it's the best thing you've done, but it's awfully close to home.'

'Not really,' he says. 'It's a fantasy.' He pours himself a drink. 'But it's taken a lot out of me. I feel quite empty. Drained.'

'You always feel like that when you finish something,' she says. 'Don't you remember?'

'I'm so sorry,' Michael says to Inge one day, 'but we have such a waiting list here that Dr Shaw wants me to limit clients to twelve sessions each if possible. It was always meant to be an opportunity for free short-term counselling as an adjunct of the practice but we didn't realise there'd be such a demand. Of course you've had more than twelve sessions already, but that's all right. What I have to ask you is how you feel about finishing in another month?'

'I don't want to finish,' she says at once. It takes no thought at all. 'I was going to ask you if I could come more often. Half an hour every two weeks doesn't seem very much.'

'I can't manage that here,' he says, 'but I could fit you in privately. I work from home in Hampstead but I do charge forty pounds an hour and I know you don't have much money to spare. If I could do it for thirty, would that help? I'm saying the same to all the clients here that I'm having to hurry away. I don't like feeling we have to rush our endings.'

Inge considers this. 'No,' she says finally. 'I think I should pay the correct amount like everyone else. If I have a month to get ready, I think I might be able to find a job.'

Elizabeth is surprised how quickly and easily she adjusts to her new life. Living with Felix again and still visiting David makes her feel adventurous and young. It all seems remarkably harmless: no one is jealous and no one is hurt. It is not a way of life she ever imagined could work for her, yet somehow it is working.

The biggest surprise is that making love with Felix makes her enjoy sex with David at last. David himself seems less than thrilled about this. 'He's turned you on,' he says resentfully, when she now joins in with enthusiasm, and the implication is that Felix has succeeded where he himself has failed. Felix by contrast seems excited by the thought of her with another man and always questions her closely when she gets home from seeing David as to what they have done together. 'I can smell him on you,' he says. 'Tell me about him.' Sometimes she actually has to lie, because sometimes she and David have merely sat and talked about Kate and his children and the problems with his second novel, but she doesn't think that is what Felix wants to hear. David has become the phantom third in their bed and he won't be very erotic if he is merely a friend. Felix keeps suggesting that she should invite David to join them and she is not entirely sure if this is a serious suggestion or just a useful fantasy. When she mentions it to David as a joke, he is disgusted.

'I'm surprised Felix has lived so long,' he says thoughtfully. 'I'd have thought some jealous husband would have bumped him off years ago.'

'I suppose some people don't take adultery very seriously any more,' she says. She feels a little shiver of alarm: she doesn't like David joking about Felix being dead. After all, it nearly happened once.

'I do. I'd have bumped him off if he's been messing around with my wife. I might have got away with it, too, if I'd brought medical evidence to show I was unbalanced at the time, although killing Felix would be the sanest thing anyone could do.' He stares at her intently, making her feel slightly uncomfortable. 'What would you do, Elizabeth, if Felix was dead? Would you come and live with me?'

So it has to be Inge. With Sally gone, there is no one else he can have so fast and he won't be at ease with Elizabeth till he's broken the ridiculous promise she extracted from him under duress. Any man would say anything to get back into his own house, he thinks. He finds himself looking at her with positive hatred sometimes, but she doesn't appear to notice. And the terrible sadness he feels at the way she has wrecked their marriage, she doesn't seem to notice that either. He must be an even greater dissembler than he thought, or she must be very stupid, which is a depressing idea. And it is hard to stay buoyant and cheerful while sharing her with someone as insignificant as David Johnson.

'I didn't expect to hear from you again, Felix,' Inge says over lunch. 'It was a very nice surprise when you rang up.'

'Well, I've missed you, Inge,' he says. 'And we didn't exactly quarrel, did we?'

'No,' she says, 'you dropped me when I rang up at midnight.'

'Well, we all do silly things. I've often thought about you but I could hardly ring you while Richard was there, could I? I've only just heard you've separated.'

'And now you think I need consolation?' she says. 'Well, perhaps I do.'

That sounds encouraging. Inge is so straightforward; he has always valued her directness. Until she overdid it.

'You look wonderful,' he says. In fact he's surprised how well she looks; he expected a heartbroken wreck. Instead he sees a woman blooming and blossoming. He hasn't seen her like this since the early days of her marriage.

'I'm in therapy,' she says, with the air of someone announcing a new religion.

'Oh, good,' he says, since she clearly thinks it's wonderful.

'He's called Michael Green and he's taught me about growth and change,' she says, eating heartily. Her appetite at least is unchanged. 'Maybe you should see him, Felix. You don't look happy.'

He feels shaken to be so transparent. 'I've had a difficult year,' he says cautiously.

'I think it's the same for all of us. It's part of getting older, isn't it? We don't bounce so easily.'

'Perhaps.' He is not quite sure what she means.

'I thought life was over for me when I lost my little girl,' she says. 'But I'm learning with Michael's help that you can survive anything.'

'What little girl, Inge?' he says, startled.

'Oh, I had a miscarriage in February,' she says. 'Didn't you know?'

'No, I only heard you and Richard had split up again. I'm sorry.'

'Oh, it was terrible. I thought he had given me this wonderful present of a new life, and at last we are going to be happy, and instead we have nothing but death – the baby and the marriage. I was very depressed.'

'Yes, I can imagine.' He thinks how glad he is that he wasn't there at the time.

'But now I think perhaps it was meant to be that way. We had to work things out to the very end and kill everything so we could start again separately, you know?

Only Helen won't have him back and I'm very worried about him. He looks so sad.'

'According to Sally, she's got someone else,' he says. It's rather fun to be gossiping with Inge after all this time.

'Really? Oh, poor Richard. No wonder he looks sad. But what can I do? We had to make an ending. It's a question of boundaries, you see, where Richard stops and I begin. He just isn't my responsibility any more. I have to put myself first now, it's a matter of self-esteem. Michael says that is the most important thing. To love myself before I love anyone else. Isn't that nice? He's wonderful, he's helped me so much.'

Really, Felix thinks, it's as if she's talking a different language, as if she's picked up some weird psycho-babble from the States, exchanging one obsession for another. But she looks very appetising indeed.

'We went to see him together for a while,' she goes on, 'but Richard didn't like him, I think he was jealous. It was free at the health centre but we could only have half an hour once a fortnight and I need more, so now I go every week for an hour and it costs forty pounds so I have to get a job to pay for it.'

This is a revelation to Felix. The idea of Inge with a job quite takes his breath away. He imagines it must be a revelation to Richard too. 'What are you doing, Inge?' he asks with real interest.

'Well, I have two jobs. Two little part-time jobs. It's fun, I like it. One is I teach people to speak German and another is I work in a shop. It's near my house, so I don't have to waste money on the bus. I sell scarves and jewellery and joss sticks and astrology things. Well, mostly I don't sell very much because people come in and wander round and then they go out again, but I get paid anyway so I don't care. Sometimes I sell things. It's just so the woman who owns it doesn't have to stay there all the time. And it smells of incense and we play funny music from Thailand. It's nice, it reminds me of the sixties or maybe it's the seventies, anyway, it makes me feel young again.'

'Yes,' he says, 'you certainly are looking young.'

'You should come in some time, Felix, you might like it. You could buy a present for Elizabeth.'

'I'm not sure Elizabeth deserves a present. We had a separation because of Sally, and now she has a lover.' He hadn't meant to tell Inge so much, but there is something about her frank, confiding face and all the rubbish she has been telling him that he finds oddly endearing. And for once in his life he feels the need to confide in someone, which surprises him. So why not Inge? With Richard gone, she is probably the nearest thing he has to an old friend. It's a strange thought.

'Oh, Felix. Are you jealous?'

'Not exactly. But he's a bloody awful writer and that hurts my pride.'

'Maybe just a little bit jealous,' she says, managing to look both sympathetic and amused.

'Let's go to bed, Inge,' he says. 'Shall we? I really want you.'

'I'd like to. It was always so good with you. But I don't want you to drop me again so suddenly. I get used to sex and I don't like it to stop.'

'And I don't want you to ring up at midnight.'

'All right.'

They shake hands across the table. Then they kiss.

'Let's have a wonderful summer,' she says.

He thinks how simple it can be with the right person.

After he tells her of his separation from Inge, Kate seems perceptibly friendlier. She has always been pleasant and helpful, but strictly as a colleague and his immediate superior. He liked her from his first day at the school when she said, 'Don't shoot till you see the whites of their eyes.' But she has always kept her professional distance until now. Now, through the summer term, she begins to linger in the staff room for a cup of tea and a chat at the end of the day. Just occasionally. Never often enough to create a pattern. And at first they only talk about school matters: problem children, the deficiencies of the timetable, the new exams, the foibles of the head. Then one day she says casually, 'How's life in your new place?'

He is startled. It seems like a very personal question in the context of work. 'All right. Not too bad.'

'Only the kids and I were wondering if you'd like to come to us for Sunday lunch some time – maybe next week?'

'I cooked the lunch,' says Annabel. She is a leggy thirteen-year-old who may be going to break into beauty quite soon. But at the moment her features are just loosely assembled, with the smooth skin and clear eyes of youth, waiting for their moment to arrive. The chrysalis stage, he thinks. And there is an air of being eager to please about her that he remembers from Sally, an anxiety about the way she glances from Kate to him and back again, while acting desperately casual.

'You cooked it very well,' Richard says. She has done roast chicken and sweet corn with roast potatoes and it's really quite good. He's impressed.

'Mum's a rotten cook,' says Thomas. He's a robust ten-year-old who manages somehow to be both cheerful and wary. Impossible not to think of Peter at the same age.

'It's true, I'm afraid,' Kate says.

'No, it's not,' Annabel says, looking at her plate. 'It's just that Dad used to do all the cooking so Mum didn't get any practice.'

Both children have dark hair and eyes and are much better-looking than Kate. In fact they hardly resemble her at all. When he looks at her kind, plain face, her straight sandy hair and eyelashes, he can hardly believe she is their mother.

His bedsit seems bleaker than ever after lunch with Kate and her children. The sensation of being in a real home again was deeply seductive. When he visits Inge she is pleasant and friendly, but he has no contact with Karl, and Peter is very awkward with him now. The affection is still there, he is sure of that, but the trust has gone. It is so painful to go on visiting the wreckage and trying to repair it, being reminded of his crimes. Perhaps he lost them both years ago, when he left them the first time. So much easier to turn somewhere else where as yet he has done no damage. He longs to be part of a family again; he wants to make friends with Kate's children but he feels he has no right to, tainted as he is by desertion. He thinks he must ask Helen if she'd mind if he got in touch with Sally. He's been wanting to do that for a long time.

Michael's flat is on the ground floor of a leafy street in Hampstead. It is very different from Camden Town and it becomes the highlight of her week to go there. Everything about it is pleasurable, even if they talk about painful things when she arrives: getting ready, the journey by bus and tube, the walk, all give her joy. The flat is cool and rather dark and he sees clients in a small room next to his living-room, which is vast. Both rooms face on to the garden and he sits with his back to the window. It touches her that he gives up the view to concentrate on her.

One day she spends the whole fifty-minute hour talking about her grief for her daughter. It is June. He says to her, 'This must be about the time your daughter would have been born.'

'Yes.' She's so grateful that he remembers. 'I don't know if you can imagine what it was like to lose her. I'm sure Richard thought I made too much fuss. You're very understanding, but it's such a special thing to lose a child, even before it's born.'

He hesitates fractionally and then says, 'Well, I did lose my only daughter, as a matter of fact.'

'Oh.' This is such a shock that she actually gasps. 'I'm sorry. How terrible. When?'

'A few years ago now.'

'How old was she?'

'Seventeen.'

'My God.'

It is the second personal thing he has told her. Another glimpse into his life. She stores up these fragments to examine later. And then she feels the door has closed again: it doesn't seem as if she can ask any more.

They have one of their long silences. She no longer worries about these, or waits for him to break them, knowing now that he won't; she just relaxes into the feeling of timelessness, of total acceptance, aware that she can speak or be silent, that anything she says or does will be all right, that this is her time to use as she chooses. He has taught her that. She sits there looking at the flowers and trees in his garden. Presently she starts talking about herself again. Sometimes it is too intense to look at him. It feels different to see him in his home. Slowly and imperceptibly she realises she is falling in love.

PART FIVE

'How am I going to manage, Felix?' Inge says. 'Michael is going to be away for the whole of August.'

'Never mind. Think of all the money you'll be saving. A hundred and sixty quid to splurge on yourself for a change.'

'You'll have to be extra nice to me. I'll have to talk to you instead. You won't charge me, will you? I'll do special things for you in bed.'

'How do these shrinks imagine their patients can cope when they piss off on holiday?' Felix enquires. 'One minute they're making out they're indispensible, the next it's bucket-and-spade time, cheerio.'

'They're only human, Felix. They need holidays too, more so really. They have to recharge their batteries. Anyway, he's not a shrink. A shrink is a psychiatrist and that means a doctor first before you specialise in psychiatry. He's a counsellor and psychotherapist. That means—'

'I know, you told me all that. I think if I was getting forty pounds an hour,' Felix says, 'I might soldier on through August. I might just settle for a long weekend.'

'Well, I was cross at first when he told me. But we worked through it. It's useful for me to be able to express anger freely in a safe environment.'

'God, there's a lot of jargon goes with this, isn't there? Sometimes you sound as if you've come straight from California. Any moment you'll be telling me it's a learning experience.'

'Well, it is, Felix. You're right. That's exactly what it is.'

'Maybe it sounds less pretentious in German, although I don't see how it could. More so, probably. What's this music, Inge? I know it so well but I can't pin it down.'

'It's Brahms, one of the symphonies. I'm not sure which one. Shall I get the paper?'

'No, don't bother. Of course it's Brahms, I should have known. When it sounds like Beethoven and you're surprised how much you're enjoying it, it always turns out to be Brahms.'

It's July before Helen feels relaxed enough to invite him to the studio. She tells herself she doesn't want him to see her new work in progress but perhaps even then it's more because Sally's home, and it feels somehow indecorous to have him stay over at the house or to go to his flat and leave Sally alone overnight. And perhaps she is shy of doing something that will seem so obviously like an attempt to remind him of the past. But eventually she does it and he comes and look around.

'Just like old times,' he says predictably. He seems very relaxed: perhaps it means much less to him to be there than it does to her to have him there. 'But your work's changing a lot.'

'Yes, it is.' And so am I, she thinks.

'I like it,' he says.

'Does that mean you didn't like it before?'

'Oh no,' he says, laughing, 'I'm not getting caught like that.'

He takes her out to dinner and they go back to the studio to make love before they go off to their separate homes.

'We must do this again,' he says, 'in the afternoon.'

And they meet several times that month, more than they ever have before, and she can't believe her luck. Making love very gently in the hazy warmth of the summer afternoon with street noises outside, the smell of the studio mixed with their own special scent.

'You know what we're doing,' he says. 'We're pretending to be young again. Now all we need is some fruit and Sally aged four coming back from nursery school.'

She feels acknowledged: he hasn't forgotten their shared past. 'And you *not* going home to Laura,' she says, greatly daring. 'Just to make a change.'

'Oh,' he says with a long sigh, 'if you only knew how often I nearly didn't go.'

Later when she thinks about it, that must have been when it happened. On one of those dreamy afternoons.

Kate is often angry and he finds her anger attractive, making her a more interesting person. He thinks of the old film cliché: 'God, you're beautiful when you're angry, Miss Jones,' with the hero removing the heroine's glasses and a few hairpins, letting long hair spill out from a confining bun. It isn't quite that, for nothing can make Kate beautiful, but anger causes her plain face to light up with energy, as if someone has switched on a lamp inside her. He remembered Felix saying with envy in his voice, 'You always marry such beautiful women,' and how the realisation warmed him, that Felix could want something Richard had and be obliged to do without it. Well, Felix had finally had Inge, briefly, but that doesn't matter now; he will never have Helen, that is certain, and Richard is savagely glad. But it disturbs him to be thinking about Kate in this context. Surely he isn't regarding her as a potential wife? And surely he isn't still bonded in some way to Felix, with all his destructive charm? It worries him that thoughts like that can come into his mind at all.

Kate is angry about life and politics and the state of the world. She is angry with the government and their educational policy, or lack of it. She talks a lot about this and he listens and agrees with her, admiring her energy. He thinks she is right but he is too exhausted to express himself so forcefully. One day they talk about writers and he discovers she is angry with them too.

'I don't think I like writers very much,' she says. 'They think they own the world and ordinary rules don't apply to them. Perhaps all creative people are like that but writers are the worst. Everything is grist to their mill. They cannibalise everyone they meet.'

'It's ironic for two teachers to think like that,' he suggests. 'All those authors we have to recommend.'

'It's not ironic at all,' Kate says. 'Most of them are dead. I prefer them that way.'

He laughs. He has a sudden memory of Felix lying unconscious on the floor and wonders if he really wanted him to die.

'The best of them goes into their books,' Kate says.

'I suppose so.'

'Living with them simply doesn't work,' she says. 'The magic wears awfully thin after a while.'

She smiles at him and pours more tea for them both. They are becoming friends.

Encouraged by all this Helen says, 'I suppose you wouldn't fancy a holiday with me? Sally's going to Greece in August, she'll be away a couple of months. I thought maybe we could go somewhere for a few days.'

'Oh, I'm going to the States for six weeks,' he says, without apology. 'I promised Susie a trip. We're going to stay with Mara in New York and then drive across and see Jake in L.A. It's about time I checked up on them both.'

'Very nice.' She's disappointed, and angry at the casual way he mentions it. She wonders when or even if he would have told her, if she hadn't brought up the subject.

'You wouldn't like me on holiday anyway,' he says. 'I'm no good at relaxing. I get very moody away from the studio.'

'Poor old Susie.'

'Oh, it's different for daughters. They know how to handle me.'

*

212

'Fancy a drink?' Kate says after the PTA meeting, and they stroll down the road to the pub together. This time last year, he thinks, he was at the end of his first term and Inge had just suggested therapy. Sometimes he still feels dizzy with disbelief at the way his life has changed.

'D'you have any plans for the summer?' Kate asks when they are settled in a corner with a pint and a half of bitter.

'Not really. I don't think I can afford a holiday this year.'

'I know the feeling. The kids and I are going down to Suffolk to stay with my parents for the whole of August, that's the nearest I'll get to a break. At least my mother will be on hand to help, and there'll be country things for them to do. They get bored in London, they aren't old enough to be cultured. Then David's having them for the first week in September, so I'll get a few days to myself before term starts. I shall have a feast of theatre, I think.'

'Very nice.'

'Well, it will make a change.' She hesitates. 'If I have any spare tickets would you like to come?'

'Yes.' He's surprised. 'I'd love to.'

'I thought maybe something at the National or the RSC. Well. Good. I'll give you a ring during the holidays then.'

What they have just said feels like such an enormous step, planning a date in September and arranging to telephone in August, that they absolutely must not draw attention to it with silence. They both rush into the empty space and collide.

'Do you think—'

'Have you been—'

'Sorry.'

'Sorry.'

They laugh nervously.

'Go on.'

'Oh, gloomy thoughts, I'm afraid,' she says, smiling to lighten the words. 'I was wondering if our children will ever recover from all this and what sort of marriages they'll have. I mean, will it make them try harder or will they just think that breaking up is normal and doesn't really matter?'

'I don't know – but I've often thought the same thing.'

'I mean our parents' generation stayed together mostly, didn't they, and yet nearly all my friends have split up like me and some re-married. Some have even split up twice. What is it? Do we all expect too much or what?'

It's a chance he may not get again, an easy casual route to his guilty past, and he must take it if they are to become friends. The longer he leaves it without telling her, the more it will look like deceit. 'I don't know. I wish I did. But I'm afraid I'm one of the ones who've split up twice.'

'Oh, Richard.' He can see her struggling with compassion and disapproval and surprise. 'I'm sorry. That doesn't seem like you, somehow.'

'No, that's exactly how I feel about it. In fact the highlight of my holiday will be seeing my step-daughter next week, if all goes according to plan.'

'I didn't know you had a step-daughter, I thought you just had two teenage boys. How old is she?'

'She's twenty now. And I've known her since she was eight.'

'Heavens. So she really is like your own.'

'Yes. More than my own, I sometimes think.' Tears prick his eyes at the mention of Sally and he feels foolish. He thought he'd got over that but it still happens sometimes, taking him by surprise. 'She's at Sussex, reading English. Her mother is my second wife but when I separated in April that was from my first wife . . .' He stops. It sounds terrible. Both complicated and damning. 'I couldn't explain at the time.'

Kate says gently, 'Perhaps it would be easier if you tell me their names.'

'You're very understanding.' He's surprised how much he wants to tell her now. 'Well, Inge and I got married too young. We had Karl and Peter, but it was never really right. And then I met Helen.'

He pauses. Kate says nothing; she has a listening expression. He tries again.

'I was entirely to blame. Inge didn't do anything wrong. Well, I felt devoured by her but that wasn't her fault. I just fell in love with Helen. She was divorced when I met her, she's a painter, she was living alone with her daughter.'

He pauses. So many memories rush back. His first sight of her at the exhibition. That cold Nordic face that encompassed all his dreams. Going to the studio. Making love. Meeting Sally. Two years' hard deception and then telling Inge. The blood on the sheets and the ambulance siren. He drags himself back to the present.

'I don't think I'd ever really been in love before, it was such a shock. We lived together for eight years. I thought it was for ever. Then when we split up I went back to Inge and the boys. But that didn't work either, it was for all the wrong reasons . . . well, that's where you came in.'

He still doesn't feel he's been honest. Perhaps he never can be. It's all too painful. It would take too long. And it would show him in a very bad light. Perhaps it already has.

'Yes,' Kate says softly. 'What a shame. Poor you.'

'Well, poor everyone.'

There is a long silence. He looks at their empty glasses. 'Same again?'

'I do hope not,' Kate says, and they manage to smile. 'But I could use another half. Let me get them this time.'

'Not at all.'

When he comes back with their drinks she is looking thoughtful. He feels embarrassed. He says, 'I'm sorry, I've been talking too much.'

'No. It's just so sad. All these poor kids we're all dragging around with us while we make our mistakes.'

'Or leaving behind.'

215

'Yes. It's worse for men, I think. The guilt. I don't think they ever recover, some of them.'

He doesn't know what to say to that. 'Do you see much of your ex-husband?'

'As little as possible. It was a great love and when that turns sour . . . Well, you know.' She makes a little helpless gesture with her hands. 'He's a writer and he's manic depressive. Well, I think he is. His moods were quite terrifying but he wouldn't admit there was anything wrong, just his artistic temperament and all that. He'd be all over me one day and ice cold the next. The poor kids never knew where they were with him. In the end he became a sort of house-husband. I had to earn the money while he wrote his book. Everything I did at home was wrong. He wrote all night so we had to creep about all day. It took him ten years to get anything published. Frankly, when I read the book and remember what we all went through, I don't think it was worth it. But that's just my opinion.'

Richard says, 'I used to have a friend who was a writer.'

Kate has on her most severe face. He can see why she never has any discipline problems at school. 'I think they're a breed apart. Really. There's a coldness at the centre, a sort of greed for experience, a basic selfishness. I don't know, perhaps it's unfair to generalise. David was like that, perhaps your friend was lovely.'

What can he say to that? He doesn't want to tell her any more; he feels he's said too much already.

'No, I don't think I'd call him lovely,' he says, 'but I miss him.'

'What happened – did you quarrel?'

'Yes, in a way.'

'Well, maybe it wasn't meant to last. I used to think all friendships were for ever but now I think they have a natural lifespan, rather like house plants. If marriage doesn't last for ever, even with children, why should friendship? I've lost a few along the way. But you make new ones eventually.'

She sounds so calm, as if she has got her life under control at last. He wonders if she will phone him in August, if they will go to the theatre in September. He thinks it's not at all by chance that they have had such an intimate conversation at nearly the end of term. They will have six weeks to get over it.

'Stay with me, Elizabeth,' David says, just as she's leaving.

'You know I can't.'

'Why not?'

'Felix would worry.'

'Doesn't he stay out?'

'No, never.' She hears herself sound proud of this fact; she also remembers the night when he did stay out, because Richard had tried to kill him. She re-lives it fast, like a clip from a film, or an old recurrent nightmare: Helen at her door with bad news, breaking it gently, terrifying her – Felix in the hospital and the doctor being kind. She shivers and thinks for a moment, What am I doing here with David? I made a bargain with God. If he let Felix live I'd never complain about anything ever again. I'm behaving like an ungrateful child.

'You could phone him.' Now David sounds like a sulky little boy. He looks like one too, with his heavy bottom lip almost pouting. She sits on the side of the bed and pushes his dark shiny hair back from his forehead, which feels hot and damp. She kisses it. Now she's a mother who should be dosing him with junior aspirin, considering a day off school. She can't believe they've just made love. Surely he's the child she never had. She wants to laugh and cry at the same time. But most of all she wants to go home. In this context Felix suddenly appears grown up, undemanding, reliable.

'He knows about me. What's the difference?' David says.

'It's just not something we do.' She sees him flinch at the 'we'. 'Anyway, you work at night. Don't you? Those are your best hours, you told me. You don't want to waste them on me, snoring away beside you.' She wants to make him smile now, to jolly him along.

'You've got time for a drink,' he says authoritatively. He puts on a dressing-gown, as if he doesn't want to be naked any more now she is clothed for departure. She watches his skinny body disappearing into the towelling-robe, thinks how vulnerable a limp cock always looks, his or Felix's or anyone from her past. Just hanging there, at the mercy of any passing predator, with no hint of the miracles it can perform. She wants to protect it. She gives it a swift kiss while he's tying the belt of his robe.

'Cupboard love,' he says, and they both laugh.

'Just saying goodnight,' she says. 'Just being polite.'

'He's off-duty now. He doesn't recognise you with your clothes on.'

'Oh, really? I thought I detected a reminiscent twitch.'

'You make him nervous. He's afraid he might get too attached to you. He doesn't want to get hurt.'

It's all getting heavy and sad again. She does a mock snarl and snaps her teeth together. Now she's reminded of coaxing a puppy to eat, pretending you're going to steal its dinner. 'I'll have it. Grr.' The early days with Felix when, he loving cats and she loving dogs, they tried having both, the perfect compromise, before ending up with neither. Animals were a tie. If you didn't have children it was crazy to have animals. It meant you couldn't travel. Even plants were a nuisance, needing water, making you feel guilty when they died. All this freedom, she thinks. All this carefully structured freedom.

She has Perrier because she's driving. David has brandy. They sit in his stark black and white living-room with its minimal furniture and subdued lighting. It still doesn't seem like a home. More an advertisement for its designer.

'God, what do women want?' David says suddenly.

'Come back, Sigmund, all is forgiven. Here I am, in love with you, monogamous, devoted, and you can't wait to scuttle back to your unfaithful husband.'

She's embarrassed. Put like that it does sound unreasonable.

Finally there's a knock at the door and it's Sally. He has been looking forward to this moment so much. He is so pleased to see her he feels tears starting and has to blink them away. She has grown her hair again so that she looks almost the way he remembers her from the happy days and not how she was when she came to see him in prison. She looks like the child he loved and cared for all those years; she smiles and hugs him like a daughter. He wishes so much she was his own.

'Richard,' she says, 'it's so lovely to see you. I should have come before.'

'Never mind,' he says, 'you're here now. What can I offer you? Tea or a proper drink? I've got a bottle of wine, or there's some beer.'

'Tea, I think,' she says vaguely. 'I don't seem to drink much any more. I want to be thin, thin, thin.'

'Well, you are,' he says.

She screws up her nose. 'Not properly.' She thumps her narrow thighs, her flat stomach. 'I'm all flabby here. I need to lose at least ten pounds.'

He knows better than to argue. 'So it's no good offering you a toasted tea cake then. I bought them specially.'

'Well . . . maybe half a one.'

He gets them out and puts them under the grill while he makes the tea.

'I'll keep an eye on them, shall I?' Sally says.

It feels comfortable, companionable, to have her with him. He has forgotten to be ashamed of his surroundings, to apologise for the room.

'I nearly bought a fork to toast them in front of the gas

fire,' he says. 'That would really have felt like being back at college. But I didn't. I thought I was being a bit silly.'

'Are you all right here?' she says. 'You don't mind living in one room?'

'Well, it's all the same if I do,' he says. 'This is all I can afford. But no, I don't really mind. I don't have a lot of stuff, just books and clothes and records, so I don't feel crowded.'

'No,' she says, rescuing the tea cakes just in time, 'it's quite a big room as bedsits go. It's a lot bigger than mine.' She smiles at him as if they are both students now, comparing notes on college facilities.

'And I don't mind sharing a bathroom and kitchen. The other tenants are quite nice.' He feels safe talking about the room; it is a neutral subject, not emotionally charged like almost everything else he can think of. 'I get a proper lunch at school so I don't need to cook much. Two burners and a grill are all I need mostly, and it helps to have a fridge and a wash-basin. It could be a lot worse. It's quite peaceful in a way, to have life reduced to something very simple.'

'You could pretend you're travelling,' she says cheer-fully. 'Living rough. Seeing India or somewhere. Especi-ally now it's summer.' She sits cross-legged on the narrow single bed. 'This mattress is a bit soft but you could put a board under it. That's what I did with mine. And you could throw some material over that chair so you wouldn't see the pattern.'

'And change the curtains,' he says, 'and put a rug over the carpet. And paint everything white.'

'Or you could just pretend you like heavily varnished plywood. It'll probably come back into fashion any day now.'

They laugh. He pours the tea. He puts butter and jam on the toasted tea cakes and she has a whole one, as he knew she would.

'It's really weird seeing you like this,' she says abruptly, braver then he is, as if she can't avoid the subject any

220

longer. 'I mean, not with Mum. D'you think you'll ever get back together?'

He shakes his head, relieved that she's mentioned Helen first. 'I'm still hoping but . . . Oh God, I'm still hoping.' He hadn't known it would come out that like. 'I've asked her, well, I've begged her really, but she says no. She always says no.'

There is a silence while they drink their tea and eat their tea cakes.

'I was so angry with you,' Sally says. 'When you left her, I mean. When you went back to Inge. I couldn't believe you'd do that. That's why I haven't seen you. Mum was so miserable. I felt you'd left me to pick up all the pieces and I hated you.' She actually blushes. 'I'm sorry, Richard. That's not how I feel now or I wouldn't be here.'

'No, *I'm* sorry,' he says. 'What can I say? I'm very sorry. It was a mess and at the time that felt like the only thing I could do.'

'Well, it's a bigger mess now,' she says severely.

He is conscious of her talking to him like an adult. He has never seen her like this before. She's twenty and she's grown up. She looks the same but she's changed. It's impressive but also alarming. He doesn't know how to react to her any more.

'I do know she's got someone else,' he says in case her silence means she is trying to be tactful. 'She told me. Have you met him?'

She frowns, as if this is a difficult question to answer. 'Yes, but he's hard to get to know. I quite like him but . . . oh, I don't know, he's nice but he's got all these ex-wives and children and a dead wife he's depressed about, so I don't know if he's going to be good for Mum long-term, although he's cheered her up a lot. It's just that if he lets her down I can imagine having to prop her up all over again and I feel I've been doing that all my life.'

He finds it hard to talk about this unknown man who is standing in his light. He has to take deep breaths for the pain. He hadn't expected it to be so painful, but to see Helen's lover as a real person through Sally's eyes hurts very much. Sally won't be as discreet as Helen would. But then he did ask her about the other man so he can't blame her for answering. He suddenly wants to ask her not to tell him too much, to spare him details that will haunt him later, but he can't.

'I know it's nice for Mum that he's another painter,' Sally says in a matter-of-fact tone, as if she had no idea she was causing him such distress, 'but there's something about him that reminds me of my father. He's got that look about him. He's lived a messy sort of life and I don't know if I can trust him. D'you know what I mean?'

He says yes. The pain goes deeply into him and spreads everywhere. He feels quite light-headed with it. He wonders why she doesn't say Helen's lover reminds her of Felix. Can she be so young and stupid it simply hasn't occurred to her? For a moment he is very angry with her and he wanted to feel only love.

'Anyway,' she says, 'there's nothing I can do about it. She's supposed to be grown up, isn't she?'

'Yes,' he says, trying to smile. 'You're sounding a bit like her mother.'

'God, I feel like her mother sometimes. I thought I could stop worrying about her when you two got married but here she is all over the place again. Honestly, I think sometimes I'm more independent than she is. She needs someone *so* much.'

'I never really saw her like that,' he says. He remembers Helen telling him she was afraid of being lonely for ever but he never quite believed her. There always seemed to be a hard core of self-sufficiency inside her which he could never penetrate, which was part of her attraction for him. He thinks it's still there. He thinks she can survive anything. He thinks she will always put her work and Sally first. Or Sally and her work. Never a man, himself or another. But maybe he's wrong. Maybe Sally knows her better.

'You weren't fooled by her big act, were you?' Sally says. 'You couldn't have been, surely, not for ten years.'

'We just see her differently,' he says.

Sally shrugs. 'Oh well, there's nothing I can do about it. I'm going on holiday and I've got so much work to do. Less than a year to finals now. I can't believe it's gone so quickly. This time next year it'll all be over, imagine that. D'you know, my tutor said I might just get a first if I work really hard. Wouldn't that be amazing? He's rather nice, actually, he's called Jonathan. I've got a sort of thing about him. Or I would have if I hadn't given up men. It's just easier at the moment not to have anyone. Maybe you'll find that when you get used to it. Sort of peaceful.'

She smiles at him kindly, as if she is older and wiser. He feels such love for her again that it tugs at his heart like a physical thing.

'I'm glad you're all right,' he says inadequately. 'And it would be lovely if you get a first.' He longs to ask about Felix, how she feels about everything, if she's in touch with him, but he can't: it would feel like intruding on her privacy and he has done enough of that in the past. And he's ashamed to admit he misses Felix. 'I'm sure you'll meet the right person one day.'

'Oh well,' she says fiercely. 'It doesn't matter if I don't. Depending on people only means you get hurt when they let you down and they always do eventually. Look at you and Mum. And my father, he's turned out disappointing, he doesn't have any time for me, not really, he's just submerged under all those other children and earning enough to keep them all. I'm better off just relying on myself.'

It sounds very bleak and stoical for someone of twenty but he tells himself it is probably just a phase. 'I *am* sorry,' he says, 'about everything that went wrong.'

She shakes her head. 'I was just bloody stupid, wasn't I? Serves me right.'

'Don't be too hard on yourself, you had a rough time. I'm just sorry I let you down when you needed me.'

'You didn't, not really. Anyway, I'm sorry I said all those horrible things to you when I came to see you in that awful place. That's what I've been waiting to tell you. I didn't mean any of it, you know.'

'I know,' he says.

'So we're all sorry,' she says, laughing slightly. 'We're all going round apologising to each other. Bit of a joke really.' She gets up, brushes tea-cake crumbs off her jeans on to the brightly patterned carpet. 'I'll have to be going. It's been lovely to see you again.'

He gets up out of the hard armchair. They hug. 'Take care,' she says. 'Don't get lonely now.'

'Let's keep in touch,' he says.

'Course we will.'

He watches her leave. The room feels empty without her, yet full of her presence. He has a sense of anticlimax like someone on a station platform after the train has pulled out, at a loose end now he has seen her off. So many memories stir. He switches on the television for company.

They do indeed have a wonderful summer. Sex with Inge seems marvellously simple, with no guilt or anxiety to foul it up, no hang-ups, no illusions. She is the same as ever: greedy, selfish, generous and skilled. The ideal mistress. And now there is the added bonus of her new cheerfulness. He can relax with her. Nothing will be demanded that he cannot give, nothing offered that he cannot match. And she balances his life at home. She is his delicious secret that Elizabeth does not know, that would make her terribly angry. When he teases Elizabeth about David Johnson, who he suspects is lousy in bed, it is Inge he caresses in his mind. You think you're control-

224

ling me, he says to Elizabeth in his head, but you can't and you never will.

'Isn't it strange?' Inge says one afternoon when they are lying drowsily in bed recovering from all their exertions. 'We've known each other twenty years, on and off, and it's taken us all this time to have an arrangement that suits us both. It didn't work two years ago. All those years I was in love with Richard and he never really loved me at all. What a waste.'

'I'm sure he did love you, Inge,' he says tactfully. 'Some of the time, at least. In his way.'

'But not in my way. Not the way I loved him. And then when he left me I was alone for such a long time but you didn't come near me, you were still being the loyal friend, and then you went abroad, and all that time I was so in love with Richard and I had to pick up people for sex and sometimes they were people I didn't even like. And we could have been having all this pleasure for all that time. Isn't it strange?'

'You're a philosopher, Inge,' he says, and she kicks him in a friendly fashion under the duvet.

Helen knows long before her doctor confirms it. The physical symptoms are slight but unmistakable, the same ones she had with Sally and the child she aborted: a vague soreness, a tingling in her breasts, faint nausea, sudden fatigue. They are so low-key as to be hardly worth mentioning; they could all be summed up as not feeling quite herself. A missed period is enough to alarm her but she could pass that off as the start of an early menopause perhaps. Not the rest of it. She has felt like this before and she knows what it means. She knows before the missed period, in fact. It can't be anything else.

She's amazed how quickly panic turns into joy. An extraordinary excitement, a sense of having a secret that she longs to tell but also longs to keep to herself. She is actually glad that Jordan is away and so cannot be told. She doesn't want to tell him yet. He doesn't deserve to be told. This is something for herself alone. And yet she also wants to boast about it.

She imagines telling him on the phone, if he rings her. She imagines writing to him, if she had an address. Neither way seems very satisfactory: such important news should be given out face to face. She pictures the scene and it alarms her. She has no idea how he will react: she knows he loves children but that doesn't automatically mean he will want a child with her. It seems a huge step in a relationship where the word love has never been used.

But all these considerations are nothing compared to the problem of Sally. Anxiety over the coil, which her doctor reassures her about, is replaced by anxiety over Sally, which no one can take away. It is probably because of Sally that she finds herself talking to Richard. She doesn't mean to, but she has got used to his occasional phone calls and visits, and there is no one else she can talk to about something so important. Since she told him about Jordan back in April, when she refused to try again, he seems more relaxed with her, as if knowing there is no hope allows him to be himself. 'You don't mind if I ring you now and then?' he says at first, tentatively. 'Maybe we can meet sometimes? It's such a help to me and, I mean, it's not as if you hate me, is it?'

No, she agrees, she certainly doesn't hate him. So she gets used to this casual contact, this keeping in touch; she even finds it comforting. There are months when she sees more of Richard than Jordan. That is more ironic than ideal. But there is something very companionable about seeing someone she knows well and has known for many years and used to love. They have history together. And it's flattering to be adored and not have to respond: like sitting in the sun or in front of a fire. Is that how Jordan feels about her? she wonders, not a pleasant thought. Anyway, it seems to balance up her life. Adoring Jordan and tolerating Richard gives her an equilibrium. Loving and being loved. Sometimes he asks about Jordan and she has the extra pleasure of talking about him. She even lets herself think ahead to a time when Richard gets over her, and knows, unfair though it is, that she will be sad.

August oppresses her, the feeling that everyone else has gone away, Jordan to America and Sally to Greece, the heat and dust and noise of the city, which seems unsuited to summer, being slightly unwell, being alone with a problem that is also a joy. Most of all the fact that she needs someone and Richard is quite simply there.

Sometimes he just phones her; sometimes he comes round for a drink and a chat. Probably he finds August oppressive too in his bedsit, on holiday but unable to afford to go away. On one of these evenings when they have been getting on well and seem to be quite relaxed with each other she thinks she sees hope in his eyes again and she realises how cruel it would be to say nothing and let him find out visually as the months pass. It's not just a matter of needing his help with Sally. He has to be told on his own account, and he must surely be the easiest of the people she has to tell. Even so, it takes her so long to get up her courage that it's only when he says, 'Well, I suppose I'd better be going,' that she suddenly manages to say, 'Richard, I need your help, there's something I've got to tell you.'

He looks alarmed and she panics then and wishes the words unsaid. What is he imagining: terminal illness? Now she has to go on and she'd much rather not.

'It's not easy to say but it's going to be worse telling Sally. I'm pregnant.'

He looks as shocked as if she had hit him.

'Sorry,' she says. 'I didn't know how to break it gently.'

She is watching his face anxiously and she sees a whole range of emotions follow the shock: anger and jealousy and pain. She feels for him but it's a relief to have it said.

He says eventually, 'You of all people.'

'I know.'

'D'you want a divorce? Is that what you mean?'

She shrugs. 'I haven't even thought that far ahead.'

'Well, d'you want to marry him?'

'Richard, I don't know, I haven't even told him yet, no, I don't think there's any chance of that, I don't imagine either of us want to be married again.'

'You haven't told him?' he repeats.

'I wasn't sure when he went away.'

'But now you are – and you want it?'

'Yes.' How simple it feels. The easiest decision she ever made.

He says, 'Oh, Helen, why not mine?'

'I don't know. I can't answer that. I'm sorry.'

'Did you do it on purpose?'

'No, my old coil let me down, I should have had it checked or changed, I suppose. But I haven't thought about it for years. After you left it was the last thing on my mind and when I met Jordan again, well, I just assumed it would be all right.' The words don't sound convincing: she imagines Sally hearing them, as if talking to Richard is a rehearsal. Did I really mean to do this? she asks herself, with a thrill of horror.

'Won't it damage the baby?'

'Apparently it's all right to leave it as it's plastic not copper. You remember when I had it put in I wanted something I could just forget about.' She sees him turn away from this memory, but she can't stop. It's such a relief to be talking about it. 'If they take it out now there's a risk of miscarriage. I was really worried about it but Dr Walsh was very reassuring.'

'You want it very much then.'

'Yes, I do. Look, I'm almost as surprised as you are. I suppose if I'd really meant what I said all those years ago I'd have got myself sterilised. A bit of me must have still wanted to have a choice. It's a funny feeling. I don't know myself as well as I thought.'

He shakes his head. 'I don't see how you'll ever explain it to Sally.'

'No. And the dates are the same.' She bites her lip. 'It's going to be April.'

He says slowly, 'You've really changed. He's changed you.'

'I told you, I knew you wouldn't like the real me.'

'I don't mean that. I love you. I've always loved you. The thought of you with a baby . . .' He starts pacing about the kitchen in an agitated way, making her feel tense with his tension. She begins to wish she hadn't told him. 'Look, Helen, if he lets you down, I'm here, I could help. It would be a privilege.'

'Oh, Richard . . .' She's embarrassed. It's like going back to the time when they first met, as if he finds her more attractive with a small child, even if it can't be his own. He seems to want her to be in need of protection.

'You don't sound sure of him when you talk about him. But you can be sure of me.'

'Please don't. It's kind of you and I appreciate it, but—'

'Don't be so bloody polite. God, I don't want gratitude.'

'I know, I know. But what can I say to Sally? After all we've been through and we were just getting over it. We were getting on better lately. It's going to seem as if there's one rule for her and another for me. How's she going to feel seeing me pregnant, seeing me with a baby?'

'Well, she's bound to be hurt and angry. But she'll forgive you.'

'Are you sure? I'm so frightened of losing her.'

'You won't.'

'I really think I might, and I can't bear it.'

'When does she get back from Greece?'

'Next month some time. Pretty late on, I think. About a week before term starts.'

'Well then, you've got some time to plan it.'

'I don't see how any amount of planning will make any difference.' He's not helping her, but perhaps he can't. Perhaps no one can.

'Just remember,' he says, still very much on his own track, 'it could be our last chance to be a family together.'

'Please don't.'

'Think about it,' he says.

PART SIX

In September a postcard of the Grand Canyon arrives from Jordan. It feels strange to be carrying his child, such an intimate connection, and to be receiving a postcard from him, that most casual of greetings. His handwriting, which she has so far only seen as his famous scrawled signature on a canvas, is barely legible: the beginnings and ends of words are there, the middles to be guessed. But after several readings she thinks it says, 'Nice to be bumming [buzzing?] around with my children [cauldron?] but this isn't home [here?] any more. Time I was getting back to work. See you soon. Love Jordan.' It means nothing, of course; it is just the sort of thing people put on postcards. But she reads it many times, lingering over the words see you soon, which she has often heard from him but which never mean what they say, and the word love, which he has never used. She noticed that there is no comma between the word love and the name Jordan, making it seem like a command. 'And I do,' she says to herself. 'I really do.'

In the six weeks they've both been away she's had three postcards from Sally as against one from Jordan. Each from a different island. The first one says, 'Can't think why I didn't find out about Greece before. Everyone else seems to have done.' Helen takes this to mean it's crowded. The second, from a smaller island, says, 'This is the only way to get through a reading list, on the beach with a jug of Retsina and *no tourists except me*.' And the third: 'Am working in a taverna now to make ends meet. Maybe I won't come home at all.' They all end. 'Much love, Sally,' in her large, clear writing. The third one is from the island where Helen and Carey spent their honeymoon. She closes her eyes for a moment and lets herself drift back, remembering sun and beach and wine and white buildings and making love in a shuttered room. How young she was then, and how grown up she thought she was. She treasures the postcards, thinking that Sally will never write her such natural, joyful messages again, that the child will cast a shadow between them for ever, and in a way it might be better if Sally did stay in Greece so she would never have to be told the truth. She fantasises pleasantly about endless letters and phone calls with never a cross word, while Sally lives an idyllic life in the sun and she herself brings up a child that Sally won't know exists. Either way it seems she will have to lose one child to keep the other. She wonders if Sally is happy, if she is perhaps in love. She only said she was travelling with friends but that could mean anything. How little she knows of Sally's life these days.

She tries to use the time alone to enjoy her pregnancy before she has to face Sally's rage. She feels like two people mentally as well as physically. One of these people is rapturously happy, the other deeply depressed. They co-exist snugly inside her, like the child, and she attends to both of them. She finds herself painting curved shapes for the first time in years and the crude symbolism makes her smile. Richard doesn't phone: perhaps he has had all he can take. Or perhaps he is leaving her alone to come to her senses. She daydreams about the baby. She fantasises that Sally will forgive her. She considers the serious possibility that if Jordan won't help her financially she will have to fill the house with lodgers or share it with another single parent. She can't survive without her job at college and she can't afford a child-minder. She wonders why she isn't more worried about all this. She'll be going right

back to the mess she was in when Sally was three. Is she
confident of Jordan's generosity or is she already becoming bovine and stupid? No amount of focusing on all the
known horrors, poverty, hard work and Sally's wrath,
the total disruption of her life, can make any difference.
She's regressing seventeen years to take the other fork at
the crossroads. She's in the grip of some vast hormonal
force beyond her control.

Jordan rings about a week after his postcard, catching
her at breakfast. 'Hullo, I'm at the airport,' he says
without preamble. 'Are you busy?'

'No, come on over,' she says. She's so happy. For a
moment nothing else matters. She's going to see him,
touch him again.

'See you soon,' he says, and for once it is true. She has
an hour to bathe and wash her hair, change the sheets,
consider what to wear. She's in a fever of impatience and
yet she would like to prolong the waiting time, a time of
perfect happiness when nothing can go wrong. If he's not
pleased with her news she's going to be terribly disappointed in him. Then he's outside her door getting out of
a taxi with his luggage.

'Hullo,' she says, smiling absurdly. 'Did you have a
good holiday?'

'Not bad,' he says. He looks brown and fit and wonderful.

'Well, come in,' she says. She closes the door behind
him and they hug, kissing desperately, trying to touch
each other everywhere. She's remembered his smell correctly. They go straight to bed and he's inside her at
once. It's such a relief. They lie there for a moment, not
moving, not speaking, just looking at each other.

'Good to be home,' he says.

'Nice to have you.' She thinks of the crazy accumula-
tion of contents: the coil, the child and its father, all

safely tucked up together. She doesn't care if she comes or not, so she probably will; she just wants to hold them all there. She thinks: I won't tell him just yet. Maybe next time. A little more happiness first.

He takes her out to lunch and talks about the trip. 'Really, my children are a feckless bunch,' he says, sounding impressed.

'Really?' she says. 'I wonder who they get it from.'

'Jake's dropped out of UCLA. He was meant to be doing his Masters but he was last seen selling souvenirs to tourists around Big Sur. Really creative stuff, huh? Susie's staying on with him till October, maybe she can talk some sense into him, they've always been very close.'

'Won't he listen to you?' She likes the family conversation; it makes her feel doubly linked. But she also thinks bitterly how easy it is to love large numbers of children if you don't have to bring them up yourself. Ruth and Laura have done all the hard work for him and he is enjoying the results.

'I was so relieved he's not doing cocaine any more I didn't say very much. I just hope he doesn't inspire her to drop out of Oxford, we had enough trouble getting her in, she's bone idle. A taste of lotus-eating may be too much for her. She was knocked out by the Grand Canyon, which of course I hadn't seen in fifteen years, and how she really fancies spending a couple of years driving around the States like someone in a movie. She's already got the dark glasses, now all she needs is the car.'

'How's Mara?' she asks. She has an idea that Mara is his favourite.

'She's sort of okay but she's not doing much work, she's in love and that always destroys her. He's a sculptor too, twice her age, married – what can I say? I don't like his work and I think he's more interested in sharing her studio than her bed, but there you are.'

Pride shines through the complaints. She's never heard him talk so much about anything. But after lunch he drops her back at the house and tells the cab to wait. 'Well, I must go home and crash out,' he says, picking up his luggage. 'I'm knackered.' Just at the last minute he adds, 'It was strange seeing my in-laws again.'

They kiss goodbye; he looks at her thoughtfully for a moment and strokes her face. 'Take care,' he says, not see you soon, for a change. She waits a few days, to be undemanding, then rings him and gets the machine. She leaves a message but he doesn't ring back. Back to square one, she thinks.

Sally comes back in late September, very brown and full of enthusiasm for Greece, chattering happily about her trip before breaking off suddenly to say, 'Mum, are you all right? You don't look well.'

'Yes, I'm fine.' Helen's heart lurches. 'Just a bit tired.'

'You should have had a holiday.'

'Yes, I should.'

'Is your painter back?'

'Yes, he is.'

'Maybe you can go somewhere with him.'

'Maybe.'

'You're got letting him mess you about, are you?'

'No, of course not.'

Sally's brought her interesting shells and pebbles; she's also taken some rather good photographs. She seems so relaxed that Helen thinks, Not yet, I can't tell her yet. I can't spoil all this. Suddenly there is so much goodwill around.

'Well, I'm going to disappear upstairs for a bit,' Sally says. 'I've done all the reading on the beach, now all I've got to do is write three essays in a week.'

'Easy,' Helen says.

*

She spends the week composing a letter to Sally in case she never has the courage to speak. It was bad enough telling Richard: she doesn't think she can get those words out again. This time is going to be so much worse. Each day when she goes to the studio, instead of painting she works on the letter and when she goes home she leaves it unfinished, lurking in a drawer like dynamite.

Darling Sally,
Please read this to the end. I haven't the courage to say it to you and I don't think you'd let me get past the first sentence anyway. But I'm here to listen to whatever you have to say.
I'm going to have Jordan's child. Please don't stop reading. I'm so afraid you'll be hurt and angry and never forgive me. I know how unfair it must seem that I'm giving myself the choice I took away from you. I still think that was the right decision but you may not agree. I've got no excuses for what I'm doing now. It was an accident but I want to go through with it. I know it's unfair that no one can stop me. I haven't told him yet. I wanted to tell you first. Or rather I don't want to tell you at all but I've got to. I'm sorry. Please forgive me.
I'm giving you this just before you go back to college because I'm a coward and because I'm sure you'll want to get away from me for a bit. Not too long, I hope. I love you so much. Please don't hate me. Mum.

'I don't remember much about my childhood,' Inge says to Michael. 'Just odd disconnected things. Like a lot of noise and being very hungry and cold. I was born just after the war and I never knew my father, he'd been killed a few months before. I remember my mother crying a lot and then being very bright and putting on make-up and men coming to see her. I remember being sent away to my grandparents a lot. They lived in the country, so it was very different. Then my mother got married again and suddenly I had a new father, only to me it was like a first father, of course.'

'How did you get on with him?'

'I'm not sure. All right, I think. I was very careful to be nice to him. I remember that was very important. I remember my mother saying we mustn't be alone again.'

On the very last morning, after a sleepless night, after breakfast, with Sally all packed and ready go, in fact on the very verge of kissing her goodbye, when she can't put it off for another minute, when if she doesn't do it now she really will have to post the letter instead, Helen feeling sick with fear finally manages to say, 'Sally, I wrote you this letter but I ought to have the guts to tell you the way you told me – would you ever forgive me if I had a child with Jordan?'

Her heart is beating very fast and she sees Sally's face change as she listens, from anxiety to horror. She steps back, away from Helen, as if the letter in Helen's hand can do her actual damage and says sharply, '*No.*'

'I'm sorry.'

Now the full horror strikes her as the meaning sinks in. 'God, you're not going to, are you? You can't be.'

'I'm sorry.'

'NO. You can't do this to me. You can't.'

'I know it's not fair.'

Sally looks at her with absolute hatred. 'When?'

'April.' Helen can hardly get the word out.

There is a moment's silence. 'I must go,' Sally says. 'I'll miss my train.'

*

Richard rings that evening. 'Did you tell her?'

'Yes.'

'How did she take it? You sound terrible.'

'It was bad. We didn't discuss it at all – well, how could we? She was so angry, she just rushed off to catch her train, couldn't wait to get away from me. I knew it would be like that.'

'Give her time. She'll get over it.'

She can't speak.

'Helen? Would you like me to come over?'

'No. I'm going to bed. But thanks. I wrote her a letter, in case I couldn't tell her. In case she wouldn't listen. But in the end I told her. I didn't do it very well.'

'Nobody could. Why not post the letter anyway, if you think it's better? She might read it when she's cooled down.'

'I did wonder about that.'

'It might make you feel better.'

So next day she posts the letter, adding a few more words of love and sorrow.

Jordan rings the next day. 'D'you want to come over to-night?'

'Yes. I'm not feeling very sexy though.'

'Neither am I. But I thought you might be feeling a bit flat after Sally went back.'

'Yes, I am.' She's grateful, impressed. 'Your timing's spot on.'

'Well, Susie was passing through yesterday, on her way back to Oxford, so I thought about you.'

'She's not touring America then?'

'No, thank God. Jake's shacked up with somebody and she decided to come home.'

She goes in the evening, conscious of looking her worst, driving through streets progressively more empty as she nears Dockland. She feels she is driving to the end of the world. Why would anyone want to live in such a godforsaken spot? And yet apparently it is the new trendy place to be. Her first glimpse of the river reminds her why.

Jordan greets her at the door in the oldest of old clothes, smelling of turps, and enfolds her in a hug. She can feel energy refilling her with his touch. He draws back and studies her for a moment. 'You look wonderfully wrecked.'

'Gee, thanks.' It's a big effort to be flippant, all she can do not to say, Yes, I am, and tell him why. Maybe she should.

'No, I like it. On you it looks good, as my in-laws used to say.'

She feels surprised and comforted by his mentioning Hannah's parents, as if he is drawing her into the fold. She goes in to the huge space of his living-room to be cosseted with lasagne, Chianti, Chopin on the stereo and blazing logs in the grate.

'A real fire,' she says, 'how lovely.'

'Yes. It's probably against some bye-law, but who cares? You're tired, aren't you?'

'Just a little.'

'Let's have an early night.'

Lying in bed beside him she thinks, Now is the time to tell him, when he's being so nice. But it feels like blackmail, and besides, she hasn't the energy. She didn't think anyone could comfort her for Sally, but apparently he can. Later, just as she's drifting off to sleep, he says, 'I may have got you here under false pretences. I may have to make love to you after all. If I'm overcome by lust in the middle of the night, just ignore me. I'll start without you and you can always join in later.'

Felix lets his publisher give a party for the book. He thinks publication should be marked by some event, like a cake

241

or conjuring tricks for a child's birthday, although in this case he himself is the conjuror and his rabbit has been hard to pull from the hat. There were many days when it kicked and struggled or lay around limply, with its ears flat to its head, refusing to come out, making him look foolish. Seeing copies of the book around him now, and his smiling photograph, he feels some miracle has been performed, some sleight of hand that he has already forgotten how to do and so can never repeat.

But he feels sad when asked whom he would like to invite. All the people he most wants to be there are angry with him or on the forbidden list: Richard, Helen, Sally, Inge. He has lost his extended family. And yet they had all been at Helen's ghastly show eighteen months ago, where he was not the centre of attention. He thinks this is very ironic.

He tries to relax and make the best of the party, though he is too tense to enjoy it much, as he knows that a lot of the media people present do not wish him well. Some of the other writers will be wondering how his book will compare with their own latest efforts in terms of advances, reviews, publicity and sales; and some of the journalists now eating and drinking as much as possible are already planning savage column inches being witty at his expense. There are also a dozen or so ex-lovers and deceived husbands he must charm. But mostly he is distracted by the bad reviews he is composing in his head, so that whatever the others say, he will have already said something worse, and any praise will be a nice surprise. He always does this: it's his way of taking out insurance. Elizabeth, knowing this, comes up to him and says in a low voice, 'Damn it, Thurber, stop writing,' before drifting back into the crowd. She makes him laugh; she is at her best on occasions like this. And Natasha, like a good agent, has saved up the news that she has nearly sold the film rights, so that she will have a little present to give him on his big day.

Then he sees her. She must have only just arrived or he

would have noticed her before. She is not exactly across a crowded room but in a corner adjacent to him so he must have actually had his back to her when Natasha came up to him. People are crowding round her and they are all men but they are not standing very close, rather gazing from an official distance, as if admiring a work of art. He can see why: such beauty is daunting. A sinuous body in a short black dress, long thick hair fashionably tangled and various shades of golden brown, and perfect legs that he immediately longs to have wrapped round his neck. But the face. He actually hears himself gasp when he sees the face. The sculptured wanton aristocratic beauty of the face makes him stare at her in awestruck silence, as if at a newly discovered masterpiece by Michelangelo. He has always been deeply affected by beauty.

'My God,' he says to Natasha, 'I think I've fallen in love,' in much the same stricken tone that he might have told a complete stranger in the street that he had left his wallet in a taxi.

Natasha laughs. She assumes he is joking.

'Oh, that,' she says. 'Quite something, isn't she? That's Raffaella Lucci, she's a photo-journalist. She wants to do a piece on you for a rather crappy magazine called *Ciao!* She's not very good, but as you can see, she doesn't have to be. Shall I introduce you?'

'In a moment,' Felix says. 'It's a long time since I've been struck by lightning. I need a little while to recover.'

'And now look at me,' Raffaella instructs, 'and don't smile, but think about something that make you very very 'appy.'

Felix obeys. It is almost impossible not to smile. Her English is rapid and fluent but her accent is strong and she drops all her aitches, so it is like listening to an Italian who suddenly lapses into Cockney, a disconcerting effect. She takes a lot of photographs very quickly. It is a surprise every time she reloads, as if he did not really believe she has film in her camera.

'And now look just over my shoulder, towards the window and think about something sad. And now say something to me, I want you to move your mouth.'

'How do you like London?' Felix says. He feels quite weak with longing. All his best lines in chat have deserted him. She is wearing a warm, spicy scent that seems to fill the room and have a hypnotic effect, something like cloves that calms and excites him at the same time.

'I like it. Talk some more. If you talk your mouth is very soft.'

'You don't look very Italian.'

'I come from Milan.' Her green eyes challenge him from behind the camera. It's like being undressed by her. 'In Milan we all look like this.'

'Then I must move to Milan immediately,' Felix says faintly.

'Why bother, when I live 'ere now?'

Over lunch she puts her tape recorder on the table.

'You don't mind, do you? Now, in your book, who loves the greatest, do you think, the man or the girl?'

'The man,' says Felix promptly. 'After all, he kills himself when his wife won't have him back.'

'But that don't mean 'e loves the girl or the wife, it mean 'e don't like to live alone.' Her eyes look at him speculatively, as if they know a lot about him; they are old eyes, but her mouth is childish. He tries to guess her age: twenty-seven, twenty-eight perhaps. She will be in perfect condition for at least the next ten years: old enough to be interesting and young enough to be flawless. Glossy and streamlined and pampered like a prize-winning racehorse. He feels a constriction in his throat when he looks at her, making it hard for him to swallow his

244

lunch. Every angle of her face has a poetic beauty; every movement she makes has a fresh aspect of grace.

'When I read your book I say to my 'usband, if I leave you, do you kill yourself, but 'e say, no, I kill you and then I find a new wife.' She laughs.

'It's not always that easy,' Felix says.

'So I think I don't leave 'im. I love 'im very much and 'e is very rich. Those are two good reasons. I think marriage is for ever, don't you?'

'Yes,' Felix says. 'I've always thought so.'

'So when it's for ever, you 'ave to make it very easy, don't you think? I like your book because it's all about sex and love, but in real life the man don't leave 'is wife for the young girl, and if 'e do 'is wife probably take 'im back when the young girl leave him, and if she don't 'e find another young girl or another wife.'

'Or both,' Felix says. He has never talked less in an interview but it doesn't matter. He is used to listening to women, and looking at Raffaella's face seems to use all the energy he has, with little left over for speech.

'Yes. Both is better.' She laughs. 'So you write a good book but you don't write the truth. What do you say to that? Is that why they call it fiction?'

'People do kill themselves for love,' Felix says. 'You read it in the papers every day.'

'But not people like us,' Raffaella says.

He wonders where she has picked up that particularly English phrase. 'Perhaps not,' he says.

'For people like us, love is a game.'

'Sometimes,' Felix says, 'it's the only game in town.'

'I like that. Are you a gambler then?'

'Not with money. An emotional gambler perhaps. But my hero is meant to be the new man, in touch with his feelings, and his feelings destroy him, the way women's feelings have traditionally destroyed them.' He thinks he must get that much on record.

'I don't believe in the new man,' Raffaella says. 'I think 'e is just the old man dress up like the wolf when 'e

245

pretend to be Red Riding 'ood's grandmother. The old man is like American Express. He will do nicely. Don't you think?'

'I certainly hope so,' Felix says.

Later in October a letter arrives from Sally. Helen opens it nervously. A lot depends on this.

> Dear Mum,
> I read your letter. I can't answer it. The whole thing is so horrible for me. I can't bear to see you while you're like this so I'll go to my father for Christmas. I don't think I can see you till the whole thing is over and I don't ever want to see it when it arrives. I know you've got your reasons and maybe I'll feel better later, but right now I feel awful. Please don't write back. I've had enough. Love, Sally.

Helen reads the letter several times and puts it away in a drawer. It is a very high price to pay for Jordan's child. If he has really killed her relationship with Sally, will she ever be able to forgive him? He has given her something precious, but destroyed something even more precious. Then she thinks she is wrong to blame him. This is something she has done herself for her own complicated reasons and she must bear the consequences, in every sense of the word.

She is still brooding over the letter when he rings, quite late at night. 'You sound a bit low,' he says when she answers.

Again she is tempted to tell him the truth, but she doesn't, because now she would be telling him in bitterness and the child deserves a better introduction than that. Anyway, it can't be done on the telephone. 'Sally's not coming home for Christmas,' she says, sufficient reason to sound low, she thinks.

There is a slight pause. 'Oh,' he says casually. 'Shall we go away somewhere then? Would you like that? I would.'

She is so surprised she hardly knows what to say. 'But what about your famous moods?'

'Oh, I'll be in a Christmas mood by then. And it's only three days.'

How simple he makes everything sound. Perhaps he only ever does what he wants to do. Perhaps that is his secret. And perhaps she is already learning to be like him.

'What about all your children?' she asks, thinking, I'll have to tell him soon, this is crazy, making plans for Christmas, the new one will be obvious by then, how weird, he'll be spending Christmas with the new one. Unless he changes his mind, of course.

'What about them? I'll just tell them I'll be away. They can come for New Year instead. It's Laura's turn to have her three for Christmas anyway.'

'Are you friendly with Laura?' she asks. She has noticed that he seldom mentions her name.

'Not exactly. When Hannah died she sent me a card saying, "Now you know how I felt when you left me."'

'God.' Helen thinks this sounds like the kind of thing Inge might do.

'I'm friendly with Ruth though. As soon as I left Laura, Ruth and I got ever so friendly. She even came to New York for the wedding when Hannah and I got married. Wanted to make quite sure I'd really done it, I suppose. It helps that she's remarried, of course. I go back to Wales and stay with them sometimes. He's a nice man she's married. Suits her better than I ever did.'

How carelessly he mentions their names, these women spanning the last three decades of his life. All those days and nights together, all the rows and routine, happiness and boredom and pain, all gone, leaving only memories and children. How much feeling is there left underneath that she doesn't know about? Does she sound the same when she talks about Carey and Richard and the last twenty years? How strange to be having a child by this man she finds at once familiar and unknown. There is something comforting about the late-night chat all the same, something inconsequential but soothing, like verbal aspirin, taking her mind off Sally for a little, easing the pain. She doesn't want him to hang up yet.

'D'you think you'll ever go back to New York? To live, I mean.'

'No. I've had the best of it. I was there at the right time. It was nice to be taken seriously for a change when abstraction was still a bit of a joke in England. You should have come, you might have liked it.'

Oh Jordan, she thinks, what a thing to say to me now.

'But it's getting more ruthless. I don't know, it's all mixed up with Hannah and me, anyway. Once she died, New York was over for me.'

'I wish I'd known her,' Helen suddenly says, meaning it, not something she had ever thought before.

'Yes, you'd have liked her, she was a sweetheart.'

Suddenly a great urge to be with him, to touch him, to comfort and be comforted, to tell him the truth. And yet somehow impossible to ask him to come over. The need to be alone is stronger.

'Well,' he says, 'd'you think you'll sleep now?'

'Oh yes,' she says. 'I expect I shall.'

By the end of the month they have accumulated the usual clutch of contradictory reviews, which they assemble one Sunday afternoon, reading them aloud to each other or passing them across the table.

'Here's one you might like,' Felix says. '"The narrator, while superficially charming, soon reveals himself to be devious, immature and, when the crunch comes, fatally dependent on his wife."'

Elizabeth smiles and says nothing.

'"But the young girl, Lisa, fails to convince as a human

248

being, and more properly belongs in a masturbation fantasy."' Felix checks the by-line. 'Well, he should know.'

'"*Anatomy of a Love Affair* is a moving analysis of man's inhumanity to woman,"' Elizabeth reads out. He thinks she sounds a little smug.

'How about this?' he says. '"Cramer is better known as a thriller writer, but his style has an incisive lyricism that lays bare the human heart." That should do nicely on the paperback.'

'Don't get too cocky. "The man's character is well observed in all its human frailty but the girl is a fantasy figure straight out of a wet dream."'

'Another well-known wanker. But here's a man with good taste. "The young girl – innocent, louche, street-wise – is a memorable creation."'

'"The character of the wife is well-observed –"' Elizabeth responds – '"a woman of steely compassion who reaches her final breaking point." How did they know?'

'But "Cramer's flabby, pedestrian style does nothing to redeem a predictably melodramatic story that belongs in the tabloid press." Ouch. Eek. Yaroo.' He smiles, but he hasn't enjoyed the ritual as much as usual: this time it seems too laden with personal innuendo to be fun. 'Well, we've got three or four good ones,' he says. 'That'll be enough. You can bin the rest. Flabby, indeed.' He wants to make her laugh. 'Why does a novelist get middle-age spread? Because he's got too many novels under his belt.'

But she stays with the resolute smile of a woman who has a lot to forgive.

It is to Inge that he turns for advice, tantalised by Raffaella almost beyond endurance. 'It's a joke,' he says bravely. 'I ring her and I get the machine. I leave a message and she doesn't ring back. Then she sets up a meeting. Then she cancels. Then we finally meet and she makes me tell her in detail what we'd do to each other in bed. Then she gropes me under the restaurant table. Then she goes home. And I haven't even kissed her yet.'

Inge laughs sympathetically. 'Poor Felix,' she says. 'I don't understand women who tease. I could never behave like that, it's such a waste of time. What happens if you pretend you're not interested?'

'I can't. I have to see that face. I have to be close to her. She's got the most extraordinary smell – I don't know if it's scent or soap or shampoo or just her skin, but I can't get enough of it. It's a joke, isn't it?' he says again.

Inge shakes her head. 'You're obsessed – like the man in your book. Felix, I think you should be very careful what you write next. When you wrote about Tony Blythe getting hit on the head, Richard knocked you down. When you wrote about the man and the wife and the young girl, Elizabeth sent you away. Now you're doing what you promised her you wouldn't. How much trouble do you want?'

'She's not even particularly interesting. She's vulgar and selfish and aggressive, and if she wasn't so beautiful she might be quite boring, I think. The piece about me never appeared in the magazine either.'

'Well, maybe it's a good thing. It's a terrible magazine, I saw it once. They had nice pictures of clothes but the articles were very silly.'

'She says it's been postponed till the book comes out in Italy.'

'Perhaps it was only an excuse to meet you. Then you could be flattered.'

'D'you think it might be that? Do you really?'

'Oh, Felix, you sound so eager. Shall I ask Michael what you should do? I'm sure he could help. I think he'd tell you to set a time limit so you don't feel so helpless. Or maybe you should just relax and enjoy it. Maybe you need a little obsession. Maybe it's too long since you used that part of yourself.'

He doesn't like the jargon. 'And she's going to Barbados with her husband for Christmas, so if I don't go too I won't see her for a whole month. But if I do go, Elizabeth may catch us together.'

'Oh, Felix,' she says tenderly, 'You're not even listening.'

And she had wanted to talk about Michael.

When the last day comes she is still undecided what to do. Will it spoil everything if she tells him now? Will it be unethical? She has tried so hard to behave correctly. She couldn't bear him to think she is just one of those silly women who throw themselves at their therapist. Will he think less of her if she tells him? Will it cancel out all she has achieved? Or is it dishonest not to tell him? She has been wrestling with all these questions for months, but always calming herself with the thought that there was still time to decide. Now suddenly there isn't. It's her last appointment.

Today she watches him with special concentration in case she never sees him again. That favourite gesture, when he takes off his heavy horn-rimmed glasses and rubs the bridge of his nose. He always does that at least once in the fifty-minute hour and she waits for it with excitement because it makes him look so different that it's like being with two people for the price of one, or so she thought the first time he did it. Today she just thinks sadly that she may never see it again. His face without glasses is naked and vulnerable like hers without make-up. He looks tired and she wants to put her arms round him and kiss him better, like one of her children when they were small. Then she wants to take all his clothes off and make wonderful love to him, two adults on equal terms.

'I don't know what to say to you today,' she says, as the time ticks away. 'I've always had so much to say and today all I can think of is it's the last time.'

'Well, we could try rejoicing at all we've achieved.'

'We could. But I just keep thinking it's goodbye and I don't know how to say it.'

'Goodbyes are always difficult, aren't they?'

'I know we've planned it like this but now it comes to the point . . .'

'There's always the telephone,' he says mildly. 'If you have an emergency. But I think you and I both know we've done all the work we can usefully do for the moment.'

'I think I'm having an emergency right now,' she says suddenly. 'I can't say goodbye. I can't go away. I love you, Michael.' What a relief it is to have the words out. So much tension has passed out of her that she feels almost calm.

'My dear Inge,' he says. 'My very dear Inge. That's so much more than I deserve.'

'Is that why you're sending me away?'

'Is that really how it feels?'

'No . . . Was I trying to cheat again? I know we agreed to do it like this. We've done the work we set out to do and I've made a lot of progress and it's time for me to manage without you. That's what you said, isn't it, more or less?'

'I think it's a little more than managing, don't you?' he says. 'The truth is you don't actually need me any more. That means we've succeeded.'

'But I love you. Doesn't that mean anything to you? If I come over to you now and put my arms round you . . .'

'I won't respond.'

'Won't you?'

'But you're not going to do it, are you?'

'No,' she says sadly. 'I suppose not.'

'Inge, you know it's very common for clients and therapists to have feelings for each other.'

'I know, it's called transference and counter-transference,' she says impatiently. 'You explained it to me. And I've read about it.'

'We can use it, we can work through it, but we can't act it out.'

'But that isn't what I feel. This is real, Michael. You're not representing Richard or my father or anybody else. I want to touch *you*. I want to make love to *you*. I want to have a glorious affair with *you*. You've always been honest with me. Can you honestly say you wouldn't like that?'

Silence, while she waits, holding her breath.

'I'd love it,' he says.

She is so happy she just sits smiling in her chair, feeling the smile getting bigger and bigger until she thinks she will become all smile, like the Cheshire cat in the story she used to read to Karl and Peter.

'I find you very attractive and I also find you very special. But I can't be your therapist and your lover. That would be most unethical.'

'Be my lover,' she says promptly. 'You've been my therapist. We're finishing. That's why I waited till today to say it. Be my lover, Michael, please.'

'Oh, Inge, Inge.' He smiles, just a little, nothing like her wide expanding grin.

'Please, Michael. You won't regret it. I make a wonderful mistress, I really do. Felix would tell you. And I've been looking for you all my life, only I didn't realise.'

'You see,' he says, 'the problem is, I know far too much about you and you know almost nothing about me. I'm in a position of power. If we have an affair now I'll be abusing your trust and using that professional knowledge. I can't do that.'

'But I want you to. Isn't it all right if I give you permission?'

'No, I think it's a little more complicated than that. I think we have to be equals and at the moment we're not.

And we have to wait and see whether what we feel is real
or just part of working together and getting close.'

'Wait?' she says. 'Wait how long?'

'Well, some people think it's never ethical to get involved with an ex-client. But I think it's all right if we
wait. I'm going to suggest a year. Anything may happen
to you in that year and I won't know anything about
it. So you'll regain some of your privacy. Then we can
meet again and if we still desire each other I'll tell you
whatever you want to know about me so we start on
equal terms.'

'Have you done it this way many times?'

'No, never.'

'Does it mean no letters and no phone calls?'

'I think so, don't you? If you need a therapist I can
refer you to a colleague of mine.'

'Oh, Michael. A whole year. What if we get knocked
down in the street? All right. After all, I waited eight
years for Richard.' She looks at her watch to check the
date. 'I'll ring you in a year's time and you can come to
my house for a fifty-minute hour. How much shall I
charge you?'

'I should think a ten per cent increase by then to keep
pace with inflation.'

'Perhaps we should make it longer than a year.' She is
gratified to detect disappointment in his eyes. 'If we're
going to be equals I have the right to choose too.' She
pauses, to tease him. 'I suggest a year and a day, like in
fairy tales.'

He smiles. They shake hands.

Kate invites him for Bonfire Night, first to watch the
public display in the park, afterwards for fireworks in her
garden. 'We always do it. It's a sort of family tradition,'
she says. 'I try to pretend it's for the children but they're
just an excuse. Really it's for me.'

254

He's pleased and surprised. It's a side of Kate he hasn't seen before, a new, playful Kate. He likes it. And he's flattered to be included in her plans.

They leave early to get a good place. 'Mum's not very grown up,' Annabel explains. 'If she can't see properly she makes a scene and we get terribly embarrassed. We have to pretend we're not with her.' He's not sure if this is entirely a joke.

They put on warm old clothes and join the crowds surging into the park, families good-humoured in expectation of a treat, scrunching leaves underfoot, pausing at fast-food stands, waving sparklers in the air to form circles and figures of eight. Hot-dog and hamburger smells fill the damp evening air, somehow contriving, Richard thinks, to entice and repel at the same time.

'Mum, I'm hungry,' Thomas complains.

'So am I,' says Annabel. 'Starving.'

'No junk food, kids, you know the rules,' says Kate briskly, and then to Richard, 'He threw up one of those things once and I've never let him forget it. A gruesome experience for everyone in the vicinity. Besides, I believe all that stuff about it making them hyperactive and he's quite active enough already.'

The bonfire heats their faces. He is transported back to childhood, seeing shapes in the flames, remembering history lessons, thinking of victims burnt at the stake. There is always something sinister and pathetic about the guy that makes him uneasy. How long did it take to die in this way? How soon did you suffocate from the smoke or faint from the pain?

'Imagine,' says Annabel at his elbow. 'They used to do this to people.'

It's as if she's picked up his thought and it makes him feel closer to her. He's been rather wary of her so far because she reminds him of Sally at the same age and he doesn't want to get involved again with someone else's daughter. Even in the short time he's known her, her voice has changed from breathless little girl eager to please, nervously laughing, to something more confident and off-hand, a woman with opinions of her own. Girls' voices break too, he thinks.

'They're doing *St Joan* this term,' Kate says.

'I'm the page,' says Annabel. 'It's not much of a part.'

He still remembers his surprise that Kate, militant Socialist Kate, sends her children to private schools, financed by her parents. How nearly they had argued about it, when he gently suggested that made her a bit of a champagne Socialist. 'I wouldn't sacrifice my children for my principles,' she'd said, 'would you?' But all he'd been able to think of then was that he had sacrificed them for Helen. 'They didn't learn anything, they were being bullied senseless, and there were drug pushers at the gates,' Kate went on. 'It's enough that I teach in the state system. There's no room for any more sacrifice in this family, I've cornered the market.' He had teased her that she would be into private medicine next and she answered sharply that she already was. 'While I'm working to change the system,' she said, 'I'm damned if I'll let my kids suffer from it. Wouldn't you jump the medical queue for your children if you could?' He'd hesitated and said finally perhaps, but he hoped not. Kate had looked quite shocked. 'I'm a pragmatist,' she said. 'I don't believe you should inflict your ideals on everyone else.' He wanted to tell her that was exactly what Socialism at its best was all about, but it suddenly occurred to him, thinking of Kate both as a woman and as his head of department, that this was an argument it might be prudent not to win.

Now, standing beside Kate and her children, he remembers such moments tenderly, like fragments of a shared past, and he thinks that anyone in the crowd who sees them all together would assume they are a family.

The display begins and colours erupt into the night sky.

There are little gasps and murmurs of approval from the crowd. After a while some become blasé, begin to have favourites. His neck soon aches from straining back so he can stare upwards; he listens to the people around him. 'That's a good one,' or 'Don't reckon that much.' More often they just sigh with satisfaction. He glances across at Kate, watching silently with rapt attention, lips parted, face lit by the fire; she looks young, almost childish, as he has never seen her before. Smoke drifts; the pungent acrid familiar smell of gunpowder floods the air and he breathes it in. There are set-pieces across the no-man's land in front of him: beyond the wire, fountains cascade down a trellis, Catherine wheels spin in perfect circles, the way they never do for him in the garden. He thinks of St Catherine revolving in death. More images of torture and martyrdom; strange how they run like a theme through all this pleasure. Rockets penetrate the sky. The bangs are very liberating, taking him by surprise each time, sharp firecracking explosions that seem to release a little of his own anger at Helen, at Felix, at himself. Colours dance in the air, flashing like splinters of jewels, forming shapes in the dark, falling like flowers through space. He wonders what it would be like to make love to Kate.

Finally it is over, the word goodnight burning ahead of them. 'Imagine how much all that must add to the rates,' says Kate, smiling. 'I must be mad to approve.' The crowd begins to break up, drift away, head for home. 'Just one go on the funfair,' Thomas pleads. 'All right, just one,' says Kate. Thomas and Annabel go on the Dive Bomber, spinning and swooping relentlessly in their tiny capsules high on the end of its long arms while he and Kate stand and watch. He remembers the year there was an accident and involuntarily crosses his fingers. 'Now you see what I mean,' Kate says. 'Imagine doing that after a hamburger or two.' And then, in a different, private voice, 'My divorce came through today. It's also my wedding anniversary. You couldn't arrange that if you tried, could you?' He doesn't know what to say; he feels honoured by her telling him, anxious to respond appropriately. He says, 'How d'you feel about it?' and she says, 'Oh, fine. Absolutely fine.'

They go back to burnt sausages, baked beans and jacket potatoes in Kate's kitchen. Afterwards he lets off pretty fireworks in her garden. Roman Candle, Chrysanthemum Fountain, Golden Rain, Mine of Serpents: the names often more elaborate than the contents, reminding him of the glorious names of paint and their almost edible beauty: burnt sienna, yellow ochre, cadmium red, ultramarine, vermillion. He feels it's a compliment or a masculine privilege to be put in charge of them, like being asked to open the wine. 'Mum won't have bangers,' Thomas complains. 'Bangers outside and bangers inside,' he adds, snorting at his own wit. 'You've had enough bangs for one night,' Kate says. Annabel watches the show with a tinge of boredom. 'I think we should have fireworks several times a year,' she says. 'Like for birthdays and Christmas. Then it wouldn't be such a big deal.' The Catherine wheels stick as he knew they would, spitting their fire at odd angles as they fight to revolve and fail. He prods them vainly with a stick. He apologises. Kate says, 'I think I like them better that way. They seem more angry. And less perfect.' When he says goodnight to her at the door he feels they have shared an important experience but he is not sure what it means. 'Well, I've had my fix for another year,' she says.

Elizabeth knows at once it's bad news. David's face has that shut-down look that she has learnt to dread over the past few months. It reminds her of a house with its blinds drawn or its shutters closed for a siesta. It is not even openly hostile. Everything is blank and she is excluded. He doesn't look at her but past her or down at the floor. His face has no expression. He is dressed all in black. Part of her wants to tell him not to be so theatrical, but part of her is scared.

He says, 'Hullo, Elizabeth, sit down, let me get you a drink.' He doesn't kiss her. Obviously there is no chance of massage or love-making tonight. It is going to be one of those grim evenings. She is quite disappointed: she has grown used to her treats.

She says, 'Is the book going badly?'

'Oh yes,' he says, 'but I'm used to that.'

He has given her brandy, without asking. She presumes he thinks she is going to need it. He is not having a drink himself, which somehow alarms her more, as if he is keeping himself sober for some precision work.

She says, 'D'you want to talk about it or let me look at it? Maybe I can help.'

'Is that what you do for him?' he says in a tone of deep disgust.

'Well, yes. Sometimes.'

'I never show work in progress to anyone. Anyway, that's not it.'

Outside there are sudden explosions and bursts of colour, the glow of a bonfire from someone's garden. She thinks of the people enjoying themselves, families in a good mood, letting off fireworks, having fun.

'My divorce came through today,' David says.

She has no idea what she is supposed to say to that. Obviously it must be a big event, but at the same time it can hardly be a shock when he knew it was coming.

She says tentatively, 'Are you very upset about it? I was hoping it might be a relief to have it finally over.'

He is staring at the floor. He says, 'It's like a death after a very long illness. It's a relief but it's still a tragedy.'

She keeps quiet then, out of respect for the bereaved. It feels appropriate, like the two minutes' silence at the Cenotaph. She also has a suspicion that anything she says will be wrong.

'And I've been thinking about Christmas.'

This sounds really ominous. She can feel her heart beginning to race.

'I don't know how I could ever have agreed even to think about it. You and I and Felix, all together in Barbados. It's a disgusting idea. I suppose I must have been desperate to be with you.'

She thinks the word disgusting is a bit strong. And she feels threatened by his use of the past tense.

'We could stay in different hotels, of course,' she says mildly, placatingly. 'It's just a way for us to be together over Christmas.'

'There is another way,' he says, looking at her for the first time. 'You stay here.'

'You mean *here*,' she says. 'In this flat?'

'Would that be so terrible?'

'No, of course not, it's very nice. But what about Felix?'

'Well, what about him?' he says.

It's like a phrase in music she thinks, Wagner probably, an ominous chord, a leitmotif of terrible hostility or even death. It's at that moment she realises his feelings go far beyond mere resentment or jealousy: he actually hates Felix. She is flattered and frightened.

'I can't leave him alone.'

'Why not?' he says.

'Well, I can't. I mean, I never have . . .'

'Of course you have,' he says in a most alarmingly even tone. 'You had a three-month separation earlier this year. You actually threw him out. Surely you haven't forgotten? I did my best to help you through it but I don't flatter myself I could have made you forget it completely.'

She takes a deep breath. 'Please don't be sarcastic.'

He gets up and stands over her. She feels quite threatened. She has finished her brandy and she wants another one but she doesn't like to ask: she thinks it would put her at a disadvantage.

He says, 'I'm sick of being used, Elizabeth.'

'But you told me that was all right, that's what people do. You said you didn't mind, we were using each other. You said it was mutual.' She particularly remembers that conversation: she had found it very touching.

'Oh, that.' He sighs impatiently, as if she were a stupid child. 'I might have known you'd remind me of that. The things one says at the beginning, in the first flush of love.'

There is something about his use of the word one that makes her extremely angry. 'Don't be so pompous,' she says. 'Anyway, I haven't been using you. I've always been honest with you. You knew exactly what you were getting into when we met.'

He laughs. 'I expect your husband makes speeches like that to all his women. He never deceived them so that makes it all right. It doesn't matter what harm he does so long as he warned them in advance. He's really trained you very well.'

She says firmly, 'I'd rather you didn't talk about Felix like that.'

'I'm sure you would. But what about me? What about what I'd rather? I've lost my wife and kids and now I'm going to lose you too. Why shouldn't I say what I like? I'm losing everything – I'm going to have nothing left soon. I can't even write the bloody book.'

As he gets more agitated, he sounds younger and younger, more like a sulky little boy, and she feels less threatened, more in charge. She says, 'It's all right, darling, you're not losing me.' She frowns; she doesn't like to think his distress can pull out of her a word reserved for Felix. 'I'm just going to Barbados for Christmas and I'd like you to come too. That's all it is.'

He looks really shocked and backs away from her. 'You haven't heard anything I've said.'

'Look, David, I'm sorry, but I can't stay here at Christmas and leave Felix alone at home or let him go to Barbados without me. You must see that. I know it's very difficult for you but I just can't do it. But if you come too we can all be happy.'

'Oh yes,' he says, 'why don't we all share a bed and have done with it. That's probably what he has in mind.'

She can feel herself blushing: he has got uncomfortably close to one of Felix's favourite fantasies.

'You're blushing,' he says. 'I'm right, aren't I?'

'For God's sake stop watching me, you're like the bloody thought police.'

They both pause, breathing rather fast, and look at each other, like boxers judging where next to strike. Hoping to break the tension she says, 'Could I have another drink?'

'No, you drink too much. It stops you listening. I know about drink. You get all blurred at the edges and you don't hear what I say. I can't live like this any more, Elizabeth. Your life with Felix is a cesspool and I'm trying to drag you out of it. Can't you see that? Don't you feel anything for me? I'm offering you love, real love – d'you really want to go on living that mucky life? Haven't you had enough pain? Haven't you let him degrade you enough?'

She's insulted, but worse, she can't help thinking that if Felix could hear all this he would roar with laughter and make some extremely rude remark about David's prose style. God knows why they gave him that prize, Felix would say, but it certainly wasn't for his dialogue. So now she feels the scene they are having is comic and yet she knows David is in pain and she has caused it, so she feels guilty as well as for thinking of Felix making a joke at David's expense.

'Don't let's talk about this now,' she says gently. 'It's so difficult and you're upset about the divorce. We're only going to offend each other if we go on. We can decide about Christmas another time, there's no rush. I know you don't like the way I live but I can't change everything overnight.' Perhaps if she can placate him now, on another day, in another mood, it can all be different. She has noticed before, over smaller things, that if she is patient the danger often passes. What was a big issue can simply fade away.

'I can't go on propping up your marriage indefinitely,' he says. 'I thought I could but I can't. I had so much pain with Kate, I can't bear any more. If you leave me at Christmas, I can't be sure I'll be here when you come back.'

Jordan says, 'When are you planning to tell me?'

It's a shock. They are lying side by side in his big bed and she had thought he was nearly asleep. The sounds are different at his place: river sounds instead of traffic. Earlier tonight there have also been lots of bangs from other people's fireworks and they watched some of the coloured lights exploding across the water as they had their supper. Now it is late and quiet again.

They haven't made love tonight; they often don't these days, just curl up together like an old married couple. She's both pleased and sad about that. She values the affectionate familiarity but misses the first rush of excitement, the overpowering desire, the all-consuming appetite: it will come on again, she knows, but perhaps only at intervals, like a thermostat. It's probably in inverse ratio to how often they meet, she thinks, and she wouldn't want to meet less often. They blame working, or failing to work, or lack of sleep; she secretly blames her secret, too. Sometimes they don't bother to assign a cause, just hug each other and turn over.

'Tell you what?' she says cautiously, in case it's not what she thinks.

'About the baby.'

263

She feels silly. She's glad they're having this conversation in the dark. It's too important to have face to face, easier just to lie there touching. 'I've been meaning to but I kept putting it off.'

'So I see. I've been wondering if I could say nothing indefinitely, just watch you swell up and ignore the whole thing, you know, whether we could actually get into the delivery room without either of us saying a word about it. Be a bit of a joke now, wouldn't it?'

He sounds so casual and cheerful that she can feel herself relaxing, and yet at the same time she would like it to be more of a big deal for him. She says, 'When did you realise?'

'Oh, about September. Don't forget, I've had five goes at this, I probably know more about it than you do. April, is it?'

'Yes.'

'There you are then.'

Is that all there is to it? She's somehow disappointed. He's known all this time and he's pleased. Can it really be that simple? 'You're being very good about it,' she says.

'Well, I just love having children, I told you that. And I didn't think I'd be having any more. You do want to have it? I'm assuming if you didn't you'd have got rid of it by now.'

How casually brutal that sounds. Is that how she made Sally feel? She says, 'Yes, I do want to have it. I'm quite surprised how much. I never thought I would. But I didn't know how to tell you. You might have felt enough was enough, or I was the wrong woman, or it was too soon.' She is aware of fishing for compliments now, and a bit embarrassed at herself.

'It's fate,' he says matter-of-factly, not taking the hint.

'No, it's coil failure actually.'

'Same thing. That's happened to me before too. And it didn't happen to you with Richard now, did it?'

'No,' she says, 'it certainly didn't.' She thinks he sounds smug.

'Poor old Richard. How's he taken it by the way?'

'What makes you think I've told him?'

'Well, you must have told someone. Even you couldn't have kept it entirely to yourself. And you'd hardly wait till he noticed, now would you?'

'He was very upset,' she says. 'Jealous, I think. Then he offered to stand by me if you did a runner.'

'I say.' He puts on an upper-class accent, theatrically exaggerated, almost submerging the Welsh and the American. 'Jolly decent of him, what?'

She doesn't like him making fun of Richard, although the offer had irritated her. But it does occur to her that he may feel ever so slightly threatened. She hopes so. She thinks it would be good for him not to take her so much for granted; then she is shocked to find herself even tempted to play games. 'Yes, I thought it was very kind. But a bit encroaching as well, like trying to take me over.'

'Well, no danger of me doing that,' he says.

No, she thinks, and it would be all the same if I wanted you to.

'You don't mind about not living together, do you?' he says after a pause, adding before she can answer, 'It wouldn't work.'

'No,' she says carefully. 'I've never said I wanted to live with you.'

'We're all right as we are, aren't we?' he says. 'I don't think I could live with anyone ever again. But I can help. You won't be poor the way you were with Carey, and that makes it easier, doesn't it? I can throw money at you. I'm good at that.'

'I'd like that,' she says. 'That would make a nice change.'

'We can hire people to do all the hard work and you and I can just have the fun.'

She says, 'How simple you make it sound.'

'Money makes everything simple,' he says comfortably.

She remembers Carey telling her only two years ago, although it seems like another lifetime, that money would have made all the difference to them too. She thinks of Jordan's recent paintings, the ones she felt were tipping into self-parody, and wonders if he knows what a high price he is paying for money. Perhaps he thinks it's worth the sacrifice. Or maybe he doesn't think it is a sacrifice. Perhaps she is wrong about his work. Anyway, it's not her business. She has more important things to worry about.

'Money won't make Sally come round,' she says.

'Ah,' he says, 'is that what you're sad about?'

'Yes,' she says, 'very sad.'

'When did you tell her?'

'A month ago. Just before she went back to college.'

'And it was bad.'

'Very bad.'

'D'you want to tell me about it?'

'No. I want to forget it but I can't.'

He puts his arm round her then and she wishes he'd done it sooner. 'She will come round,' he says. 'All my children did, after I went away. Just give her time. Children are very forgiving.'

'They have to be, don't they,' she says bitterly, 'the things we do to them. Sally's lost her father and her step-father and her baby, and all thanks to me.' But she is also thinking of him and wondering how she can trust a man who has already left two wives and five children. How can she want to have a baby by such a man, when there are no guarantees that he won't go off and leave her too? And yet she does want to, very much. She doesn't trust him but she loves him. She has gone right back to her other self, her younger self, the Helen she thought had gone for ever.

'You did your best,' he says. 'You did the right thing at the time. Didn't you?'

'I thought so, I really did. But we were just getting over

266

it and it's taken so long and now this. Even the dates are the same. It's like a slap in the face, as if I'd done it on purpose, as if I'm saying to her, I wouldn't let you have your baby but you can't stop me having mine.'

There is a long silence. 'Well,' he says, 'I don't think I can make you feel better about it, any more than you could make me feel better about having that woman while Hannah was dying. But I can almost promise you she'll come round.'

'Almost promise,' she repeats. 'That's the best we can do these days, isn't it?'

'Don't spoil it,' he says. 'We're going to have such a lovely baby. Born with a coil in one hand and a brush in the other.'

In spite of herself she laughs. 'I feel it's fallen rather flat, my big news. There was I dreading telling you and you knew all the time.'

'I don't think flat's quite the word,' he says. 'Not for a baby. But as I've known since September and you must have known since August, you might say we've had plenty of time to get used to the idea. Still, it's not too late to celebrate. Shall I get up and open a bottle of champagne, would that help?'

'No, I don't think so,' she says. 'It's a nice idea but it feels a bit over the top.'

'Well, how about this,' he says, moving her hand, 'how does this feel?' And presently, to her surprise, in a gentle, leisurely way they start to make love, as if to seal a bargain.

PART SEVEN

In December a letter arrives at the flat from Sally.

Dear Felix,
I thought we said goodbye on fairly good terms back in April and I was even starting to feel okay about you again as an important part of my growing up. But now I've finally got your book from the library and I'm very upset. I can see why you never sent me a copy. It's so obviously about me and full of really crude details that I thought were private. I don't understand how you could do a thing like that to me when I've never done anything to hurt you, even when I could have done. Why do you have to write about me at all? Haven't you got any imagination? It really hurts to know I'm there for everyone to see, as if you had taken pictures of me naked and published them. It's not fair and it makes me very angry. Sally.

He hesitates before replying. He is already busy planning the script and the holiday is almost upon him. He even wonders if a dignified silence might be more appropriate. But the letter seems to demand an answer, so he forces himself to write. He does so hate letters.

Dearest Sally,
I'm so sorry you're upset about the book. If we'd still been together I'd certainly have sent you a copy because I really thought you'd be flattered. I would never write about anyone I didn't care for deeply; it

is much too hard work. Any details in it that remind you of us are written with love and intended to be a tribute to you. But to send it to you after you left me would have felt like an attempt at getting you back and I know you don't want that.

Let me also explain that although it may seem to you to be all about us, a lot of it is in fact fiction. This is not the time or place to go into that torturesome process whereby life becomes art (or often the reverse), but taking a few details from someone you love for a novel is not at all the same thing as presenting a naked portrait of them to the world. If you think it is, then you must admit I have exposed myself just as blatantly, and in a much more unflattering light. But in fact there are only a very few people who even know that we were together for those unforgettable months and they are people already close to us both.

I hope in time you may come to see the book as I do, an attempt to create something new out of a vital spark of life, as well as to give some important memories a measure of permanence. It may be an unworthy attempt, or even a failure, but it was certainly never meant to hurt you, rather to remind you how precious you were and still are to me.

With love,
As ever,
Felix.

A week before she is due to leave on holiday a huge basket of flowers arrives. Felix, looking at them, says, 'Persistent little chap, isn't he?' She opens the envelope and reads:

'The pain of loving you
Is almost more than I can bear.'

And below David has written: 'I don't think DHL can help me any more, if indeed he ever did.'

She feels a loss, a missed opportunity, a friend turning his back, and yet what can she do? She puts the card in her handbag to avoid ridicule but she must be looking sad because Felix, with a victor's generosity, puts his arms round her and says, 'Not coming then?'

She shakes her head.

'What a shame. He'd have done much better just to pack his bags and sort out the small print later. Never mind, we're going to have a lovely time, you and I, and when you get back you can tell him what he's missed.'

She can't bear to admit it's over: it will weaken her position. And perhaps it isn't over, she thinks, to give herself courage. Perhaps he will change his mind.

Kate invites him for supper at the end of term. It's a week before Christmas and they're both exhausted from school and aware of having done no shopping.

'I suppose it'll happen anyway,' Kate says, slumped at the kitchen table. 'Christmas, I mean. Sometimes I have this fantasy that if I do nothing at all, just sit here in a stupor staring at the wall, it'll all happen without me and I can turn up one morning and say, "Well, fancy that, it's Christmas again, terrific."'

'She means if I do it all instead,' says Annabel.

'She likes it really,' Thomas says.

'And if anyone in the shops says, "Oh, are you on holiday again?"' says Kate, 'I may just do violence to them.'

Kate has made a stew. She serves boiled potatoes and cabbage with it and it is all truly disgusting. He doesn't understand how anyone can make such a simple meal turn out so badly. And he is forced to assume this is one of Kate's best efforts, since he has been invited specially to share it. The children eat it calmly, matter-of-factly, even with the appearance of routine enjoyment. Richard wonders if it is time for him to invite Kate to supper. He has been too ashamed of his bedsit and unsure about the relationship, but he knows he can do better than this on his two burners and grill. He thinks Kate needs him to cook for her. And he would like to have someone to cook for again. They finish with baked apples. Something has gone wrong with them too, but he is not sure how Kate has achieved it. They are burnt on the outside but hard on the inside and they taste of soap.

'Bath, Thomas,' Kate says after supper.

'Oh, *Mum*.'

'I know, you had one last Friday. Bath, Thomas. Before I come and scrape the dirt off with a knife.'

'She's an awful bully,' Thomas says. ''Night, Richard.'

'Goodnight, Thomas.'

Annabel lingers, helps with the washing up, watches some nonsense on television. He and Kate sit and chat about school. There's an odd mixture of tension and relaxation in the atmosphere. When Annabel goes to bed she hesitates as she passes him, then kisses him swiftly on the cheek for the very first time. ''Night, Richard.'

'Goodnight, Annabel.' He's quite unnerved, touched, even moved to tears. He blinks rapidly, aware of Kate watching him.

'Have another drink,' Kate says. She pours two more glasses of wine. The silence is suddenly awkward. She seems embarrassed about something, fidgeting, hesitant. 'D'you have any plans for Christmas?'

'No, not really.'

'Only we were wondering, the kids and I . . . if you'd like to spend it with us.'

This is so unexpected he doesn't know how to answer.

'Only if you've nothing better to do,' she goes on hurriedly. 'We just thought it might be more fun than being on your own. And they'll be going to see David part of the time, so I'll be on my own a bit as well. Anyway. No need to tell me now. We just had a sort of family conference and I promised them I'd ask you.'

'It's a lovely idea, Kate. I really appreciate it.'

'I'd better go up and say goodnight to them. Inspect Thomas's ears and all that.' She goes out of the room very quickly.

He knows he must think fast to be ready with an answer when she comes back, but he is still so surprised that his brain moves slowly. Christmas with Kate and the children. It doesn't seem like a casual offer: it feels heavy with significance. And in a way he is tempted. He is not looking forward to Christmas alone. Helen has made it clear she doesn't want to see him over the holiday and may even be going away, presumably with her lover; Inge has invited him to call in but somehow made him feel that this year it is she who is doing him a favour. After being loved by both of them for so many years he is finding it hard to accept that neither of them loves him any more. It is a bleak, unreal feeling, like a physical chill, a psychic shiver at the withdrawal of so much warmth. He had relied upon both of them more than he realised. And the pain of knowing that Helen is having a child by someone else is sometimes almost more than he can bear. He feels exhausted and bereft; he knows he needs someone but that doesn't necessarily mean that Kate is the right person or even if she is that he is ready for her. Is she expecting him to make love to her? How can they go on working together if Christmas doesn't go well? And is there any way he can manage to eat a turkey cooked by her?

'Well, that's them settled,' she says, returning. 'They wanted to know what you said but I told them I hadn't asked you yet, so there's no hurry to decide. Honestly. It was just a thought. I won't be at all offended if you say no. I won't throw a tantrum in the staff room next term or anything like that.'

Felix would say she is protesting too much. Why should he think of Felix now? Another aching loss. He can't afford any more. He says, 'Kate, I'm grateful, I just don't know what to say. I've got to see Inge and the boys but –'

275

'Yes, of course, they're your number-one priority, I realise that.'

'– but I'm doing that on Christmas Eve.' He thinks how ironic it is that this year he is willing to go on the special day and Inge no longer cares when he visits. 'After that I'm free as air.'

Kate says hesitantly, 'I thought you might be seeing Helen.'

'No, she's probably going to be away. And she doesn't want to see me anyway, not really. She'd only be doing it to be polite. I just don't know if I'll be a very good guest, I'm not very cheerful these days and I don't want to put a damper on things for you.'

'Well, it's harder for you than for me,' says Kate generously. 'You've had a hell of a year, no wonder you're shell-shocked. Eighteen months at our school would have been enough on its own. But I'm used to that and I've had two years to get over David, so I'm fine.'

'Every time you say that,' he says, glad to focus on her instead of himself, 'I wonder a bit more if you really are.'

'Yes, I really am,' says Kate, sounding angry. 'It was a dream and it turned into a nightmare. I'm glad it's over and I don't ever want to go through anything like that again.'

'Right,' he says. 'Okay.'

'I'm going to see as little as possible of David, just enough to hand over the kids and pick them up. None of that civilised divorce, best pals stuff for me. I'm going to cut my losses and start again. And I'd like to start by spending Christmas with you. Nothing heavy. Don't look so worried. I'm not going to rape you or propose marriage.'

'I know that,' he says. 'I'm not looking worried, am I?'

'Oh, Richard,' she says, 'that was a joke. Well, sort of. A very small one. I want to have a jolly Christmas, that's all.'

But he thinks she still sounds angry. 'What if I cook for

276

you?' he suggests. 'Just to give you a break. Then I might feel I was making a contribution, not just freeloading.'

'That would be lovely. I know I'm a rotten cook.'

'No, not at all, I didn't mean that. I just thought it might make a change for you and I rather miss not having a kitchen.'

'God, you're welcome to mine. David never let me go in it so I never got any practice. Any time I did try to cook something he told me how ghastly it was, so I gave up.'

'That's settled then.' He feels relieved and yet resentful too, as if he's never really had any choice in the matter.

'You know,' Kate says, suddenly gentle, 'I do understand. Helen was magic for you, wasn't she? It was the same for me with David, so I think I know how you feel. We've both had to let go of a magic person. But now I've had time to get used to it, I honestly think life can be better without illusions.'

He wonders if she is right.

It is hot in the small stuffy bedroom. Felix lies beside Inge in a drowsy post-coital stupor, breathing in her ripe familiar smell. He has had so much pleasure that he feels quite satiated and full of goodwill. 'You know,' he says to her, almost with affection, 'you really should take this up professionally, you could make a fortune.' Some women might find this remark offensive, but he's pretty sure Inge will take it as the compliment he intends.

She smiles, as far as he can tell under the tangled mess of hair and duvet. 'It's too late for that, Felix, I'm too old, and besides, I'm always in love.'

'But not with me,' he points out. 'Never with me. First Richard and now Michael. Every time I meet you, you're in love with someone else.' He has often thought about this and how it makes everything much easier. God knows, no man in his senses would want to be loved by

277

Inge, to be the object of all that obsessive yearning, and yet there is something about the harsh light of reality that doesn't please him. It's relaxing but not flattering that Inge sees him as he really is. He misses the soft-focus mezzotint of love, the adoration that Sally used to give him. He misses the drama of a grand passion, the operatic excess. It makes for trouble but there is still nothing like it. He wonders if he can make Raffaella fall in love with him.

'Well, you can't expect me to fall in love with you,' Inge says pleasantly. 'I know you too well.'

He reaches under the bed where he has hidden her present. 'Look what I got you for Christmas, Inge,' he says. 'Would you like to open it now?'

'No, I want to save it for Christmas Eve.'

'Open this one now,' he says. 'I got you something else for Christmas Eve. You can't open this one in front of the boys.'

Her face lights up and she tears at the wrapping paper with childish glee. 'Oh, Felix,' she says, real delight in her voice, 'you're so kind, you got me a new vibrator.'

'Well, I remembered you saying you'd lost yours.'

'I didn't lose it, somebody stole it from my handbag when I went to that party and I was too embarrassed to ask about it. Shall we try it out?'

'Not now. I've really had enough for one day.'

'I never thought I'd hear you say that. Next time then. Isn't it nice, Felix, that we can give each other so much pleasure?'

He still isn't used to the change in Inge. It goes against his fundamental belief that character, his own and other people's, is formed at an early age and stays much the same through life. But Inge has actually changed. She looks and tastes and smells and feels as she always did, she behaves in the same way, but she is so cheerful that he fancies she has been cloned and reprogrammed. Like everything else about her, this new cheerfulness is excessive and he is not sure he can keep pace with it.

'I'm going to have such a happy Christmas,' she says. 'I shall play with my new toy and think about Michael. It's going to be wonderful. Thank you, Felix.'

She kisses him on the cheek. He notices she is not going to fantasise about him.

'So you won't be lonely this year?' he says.

'No, the boys are here and Richard is coming on Christmas Eve but it really doesn't matter. I'm not going to be lonely anyway, I'm going to help in a hospital. Once Christmas is over it's the new year and then I can think it's only ten months till I see Michael again. Just think, Felix, once the year has turned the time will pass so quickly and then we can have a glorious affair, Michael and I. It's going to be so wonderful. If I want to be faithful to him you won't mind, will you? I may have to give you up then.'

He really doesn't know if she's ludicrous or pathetic. Perhaps there is even something faintly magnificent about such lunacy. Madness on an epic scale rather appeals to him. 'Well, of course you must do what you like. I'm certainly not going to worry about something that may or may not happen in ten months' time. I just hope you won't be too disappointed if it doesn't work out with him, that's all.'

'But of course it will work out. He promised me. We're going to meet again in a year and a day, like in fairy tales, and that was November the fourth so it's only—'

'Yes, you told me all that.' He can't bear to hear it again. He thinks all this attention to detail is very German and he finds it heavy going. 'I just mean he might change his mind. Or he might not have meant it in the first place. It could just be something therapists say to their clients when they're breaking up, just to keep them happy till they get over it.'

He sees the smile fade from her face and wonders if he actually wants to upset her. 'But that can't be right, Felix. He wouldn't lie to me. That's not how therapists behave. He wants to see me again but we have to be ethical, we have to leave a space.'

'Oh well, I don't know, I was only trying to warn you. I'm sure you know best.'

The smile is back, irrepressible it seems. 'It's going to be wonderful, Felix, you'll see. Don't worry about me, I'm going to be so happy. Now what about you, have you got your Gabriella into bed yet?'

'Raffaella.' He wonders if she does it on purpose. 'No, I haven't, she's teasing me. But that's quite fun and it's only a matter of time.'

'So we're both in the same position. Isn't that interesting? We're both waiting for these wonderful people to be ready for us and meanwhile we keep each other happy. Isn't that nice?'

She's positively radiant. He has to remind himself that he used to complain when she was depressed, but it's still hard to bear. What a pity, he thinks, that there is always a snag. She's probably better in bed than anyone he's ever had, but one way or another she always ends up driving him crazy. He can't stay away from her for long but he can't stay long with her either, a familiar dilemma.

'So have you got your holiday all planned?' she asks. 'Are you going to have Christmas in the sunshine?'

'Yes, I certainly am. It won't be all holiday, though, I'm going to make a start on the script of the book while I'm there. My agent finally sold the film rights so I'm going to be quite busy.'

She looks so happy for him that he feels a beast for having tried to dampen her spirits. 'But that's wonderful, Felix, you're so clever, why didn't you tell me before?'

'Well, it wasn't quite settled and I didn't want to jinx it.'

'No, I mean today. As soon as you arrived.'

'Well, we were busy with other things, weren't we?'

'But we must celebrate.' She jumps out of bed and pulls on her clothes, leaving her underwear on the floor as usual. 'Come downstairs and have a drink and tell me all about it. Who is going to play the girl in your book? Did Sally mind that you wrote all about her? Who is going to play you in the film, Felix? Will they get someone who looks like you? Do they let you choose the actors?'

Felix gets up and dresses more slowly. He is beginning to feel exhausted. Previously she reminded him of Madam Butterfly, with Michael instead of Richard as Pinkerton. Now all her breathless enthusiasm reminds him of Gigi. He feels like patting her on the head and saying, 'Hush, you silly child.' He notices he is starting to feel affection for her again.

He follows her downstairs and she pours them two large whiskies. The sitting-room is immaculate, the way it always is these days, another symptom of the new changed Inge. Sometimes he almost feels he has come to the wrong house.

'They don't let you choose the cast,' he says, trying to answer her questions as briefly as possible to avoid the feeling that he is being interviewed yet again. 'But you can make suggestions. And I didn't really write all about Sally, she was just the germ of the idea. But you're right, she wasn't very pleased. I thought she should have been flattered, but there you are.'

'Well, if you ever write about me, Felix,' Inge says, 'don't worry, I shall be very flattered and I shall tell everyone, you must buy that book, it's all about me.'

'All right,' he says wearily, charmed and exasperated, 'I'll remember that.'

'And is Elizabeth's lover going to come on holiday with you?' she asks suddenly.

'I don't know. It looks as though he's got cold feet, he may be going to chicken out. Still, that's not my problem.'

'Perhaps he's embarrassed,' she says. 'It was a bit of a strange idea, I think.'

'I thought it was a very sensible idea. He could keep Elizabeth busy while I see Raffaella.'

'But who is going to keep Raffaella's husband busy?

You still haven't got it right, there is always one person left over, like musical chairs.'

'I don't know, he's supposed to be busy on the telephone doing business deals, or maybe he likes black girls, I can't control everything, Inge, but I'm doing my best. Some things will just have to be left to chance.'

Suddenly her face goes very serious. 'Not too much to chance, Felix.' She reaches behind a cushion and pulls out a flat thin object, A4 size, in Christmas wrapping. For a terrible moment he thinks she has written something and wants him to read it. That really will be the end of the relationship, he thinks. No amount of good sex could make up for that.

'This is your Christmas present, Felix,' she says, 'but you'll have to open it now, you can't take it to the Caribbean with you, I don't think Elizabeth would understand.'

He opens it, feeling her watching him. Perhaps it is a pornographic magazine that she has got him as a joke. He prepares his face to look pleased.

He unwraps a horoscope, a booklet of maybe a dozen pages neatly bound. He can't think of anything he wants less. He says, 'Inge, how lovely, what a surprise.'

'I got your chart done. Only I'm not sure it's correct because you didn't know your exact time of birth when I asked you.'

'I don't remember you asking me that.'

She smiles. 'Ah, I was very clever about it. We were talking about being good at different times of day and whether it had anything to do with when you were born and you told me you weren't sure because your parents are dead. Anyway, this is the best they can do with the information we have, and I've read it, of course, and the thing is, Felix, you are going to have a Saturn transit for the next two and a half years and that will separate the false from the true, so you must be very careful.'

He looks at her in amazement. She really is quite unhinged, he thinks.

'You mustn't worry about it. But it's a very important time for you and you're going to be tested. You could have a big crisis, not fatal, but serious. Relationships could be ending or beginning.'

'But they always are,' he says mildly. 'I don't think we need Saturn to tell us that.'

'No, this is something special, Felix, you must listen to me. This is something unforeseen.'

'Well, I'll remember that,' he says. 'I'm not really into astrology myself but maybe I will be now. Thank you, Inge, that's a lovely present. A really big surprise, the way presents should be. I'll keep it at the flat and refer to it often.' He takes a small square gift-wrapped box from the pocket of his jacket. 'And this is for you to have on the day.'

Her face brightens again. She takes the little parcel and examines it carefully, shaking it, turning it this way and that, suddenly reminding him of a monkey. 'What is it, Felix? Is it scent? It feels like scent. Oh, I do hope it's scent, I've run out of my favourite, well, I have to carve it out of the bottle with a nail-file, and it's so expensive. I got it before Richard came back and I've made it last too long, I think, it's sticking to the bottom of the bottle.'

It is indeed her favourite scent, for he has observed the empty bottle on her dressing-table, but he is not going to tell her that. 'It's a surprise, Inge,' he says sternly, 'and you must wait till Christmas Eve.'

She hugs him. She feels very strong and energetic. She never hugs him like that in bed. 'Oh Felix,' she says, 'you're a nice man after all, I think. Well, parts of you are nice, anyway. Would you like to stay to supper? The boys are out tonight. We can play all our favourite music.'

He shakes his head. 'I can't. I'm taking Elizabeth to *Bohème* as a treat before we go away. We won't find much opera in Barbados.'

'A treat for you or her? I thought you like opera more than she does.'

'Yes, I do, but she likes it enough.'

'Well, have another drink before you go.'

'Thanks, but I don't have time.'

She follows him to the door and they kiss on both cheeks. She says, 'Now don't forget my advice, Felix. You're such an old friend now, I don't want to see any more bad things happen to you. You be careful. Saturn is very powerful.'

'That's all right,' Felix says, laughing. 'I like living dangerously.'